The
Bookseller
of
Dachau

SHARI J. RYAN

The

Bookseller

of

Dachau

bookouture

Published by Bookouture in 2021

An imprint of Storyfire Ltd.
Carmelite House
50 Victoria Embankment
London EC4Y oDZ

www.bookouture.com

ISBN: 978-1-80019-871-5
eBook ISBN: 978-1-80019-870-8

To those who have ever endured the agony of execration. Your strength is our future.

PROLOGUE

MATILDA, 1943

The earth is not flat. I know this now. I'm unsure how anyone could think the world is anything but a mess of hills, mountains, meadows, and valleys, all of which prevent our eyes from seeing too much at once. The man-made towers, walls, and fences overshadow the grounds below, hiding a truth most cannot fathom, but to know it exists only leaves my imagination to assume the worst.

I've come up here to the highest peak of this town many times. It's a well-known spot, once intended for sightseeing. Most visit this landmark for the purpose of stealing a piece of the scenery to render on canvas or film. To be surrounded by such beauty is something of a rare commodity since our country has become the focal point of what feels like a never-ending war.

There is no other place in the world where one can stand before an eleventh-century abandoned palace cloaked by delicious sprigs of greenery while concurrently bearing witness to the ash-filled human remains funneling up into the crying sky.

I pray it's not him. Every day, I pray harder than the one before. We aren't supposed to know what the smoke is made up of, nor should we assume what is causing the pungent odor blanketing the village. Of course, without being able to recognize a scent, no one is left to wonder unless they have a connection to someone within those walls. I wish I could forget the words used to describe the ongoing atrocities brewing a mile away.

Though ignorance is not a crime, today, it is a temporary blessing.

CHAPTER 1
GRACE
2018

Our mirroring appearances gave it away—the mother-daughter connection. We had the same sunny blue, deep-set eyes, but I always thought hers sparkled more than mine. Maybe it was the way I saw her. We used to wear our hair the same way too. Both of us loved the long, tousled look since our matching ashy-blonde hair would fall into thick natural waves. I think *that* was the hardest part for her—giving up her favorite feature to the maybes of science and medicine. I haven't been able to grow my hair out that long since then. I feel a sense of guilt, so I keep my strands at shoulder length now. I straighten the photograph hanging from a pin on the wall above my desk and silently send Mom my love.

"Lucky Brew in ten?" Brian, a co-worker I share a wall with, calls out over the farm of cubicles. He's the loudest in the office and the first to start a motion for evening plans.

A succession of responses varying from, "I'm there," to hoots or catcalls echo in the glass-encased office space I feel stuck between most days.

I drop my gaze to my drawing and relax my shoulders. It's time to part with another piece of my artwork. The very moment I complete a blueprint drawing for a client, it's like I'm rolling up a part of my mind and slipping it into a bottomless tube. Before college, I envisioned my career as an architect a bit differently than what I'm experiencing now. I thought I would be working face-to-face with clients, unveiling the hours of thought and strategy I poured onto paper. Instead, I hand off the tubes and remain a silent middle person as if I'm no more than a machine generating a product. I don't think it's wrong to want more, especially after investing over a decade of my life to this firm, but it is what it is.

"Grace, are you going to join us for a change?" Brian asks, slapping his hand against the metal rail of the wall-panel connector. He's only asking to keep the peace.

Lucky Brew is a college bar that smells of rotten beer, uncleaned bathrooms, and trash. For whatever reason, every male employee of this firm thinks of the place as a second home.

I twist the cover onto the last tube and bundle the three together on my desk. I force a smile to be polite. "Thanks for the offer, but I have a busy night ahead," I reply.

Brian chuckles and rolls his eyes. I'm sure they know I don't have anything going on tonight, but I'd rather get a tooth drilled than spend any more time with these men than I have to each day.

I scoop up the three tubes of rolled blueprints and walk them over to Paul's office. It's the one with the handwritten sign taped over his nameplate that reads: Boss of the Year. I clear my throat and tap my knuckles against the billowed windowpane. "Do you have a minute?" I ask.

Paul spins his chair around, leans back, and folds his hands behind his neck. His slick dark hair catches the reflection of the fluorescent ceiling light, and his smile bares more teeth than necessary. "For you, I have all the time in the world, Grace."

I take a seat on his straight-back, leather chair, parallel to his desk. "I wanted to talk about the mid-level architect position." I twist around and close his office door for a sense of privacy that seems impossible to find here. "Paul, I've been with this firm for twelve years and we both know I have the skills and experience for this open position."

Paul's arms float down to his desk as his fingers seamlessly clasp together, changing the casual tone to business formal. "I'm aware you submitted your application for the position," he says.

"Yes, but I wanted to follow up, as well."

"Yeah," he replies, inhaling sharply through his nose. Paul is no more than a year or two older than me at most and he runs this firm, which should define his level of expertise. We both graduated from college with a degree in architectural design and have been working in the field since. We're no different from one another except I'm usually here before him in the morning and the last to leave at night, and it isn't because I'm not working smarter than him. "Look, Grace, I don't want to get your hopes up about this position. We've had many great applicants and it's going to be a tough decision."

"Applicants from within the firm?" I question.

"No, but I have to treat all applicants equally, as you know."

I would enjoy nothing more than responding with laughter because I'm not sure he understands the meaning of equality. The lack of diversity and the fact that I'm the only female architect in this firm doesn't speak highly of him. "I see."

"Don't give up hope, though. I just can't say much more at this point."

"Right, of course, Paul." I stand from the seat and place the blueprint tubes down on his desk. "Have a good night."

"Grace, are you all right?" His expression doesn't change from the one he had when explaining why I shouldn't get my hopes up but, also, not to lose hope altogether.

"Never better," I reply, before walking out of his office.

It isn't until I'm out of the building and stepping onto the metro that the anger builds inside of me. I don't think I'll ever be a candidate for a promotion while competing against the men he crashes beer glasses with every night. I've been patient and worked hard, but I feel like I'm on a treadmill most days—in a race to get nowhere.

I could apply for other positions in the city. Boston has many architecture firms, but all the time and energy I have devoted to Carmello Designs seems to be worth nothing.

My thoughts carry me through the front doors of my Beacon Hill apartment building and up to my mailbox. Part of me would like to ignore the stack of bills likely waiting for me, but I ordered a new charging cord for my phone that I desperately need. It should have been delivered today.

The mailbox is full, and I pull everything out and fold the load into my arms. I take a moment to straighten the pile, but I'm distracted by an oversized heavy envelope clearly sent from a law office.

My stomach churns into knots as I hike up the three flights of stairs to my studio and fumble with the key to open the door. I drop all the mail onto my round glass dining table and tear open the mustard-yellow envelope, pulling everything out in one handful.

The sirens from police cars whistle by my window and my smart-home pod is flashing to alert me I have a package, but nothing matters as I read the first line of this letter for a second time.

Dear Ms. Laurent,

We hope this letter finds you well. The law office of Straus & Straus has been retained to handle the testament of a property you, the beneficiary, are to inherit from Matilda Ellman. It has been determined that you are the biological granddaughter to Ms. Ellman, and therefore, the eligible kin to claim the property.

There are several options for how you may transfer the property title, and we are happy to do so virtually since your residency is in the United States. Please feel free to contact us at your earliest convenience so that we may discuss how to move forward with the proceedings of this matter.

With Regards,

Attorney Brigitte Cora

Konrad-Adenauer-Straße 1080A

85221 Dachau, Germany

+49 8131 300020

I fall onto the sofa, grateful to have been standing in front of it to catch me from hitting the ground.

Matilda Ellman—I've never heard the name. Mom spent her life searching for her biological parents, but she was told the likelihood of finding the bloodline to them was nearly impossible since she arrived in the United States as an orphaned immigrant from Europe. She was sent away without even a name. Somewhere along her travels, one was assigned to her. Never finding an answer to her one lifelong question about her family—her parents, or where she came from—was the hardest pill to swallow when we found out she was sick. I did everything I could to help, but without a place to begin a search, the rest always seemed too far out of reach. For all I know, this could be a scam. In fact, I might almost bet my life on it being a hoax.

I fan through the other papers in the pile, finding a black-and-white map of the city, Dachau, with an address written across the top and a business card for the law office clipped to the side. The last of what was in the envelope is a bound report filled with photocopied documents and handwritten pages. The words look to be written in German, which is not a language I'm familiar with in the slightest.

It's a scam. I need to believe this, even if it's just for my sanity.

I reach into my coat pocket and pull out my phone, groaning as I search for Dad's number in my contacts. It's been about four months since we've spoken at this point. I should be surprised it hasn't been longer, I suppose. With his new family, he doesn't often have time to remember his firstborn daughter, but I've learned never to expect much from him after watching my parents' marriage crumble from an early age until a year before Mom was diagnosed with lung cancer.

Before the second ring, Dad answers the call. "Grace, is that you?" His question makes me wonder if my name is in his list of contacts, or if he's being sarcastic.

"Yes, Dad, it's me," I reply. "I'm calling because I have a question that I hope you might know something about." Though, I doubt it, since I was the one who sat with Mom for years as she tried to track down any hint of her relatives. Samples of her DNA must be in every genetic science lab in this country considering how many ways she tried to find information. There was never a match.

"Is everything all right? You sound frantic." I'm surprised he remembers what my form of worry sounds like, but I'm not in the mood to pull hairs right now.

"I received a weird letter from a law office in Dachau, Germany, stating that I'm the heir to a property left behind by a—" My gaze drops back down to the letter that's vibrating on top of my bouncing knees. "Matilda Ellman. Apparently someone has determined that I am her biological granddaughter."

"Matilda Ellman," Dad responds, as if he's thumbing through a catalog of names in his head. "I've never heard of her. Did you say Dachau, Germany?"

"That's where the law office is and a second address on a map is also in Dachau. I assume it's where the property must be."

A long sigh expels from his lungs. "Gosh, Grace, I don't know what to tell you, dear. You should do some research and call the law office for more information. I'm not sure what other advice to give you on this one."

"Yeah, okay. I'll let you know what happens. I hope everyone is doing well. I'll talk to you later."

"Grace," Dad says, stopping me from ending the call, "do you want to have dinner sometime soon?"

I will agree. He won't follow up with a date or a time, and if I do, he won't show up at that date or time. "Sure, Dad. Give me a call when you're free."

"Will do, dear. Have a good night and try not to worry about this too much. Your mother made herself sick with this stuff."

My cheeks burn with frustration, and I hang up before saying anything I might regret.

I carry the papers over to my computer desk and switch on the monitor. While waiting for the search engine to load, I flip through the contents again, pulling out one of the photocopied reports. It's from the National DNA Database, with an abundance of information that looks like gibberish when I'm trying to see it all at once.

I close my eyes, pull in a deep breath, and try to refocus my attention on the first section of the sheet titled: Maternal Haplogroup. Below is a list of names, including Mom's and Matilda Ellman. Except for Mom, the others are all from the Bavarian region in Germany. I turn to face the computer and type Matilda's name into the search bar, following Dachau, Germany. My eyes widen upon scrolling down the list of articles to choose from. I don't see any mention of Matilda Ellman, but on almost every link, it is impossible to avoid the bold topic of Dachau being best known as the home of the first concentration camp established during the Holocaust. The property I'm inheriting is in this city.

I'm imagining the worst before clicking on any of the links, but my imagination couldn't have prepared me for what is displayed on my screen. My immediate question is whether people still live in this place, but my answer isn't hard to find. People have always lived in this city, and yet more than thirty-thousand people died within its thirteen square miles.

The day was warmer than usual, the sky a unique shade of blue as if it were a precise reflection of the ocean. There wasn't a cloud to spot for as far as we could see. The grass was growing above our waists and wildflowers were blooming as if they all received a formal invitation from the sun. The wind was singing a song we had never heard, a lullaby to erase the unimportant hours of the day. The air smelled like freshly hung linen on a clothesline and the crisp breeze tickled our cheeks as if we were running through the damp fabric.

"That's all I have written so far," Hans says. He stands up from his spot beside me—the shaded area beneath the lonely birch tree amid this quiet wildflower field. With a shake of his head, Hans dismisses whatever thoughts are running through his mind and tucks the paper into his pocket.

I smile in return, knowing he must have changed each of those words at least a hundred times over the course of a few hours. His dream is to write a book, but every word is as important as the last, and sometimes he cannot move on until he is satisfied. "That's quite a bit for one day," I tell him.

"You lie as terribly as you dance, Matilda, you know that?"

I laugh at the truth I can't hide from.

"I suppose I could try harder," I say, arching my brow in his direction.

Sun-kissed freckles glow across Hans's cheeks, and I giggle while connecting the dots with the tip of my finger. "That's about as likely as me growing out of these silly marks on my face," he says.

"Why would you want them to go away? Have you considered the thought that you may have earned each marking for every good deed you have done? Surely if that were the case, you wouldn't be so ashamed now, would you?" My questions cause him to look away from me. Hans becomes embarrassed so easily, it's almost hard not to tease him a bit. "Besides, who else can say they have a lucky star made up of freckles on the top of his hand?" I grin, knowing he can't disagree.

Hans looks down at his hand and makes a fist to highlight the dots on his knuckle, then shakes his head. "Real lucky. Not all of us are blessed with long golden-blonde hair that shimmers beneath the sun or have large, sapphire doll-like eyes. You're flawless and I have flaws, it's that simple. Speaking of which, if I don't bring you home soon, I'll have a lot more flaws to deal with," he says. He's the responsible one of us. I'm like the wind—unpredictable and free to do as I please. He is more like the sun with one unique job to do no matter the occasion. He will rise at a certain time and set at just the same, day and night—predictable and reliable. I could be reliable too, but what's the sense in growing up faster than we must?

"Okay, but for the record, I'm not flawless. I'm far from it."

"To me, you're perfect," Hans says, allowing his gaze to linger on me for a long second. "Although I suppose I can't ignore the fact that your cheeks blush easier than other girls, but I like it." He seems to get a thrill out of making my cheeks turn red whenever we're alone, but our time together lately has become more infrequent, and it saddens me to think the rules we live by might only become stricter.

At seventeen, we should be able to live without a care in the world. People aren't given enough years of their lives to live without consequence. We aren't allowed to do much on our own until we're mature enough to know right from wrong, and by that time, adulthood is just around the corner. Then, forever until we find heaven's gates, there will be a job or task depending on us. "Every day should be like this."

"It should," Hans replies, leading the way through the tall grass, "but then we would be living in a fantastical dream rather than existing in real life."

"I disagree," I sing with a sigh.

"Well then, I suppose you should skip school tomorrow and see what happens, yes?"

"You're becoming an old man, Hans," I tease.

He stops at the creaky wooden gate; its purpose is unknown as there are no connecting fence posts—just a lone swinging entrance into a meadow. It's only proper that we walk through it, though. Hans holds the gate open for me as usual and bows as if I'm royalty. "Fräulein," he japes.

Our moment of play is over as the wooden slab claps shut against the sunken posts and Hans claims his spot beside me as we meander down the cobblestone road.

"All this fresh air has me famished. What do you suppose you are eating for supper tonight?" I ask. The moment the question slips from my mouth, I wish I could take it back. "I shouldn't have—"

"Tilly, stop worrying so much about me. I'm fine. I'm sure we're having sauerbraten and potato dumplings just like you."

My stomach groans at the thought, but then aches with realization. I already know he will likely be eating cabbage soup and stale bread. "I'll bring you some of mine. No one has to know."

Hans clenches his hands behind his head, stretching his torso. "Not tonight. I heard your papa shouting this morning. I don't think it would be wise to test him."

I often try to forget that there are no secrets between us, but at the same time I'm used to knowing most of what happens when we aren't around one another. The floor of our flat is the ceiling of his and has been since we were small children. The walls are thin, and I know from experience, a tiptoe across our wooden floors sounds like a herd of elephants crossing a bridge.

"Perhaps he'll be in a better mood after work," I offer, knowing it won't be the case. Papa is angry almost all the time now that the factory assembly line has been cut in half. He's doing twice as much work and receiving the same pay, but I wouldn't dare say this out loud, knowing Hans's papa was one of the workers forced to leave his job. Jews are no longer allowed in the automobile factory or any public workplace that hasn't been designed for Jewish-only labor. Papa's irritability makes me want to tell him how much worse it could be for him, but, shamefully, he knows this and continues to take his frustration out on Mama and me.

"It's possible," Hans says, but his words are just to fill the silence.

No one is ever happy lately. The world feels like it's caving in and it's hard to know if we're safe or will go down with it.

"You should write some more tonight; disappear into another place just for a little while."

Hans doesn't respond as we approach the front door to our building. I follow him up the stairs, reaching the door to his home first. His parents are engaged in a conversation loud enough to hear clearly in the hallway, forcing Hans to toss his head back with a groan of aggravation. "Not again."

"We won't be able to stay here, Sarah. Don't you understand? We can't go on pretending like this will all go away. It's becoming worse and we're running out of marks. We'll be left with nothing soon, and how shall we feed the children?"

"What are you suggesting, Adam? We give up our home to those Nazis?"

"This isn't what I want, Sarah. I'm afraid we're going to have no choice soon."

"No," I shout as if Hans is engaged in the conversation between his parents on the other side of the door. "You can't leave. We've been neighbors most of our lives. I can't imagine being in this building without you."

Hans is pale, his eyes downcast, and his lips parted. "I don't want to leave."

"I'll think of a plan. I will," I say.

Hans won't look me in the eyes, so I drop my hands onto his shoulders, forcing him to give me his attention. His hazel eyes lift from his staring at the creaking wood beneath our feet. There is a look of defeat, fear, hopelessness, and other feelings I'm not sure I can comprehend.

"It's only a matter of time, Tilly. We're at war. There's no saying what will happen to either of us. Plus, Hitler, the Nazis, they don't want us Jews here. It's obvious."

"Well, it's not fair. It's not, and I won't stand for this type of injustice. I'll come up with a plan. You'll see. I will."

Our gazes lock in a frozen moment in time as an ache surges through my chest. I don't know if I'm making promises I can't keep, but I won't stop trying until I have run out of options.

"You're my very best friend in this entire universe. Distance can't take that away from us, Tilly. You know this."

Now my gaze is the one to fall. Hans has already been removed from our school and sent to a Jewish-only one. Their family has had to give up all of their gold and silver, and this is on top of his papa being released from his job. They're basically starving and about to lose their home. It's all because of their faith, and I don't understand why. I have asked so many questions in school and to Mama and Papa, but no one seems to know the answers to the whys.

"I won't let you down," I tell him.

The front door to his flat opens and his papa is standing before us with a look of shock written along his lips. "What are you doing, son? Have you been out here listening to my conversation with your mama?"

"No, Father," Hans says, his voice meek and soft.

"Fräulein Ellman, why don't you see yourself home? Tell your parents I say hello, please."

"Yes, Herr Bauer," I respond.

"Go on, now."

There were times I would spend high holidays and every Shabbat with Hans's family on Friday nights. I enjoyed the stories, and the prayers over the candles, wine, and challah. Friday nights were a time of happiness despite all the troubles anyone had gone through during the week. I felt honored to be included in their weekly ritual and blessings. It was beautiful, but I haven't been invited over in some time now. There are some Friday evenings when I recite the prayers to myself in the hope of erasing all negative feelings from the week. It always works, but it's a happier time when I'm with Hans and his family.

Mama and Papa don't practice Christianity like other families. We celebrate major holidays, but I don't recall the last time we went to church. Maybe if we made more time for prayer, Papa wouldn't always be so angry.

The one flight of stairs up to our flat feels as though I'm hiking the steepest of mountains. I don't want to go home. I don't want to listen to the arguments at supper, and the gossip of what's to come in our region. I'm scared and I have no right to say so.

I'm quiet when I slip in through the door, removing my coat with as little noise as possible. I hang up my belongings and remove my boots.

"Matilda, where have you been since school let out? I was worried," Mama calls out from the kitchen.

I hadn't thought of a story to tell her like I normally would. My mind is too caught up with what Hans is going through. I clasp my hands in front of my waist and take a few tentative steps over to the kitchen, finding Mama preparing a feast with her favorite pale-yellow apron, lined with red and purple bunches of grapes. The pristine rolled curls fanned across the nape of her neck tell me she was out and about, shopping in the village today.

"I was reading a book in the poppy field. It was such a beautiful day, I wanted to take in all the fresh air I could."

"I see," Mama says without batting her lashes. "What book are you reading?"

"I was reading a book by..."

"Yes, go on."

"Do you need help with supper?"

"You were with Hans, weren't you?" Mama continues. The spoon in her hand is moving in furious circles around the bowl.

"Mama, why am I not allowed to spend time with Hans?"

"You know why. You don't need me to explain this to you again."

"But I do because it doesn't make any sense to me. He's my friend. I should be able to spend time with him as I please."

Mama drops the wooden spoon against the ceramic bowl. The clang forces my shoulders to tense, but I inhale slowly and try my best to relax.

"Go to your room, Matilda. I will call you for supper when it's ready." She runs a dishrag along her arm to clean the splatter of whipped potatoes from the dropped spoon.

"Jewish people are not monsters. They are not criminals or animals, and yet, their rights have been stolen, and we are standing here watching it happen as if we should turn a blind eye. I can't speak for you or Papa, but I'm ashamed of us. I am ashamed of all those who are pretending that this hate isn't growing worse. What have Hans or his parents done to you? You used to be the closest of friends with Sarah, and Papa was like a brother to Adam. Now it's as if we've been strangers our whole lives. It's terrible." I don't stand still long enough for Mama to reply to my statement.

"Matilda, come back here at once," she scolds.

I go against my good judgment and ignore her call. Instead, I climb up the steep steps to my bedroom in the attic and close the door behind me. The two of them only come up here if necessary. With the roof being a dormer over our flat, it's difficult for Papa to walk around the room while standing up straight, and Mama despises the narrow steps. To me, it's perfect and cozy. There is just enough sunlight during the day, and at night the tight space is enchanting, with candlelight flickering against the golden stripes of wallpaper covering.

I fall to my mattress and roll myself up within my wool blanket. The silence allows me to hear a faint hint of shouting from two floors below in Hans's flat.

There must be something I can do.

CHAPTER 3
MATILDA
APRIL 1940

Hours later, there was no way I could sleep. I scale down the stairs from the attic, skipping the third step down to avoid the loudest of creaks. I've memorized the loose floorboards, knowing which will alert someone that I'm up and about. The edges along the walls are the quietest and I make my way out the front door, swooshing barefoot along every inch I walk to the floor below. The flicker from my candle is all I have to illuminate the way, but I've done this so many times in the middle of the night, I could likely do so with my eyes closed. Hans's bedroom shares a wall with the hallway, just a few feet away from his front door.

I tap my finger against the wall three times, wait two seconds, and repeat three more times. It's a secret code we made up when we were in primary school. Back then, the only trouble we would find was the fire escape up to the roof above my bedroom, where we could stargaze on warm nights. Hans would tell stories of life which exist far beyond our reach, worlds unimaginable to anyone here on earth. He told me each star is a soul, watching over us, protecting us from the heavens and the unearthly worlds from us. His imagination is like a book full of the most vivid illustrations, wonders I could never dream up. I can't imagine life without hearing about the details swimming through his head each day.

A soft hint of a finger tapping against the wall informs me he's awake and knows I'm out here. I pull my robe tighter, blocking out the crisp draft breaking through the window beside me. My feet are becoming numb against the cold planks, but the rest of me is on fire, waiting to tell him each detail of the plan I've come up with.

Hans's front door slips open just enough to create only a whisper of a creak. He spins around to close the door and twists the doorknob all the way to the right, so the slow brush of the brass fixtures merely makes contact. "What are you doing here, Tilly? It's late." He's in a white T-shirt and his favorite red striped pajama bottoms.

Never before has he asked me what I was doing outside of his flat at this time of night. Life has changed too much for us to go back to the way we used to be. He seems to live in fear of the unknown and I want to act as though we're both safe and nothing can come between us.

"I need to talk to you. I have a plan."

"A plan for what?" he questions as if we didn't hear the conversation his parents were having earlier.

I take his hand and pull him down the hallway toward the fire escape. It's been so long since we've gone up on the roof, but it's the only place no one can hear us talk.

"It's freezing out, Tilly. You'll catch a cold," he says. It's always about me rather than him. If I catch a cold, he will too, but I believe this is important enough to chance the risk.

"Stop worrying so much about me. Come on, now."

With a soft sigh of frustration, Hans follows my gentle steps along the closest wooden panels along the wall. It takes just a few minutes to find the small metal door that leads to the roof. The space feels smaller than it did the last time we were here. I suppose we must have grown quite a bit in the last few years.

The April temperatures are relentless, refusing to give up rights to the winter's deep freeze. The air against my eyes burns as I stand up against the wind, wrapping my arms around my shoulders for warmth.

I had forgotten how beautiful it was out here at night. All the lights in the village blur into the darkness as if they are one with the stars.

After Hans takes in a breath of the fresh air, I twist to face him. The flame on my candle singes, leaving us with a small string of smoke, but the stars offer enough light. I place the candleholder down beside my feet. "Let's leave. We'll run away from here. If we leave Germany and go as far east as we can, we will be safe."

Hans's eyebrows furrow toward his freckled nose. "That's foolish,

Matilda. We don't have marks to sustain our travels. And if I'm caught doing anything I shouldn't be, I don't know what will happen, but if a Nazi were to catch you with me—trying to help—I don't want to think about what could happen to you."

I clutch my hands around his shoulders. "That's absurd. Nothing is going to happen to me. We are both going to be eighteen in just over a year. We're adults, and we need to do what's best."

Hans is quick to shake his head, rejecting my idea. "I don't think it matters how far east we go. There has been talk of what Hitler is accomplishing. Papa says the Nazis are seizing Czechoslovakia now."

"Then, leaving is our only option. How could you think otherwise?" I argue.

"We won't survive, and if anything happens to me and you're all alone somewhere, I can't fathom the thought of what might become of you."

I didn't intend to tighten my grip, but I shove Hans with my palms, wishing I could shake some sense into him. "You're just going to let them take everything from you?" My throat narrows around the words I'm trying to belt in a whisper.

"I don't see it that way, Tilly. They can try to take everything, but some things can't be obtained," he says, pointing to his mind. "I will have my dreams, memories, and the stories that live within my head... I will still have you."

My muscles tighten against the cold as shivers pulsate through my limbs. "This isn't fair," I utter.

Hans stares deeply into my eyes. I can see he wants to agree with me, but he refuses to give in to their fear tactics. "Life is about lessons and what we can overcome. I believe we can overcome this."

Neither of us can define the word "this." Europe has lost its free will, but I won't fall for the words of a dictator. No one can tell me who to love or hate.

"I don't want you to leave," I tell Hans.

"Nor do I." He wraps his arms around me, pulling me in against his chest. I recall the time when we used to be the same height, but over the last few years, he has grown so tall. Now I fit beneath his chin. "It will be okay if we believe it will be okay. Imagine a good ending to the troubling times and you'll see, we'll get to that page in the story."

I tighten my arms around his torso, breathing in the fresh air and soap from his T-shirt. "We'll always be best friends, yes?" I ask for reassurance, and the proof of his loyalty, something I've never needed from him before.

Hans takes a step back, away from our embrace, and I search his expression. He's staring down at me in a way he hasn't before. It's as if there is pain mixed with love, a pull against forces. "I'm not sure I can always just be best friends with you, Tilly. I love you in a way that means more than friendship. When I see you, there is a warmth that roots from the bottom of my chest and fires through every nerve of my body. I don't want to be around you all the time—I *need* to be."

I clutch my chest, trying to calm my racing heart. He may not be able to see the speed of my pulse or the heat blooming through my cheeks, but it's overwhelming. I've never needed reassurance of our connection, but when he speaks of it—the way he speaks of us—it sends a spark of joy through every part of me.

Unspoken words are unusual between the two of us, but his feelings match mine—ones we haven't shared out loud. I have feared losing his friendship, and maybe it has been the same for him, but if time is running out, and if we can't control what comes next, we should say everything there is to say while there is still time.

"Why do you think I want to run away with you?" I respond.

"The same reason I want to keep you safe here."

He leans down, and for the first time outside of the dreams I keep to myself, his lips touch mine. We're both colder than the night's sky and our mouths are like ice, but the warmth we share is enough to keep us safe from the coldest days or nights. My heart is beating so fiercely, I can feel it pounding against his chest. His hands loosen around my arms and skate up to my cheeks. The soft touch of his fingers weakens my knees, but I don't want the moment to end. I don't want to let go.

When our lips part, he doesn't pull away. "That's how much I love you, Tilly."

For the first time in our lifelong friendship, I'm at a loss for words. This moment will be the crux of heartache if the worst is yet to come.

"Let's get back inside before someone notices we're gone," he says. Hans is always the one to rein us in and make sure we don't land ourselves in trouble.

I don't agree, but I follow just the same. I don't want to look for more trouble with anger already potent between Mama and Papa. I imagine he's thinking the same, but for different reasons.

When we descend the steps of the fire exit, Hans holds up a finger to his lips, a warning that we shouldn't speak. He leans down and presses a soft kiss to my cheek. "I'll see you tomorrow," he whispers.

"Goodnight," I reply, reeling from the rush of static buzzing through my cheeks.

I've never been a writer, but the moment I close myself back into my bedroom, I'm filled with an urge to write down every detail of what took place on the roof as if I'll need the words to remind me of the way I feel at this precise moment. I'm not sure my description could do justice to the beauty and prose of Hans, but I must never forget this—not one detail.

CHAPTER 4
GRACE
2018

I've been sitting on the edge of my bed, biting my nails since four in the morning. Spontaneous decisions are not in my repertoire, but after everything I have read and seen since last night, I'm not sure I'll be able to sleep until I have answers to the hundreds of questions I have. The amount of uncertainty is causing more anxiety than I've felt in years. I proactively try to control each aspect of my life to ensure I know what tomorrow brings, but I didn't see this coming.

My phone buzzes in my lap, illuminating the airline ticket I purchased three hours ago. I've written an email to Paul, informing him that something has come up and I'll need to take some personal time and a leave of absence this week. The decision was easier to make knowing how unlikely my promotion is.

I'm not sure how well I'm processing plans in the dark hours of the morning, but all signs are pointing to me leaving for Europe to handle the exchange of title for the inheritance of the property.

The papers I have translated into English from German read like a novel or a personal diary, have only furthered my curiosity about Matilda Ellman, my grandmother. From what I've seen so far, Matilda seems so all-knowing and determined, especially during a devastating time in history. I can't imagine what might have happened between these first pages and the moment in time she and Mom were separated.

I press the power button on my phone, checking the time again. I've been waiting until a decent hour before calling Carla to let her know I'm leaving. I'm prepared for a lecture when I do speak to her, but that's what best friends do—make us see through the haze fogging our minds. Of course, it's too late to see anything more than Germany on the horizon at the moment.

At seven o'clock on the dot, I click Carla's contact in my phone and hit the speaker button as I stand up to pack my bags.

"Why are you calling? What's wrong?" she answers. Usually we either send text messages or barge into each other's apartments. We've been the closest of friends since our freshman year at Boston College. It was the two of us against the world and we were inseparable. During our junior and senior years, we moved off campus into a tiny apartment and thought we might just stay there forever, but after graduation and a couple of long-term relationships Carla went through, we knew we needed our own spaces. As rare as it is to find two vacant apartment units, side-by-side, we did, and it's the perfect arrangement.

I could bang on the wall if I needed her attention badly enough. If I told her what I'm doing face to face, she would raise her eyebrow and give me the motherly glare I'll be able to sense through the phone. I can answer her questions with honesty, but without further explanation, she would think I've lost my mind.

"I'm going to Germany today and I just wanted to let you know before I left. Also, can you grab my mail while I'm gone?"

Carla is racing around her apartment, getting ready to head off to her father's booming accounting firm downtown in the financial district. She is determined to work her way up the corporate ladder without any special privileges, and lives in the hope of becoming a co-owner someday. I can hear her heels against the floor, matching her quick breaths over the phone. "I'm sorry, I thought I just heard you say you were going to Germany today. Can you repeat that?" Drawers are opening and closing, and by the echoes of her words, I assume she's in her bathroom.

"I'm going to Germany. I... uh, I've inherited some property over there, and I need to go claim the title and figure out what to do with the property. It should only take a few days, I'm sure."

The heels clacking against the floor stop and her breaths slow. "Grace, meet me in the hallway, now," she says.

With a fleeting glance down at my torn cotton shorts and an ex-boyfriend's T-shirt I've had for fifteen years, I touch the top of my head, confirming the bird's nest left behind from my restless sleep. Carla has seen me at my worst, especially during the months following Mom's death a few years ago.

I drag my feet toward the front door of my studio and step into the hallway, waiting for her door to open. She's half ready for work. One side of her toffee-brown hair is smooth and curled into barrel waves, and the other is wet, but she is dressed and has a primer layer of makeup on.

"I know this is out of nowhere," I tell her.

"Well, yes, we can start there," she says, folding her arms over her chest. It's the first sign of her questioning my sanity.

"My biological grandmother somehow found me and has left me a piece of property. I received a DNA report I can't ignore. My mother spent her life trying to find her parents. I need to know if this is true. If so, I have to know the rest."

Carla closes her eyes for a moment, as if taking in each word again to truly comprehend what I'm saying. "This just happened last night?"

We spoke at lunch yesterday, and everything was as normal as an exhausting Monday should be. "Yes."

"And you're leaving today?"

"Yes," I answer again.

"Who sent this letter or whatever it is?"

"A law office in Germany."

"Maybe you should call them to find out more information before you fly to another country, alone, with no knowledge of the German language. I bet you don't even know what currency they use there, do you?"

I was waiting for each of these questions. I've had plenty of time to think everything through while sitting awake most of the night.

"I called the law office. It's already one in the afternoon there. They said all the information they could legally share was in the envelope and that someone hired them to handle the paperwork of the inheritance and nothing more. I have a translator on my phone, I've upgraded to an international calling plan, and they use euros in Germany, which I can exchange for cash at the airport."

Carla appears taken aback by the amount of research I've accomplished in such a short space of time. "But do you know anyone there? Is it a safe area?"

My gaze falls to the ground, the fresh powder-pink pedicure on my toes shimmering beneath the canned lighting. "I don't know anyone there, but it's an old village surrounding a concentration camp. I realize that's a whole other topic of conversation, but it's a tourist area because of this fact."

"Oh my God, Grace! The property is near a concentration camp?" One of Carla's arms falls by her side, seeming dumbfounded by everything I'm telling her.

"Yes, and I need to know why," I explain.

"If you wait until the weekend, I can go with you. I don't think you should go alone."

"I can't wait, and while I appreciate you offering to do something so drastic with me on a whim, I need to do this on my own, for my mom."

Her eyes are wide, filled with concern and shock. "You don't like shopping by yourself, never mind going all the way to Germany. I don't understand where this is all coming from."

My cheeks heat and tingle, and I palm them to ease the incessant nerves. "My heart is telling me to go."

"What about work? The promotion?" She's trying every angle, but I've already been down each road.

"The promotion isn't happening, and I need to put myself first for a change."

I've had my career on the front burner for so long, I've given up on even considering what else I want in life. Nothing has crossed my path to make me stop and consider the direction I've been traveling, but this—it's a gamechanger for me.

Carla takes in a heavy breath and blows a fallen strand of hair out of her eye. "You need to check in with me. I need to know you're safe and everything is okay while you're there. You're just going for a few days?"

"I'm not sure how long everything will take, but I assume no longer than a week. I'll let you know when I find out more."

Carla looks me straight in the eyes. "This isn't sitting well with me, Grace. Maybe I should be trying harder to change your mind, but I can see you're not budging on this. Still, I wish you'd let me come with you, but I understand. I'll grab your mail. Does your dad know you're leaving?"

My head cocks to the side. "Like he would care?"

"Just asking," she says. "When's the flight?"

"Eleven this morning."

"When will you arrive in Germany?" she continues.

"It'll be around six at night here, so I can text you when I land."

"Yes, please, and I want to know where you're staying, the town, and all that too."

"Okay."

Carla takes the few steps between us and wraps her arms around my neck, her wet hair falling in my face. "I don't want anything to happen to you. Please be careful."

"I promise," I say, looping my arms around her in return, while wondering momentarily if it's better to wait until she can come with me—but my heart is telling me to go now. I hand her the mail key. "Thank you for caring about me so much."

"Always besties," she coos, clasping her fingers around the keys before walking back through her open door. "Don't forget to text me. I'll come after you, Grace Laurent."

"I know you will," I reply with a soft laugh.

By the time I've gone through security, customs, and waited an hour at the international gate, I realize how much I accomplished before noon today. I'm mostly surprised I was lucky enough to snag a reasonably priced flight and secure a hotel reservation with little effort. It feels like I have lived three days in less than twelve hours. The only stress weighing on my shoulders is the lack of response from Paul. At this point, I've called, left a voicemail, and emailed him again. I should have expected he'd drag this out, knowing it would make me nervous. I've checked my email a dozen times since I arrived at the airport to see if he's responded to my unexpected leave of absence.

As if somehow timed with the flight attendant asking everyone to power down their devices, Paul's email arrives in my inbox.

Grace,

I must say, it's a shame about whatever you are going through and that is causing you to use a leave of absence. I'm aware this is unlike you, and I certainly hope our conversation yesterday afternoon isn't playing a part in your decision. Of course, we all have unexpected situations occur in life and reasons for unplanned days off. It would have been preferable to have a discussion first since there are a few incoming projects I have you scheduled to begin on, but I will spend some time tonight reworking the project plans to accommodate your absence. Perhaps one of the new applicants might like a trial project to test the waters here. There's never a bad time to prove yourself, right?

As soon as you have your situation under control, please let me know right away so I can plan our project schedules appropriately.

Lastly, I checked with Shelly from human resources, and it appears you only have four days of paid time off left for this year. As a reminder from the employee handbook: *Additional days cannot be borrowed from a future fiscal year*. Therefore, you would be docked the compensation from your paycheck.

Take care,

Paul

I should have known he'd be a professional jerk in his response. For all he knows, there has been a death in my family, but he would never care about anything that's not about him or the firm. His slick comment of offering my work to an applicant was just another ploy in his mind games. Applicants rarely agree to trial runs, especially if they have years of experience under their belt. Paul plays like a child and manages his firm like a boy with too much power in his hands.

"Miss, I need you to turn your device off now, please," the flight attendant reminds me.

I do as she asks. "I'm so sorry. Those last-minute emails always come in at the worst times, right?"

With all electronics put away, I remove the translated papers from my carry-on bag and rest them on my lap, ready to continue reading.

CHAPTER 5
MATILDA
MAY 1940

The hazy rays of the morning sun have had less than a few minutes to spill over the horizon, and there is already a commotion outside the building. There seems to be more disruptions than silence these last few months, but it's hard to say what's causing the tension in each situation. Everyone seems angry with one another. Hate is like a viral disease, sparing almost no one a chance to live as they were raised—with love for one another.

I shove the heels of my palms against my closed eyelids, rubbing away the few hours of sleep I stole. The shouting outside is growing louder by the second, and I toss the blankets to the side and race to the window. The severity of varying temperatures over the years has caused the seal on my window to decay, which leaves me with a layer of dew on the inside of the glass I wipe away each morning. The blur dries slowly, revealing the scene several stories below.

To my surprise, I spot Hans staring up toward my window. He's wearing his long black overcoat, a white button-down shirt, vest, slacks, and his favorite shoes and flat cap. It can't be that cold out that he would need to be wearing so much all at once. I also notice he has a tight grip on the suitcase dangling from his left hand. His mother is shouting at his father as he places his bag in the wooden bed of a truck I've never seen before. The nightmare of a scene makes my heart sink to what feels like a bottomless cavern within my body.

It takes a moment to come to terms with what's happening: they're leaving.

As quickly as I can find my slippers and robe, I bundle myself up and trail down the narrow steps toward my front door, then again down three more flights before I shove open the heavy door to the building's entrance.

"Where are you going?" I shout. "Hans?"

He turns to face my direction and places his hand on his heart, shaking his head. His vibrant dark-golden eyes fill with tears, an unusual sight as I've never seen Hans shed even one tear. He's scared. I can see that much.

"Matilda," a small voice calls out.

Danya, the tiny female version of Hans. She's not yet six, but wise beyond her years. Her parents haven't let her outside to play in so long, I feel like she's grown so tall since I've seen her last and we live just a floor away from one another. She runs toward me, disobeying her parents' orders to stop at once.

"Danya, it's okay," I tell her. A lie. A blatant lie. There is nothing about this moment that is okay.

She wraps her small arms around my waist. "Matilda, we must leave. Papa said we have to stay with an aunt in Krumbach. It's where many other Jewish people are gathering," she cries out. "I don't want to leave."

Chills seep through every pore of exposed skin. They're leaving Augsburg, our home—the only place we've ever known. There's nothing I can say to make this better for her or any of them. "Why must you leave so quickly?" I ask softly, hoping her parents don't hear. I act as though I'm pulling her arms away from my body, but I'm stalling to give her a chance to answer.

"I don't know. He won't tell us. I think it's because he doesn't want Jewish people to live in this building anymore," Danya utters beneath her breath.

"He—your papa?"

Her chestnut eyes widen as if she's staring at the face of a ghost. "No," she says, turning her head, peeking over her shoulder with a sense of unease. "Herr Franco." Danya points toward the landlord of the building, who is collecting marks from two soldiers. With her hand cupped around the side of her mouth, she whispers, "Herr Franco said Jews don't belong here anymore. That's why we must leave."

"I'm sure you'll be quite comfortable here. It's a pleasant community," the landlord tells the soldiers.

"Yes, it looks like it will do for now," one of the soldiers says.

The men are in field-gray uniforms pressed without a flaw. Their matching caps are slightly tilted to the side, and of course, the blood-red bands around their left arm have a white swastika emblem. I've silently referred to the insignia as the kiss of death. They stand straight as arrows, as if they are watchdogs; their eyes darting around while the rest of their faces remain perfectly still. It's like they are waiting for someone to make a wrong move.

My gaze drifts to Hans.

"I'm sorry," he mouths.

No. No, no, no, they can't make him leave—*them*.

The soldiers are staring at me. Their icy glares make my skin feel colder and hot at the same time.

"Hans, Danya, let's go," Herr Bauer demands.

They don't have all their things. Surely it won't all fit in the vehicle. I'm not sure what they have left after selling so many of their belongings, but there must be more left behind. They'll have to come back for it, I tell myself.

I want to hug my best friend goodbye, maybe earn a whisper of where he's going.

"Now," his papa says.

"Is there anything I can do?" I call out.

"Matilda, go back inside to your parents right away," Frau Bauer says. "Please, darling."

Frau Bauer—Hans's mama—has been like a second mother to me. When we were younger, she would always have vanilla Danish cookies with a thin layer of butter frosting waiting for us after what she would call "a long day." School as a young girl would feel like a never-ending day, but now, I would happily trade a few tiring hours in a classroom for whatever this life is we are living. She would often bandage up my scraped knees since Hans and I would somehow end up with matching wounds from horseplay on the cobblestone. She was gentle, kind, and as loving to me as she was to Hans and Danya when she came along.

Mama used to be similar but made it known to me she was not cut out to be a mother, not like Frau Bauer. Mama is colder and showing love has always been something she has had to work hard at. Her parents didn't treat her well, from what she has told me, but they died before I was born, so I know little of Mama's life as a young girl.

Herr Bauer takes Hans's arm and pulls him toward the truck. "Let's go, son."

"Can't I say goodbye?" I shout, immediately cupping my hands over my mouth with regret. The Nazis will not tolerate pushback from any civilian, no matter their heritage or race. They are like heartless machines, programmed to do a job and to remove anything in their way.

The gravel being displaced beneath their shoes sounds like an animal gnawing on small bones. The look in their eyes is enough of a warning to remove myself from their sights, but it won't stop me from finding out where in Krumbach they are going. I must know.

I race up the stairs, returning to my flat, exchanging my slippers for boots.

"Matilda, is that you?" Papa calls out from their bedroom.

Concern doesn't pass through my mind as I ignore his question and depart the flat as quickly as I returned, making sure I won't miss my opportunity to follow the vehicle.

My bicycle is leaning up against the side of the building. It used to be next to Hans's before he had to give up his beloved bicycle thanks to the laws preventing any Jewish person from owning one. I've noticed the number of bicycles that used to take up space here against the edifice have decreased by at least half.

The truck has left tire marks in the gravel road, but the cobblestone isn't far, and I won't be able to follow a trail once they reach it. With difficulty, I try my best to keep up, thankfully spotting the truck after a long minute of pedaling harder than I've ever had to before.

Though it has only been two hours or so since I've left Augsburg, it feels more like three before the truck comes to a stop, unloading the family with their belongings. I don't have a clue where we are, but I must remember how to find my way here when I return home.

A building stands between the truck and the corner on which I'm standing. I spot guards leading more sets of families who are lugging their suitcases and small belongings down the block too, but I can't see past the next corner. I run along the back of the building to the other side, hoping to see more of where we are, but what I see is worse than what I was fearfully expecting. Decaying brick buildings with broken glass windows in street-facing shops. People, all of whom appear displaced or homeless, are sitting in the street, leaning against the walls. Most appear haggard and worn, despondent and weak. Soldiers circulate the streets as if monitoring for a type of misbehavior I can't imagine with the frail appearance of every person in the surrounding area.

The farther I look, the more deterioration I notice. The Nazis obviously attacked this town hard during *Kristallnacht*. It's been about eight months since they destroyed all the Jewish businesses, homes, and synagogues throughout our country. Wherever the greatest Jewish population exists is where the most destruction remains. It seems no one has cleaned up or repaired a thing. To know this unfathomable sight was a punishment for one young Jewish man fighting against the hatred of his heritage leads me to wonder what will come next.

It's clear now—all Jewish people are paying a daily consequence now. Rumblings of what happened that night came in a wave of various stories. The information on the details was scarce, but it's clear the Nazis caused the damage, and are now holding the Jewish people responsible as well as forcing them to live in the aftermath. In my wildest nightmares, I couldn't expect anything to look so broken.

I spot Hans and his family stepping in through a doorway, each one of them looking around as if they are trying to digest what's happening to their lives. My feet carry me back to my bicycle quickly and I return down the same road I arrived, spotting signs so I will remember my way back.

CHAPTER 6
MATILDA
MAY 1940

Mama is sitting at the dining table when I walk through the front door. "You're in your pajamas, Matilda," she says, glancing down at her watch.

"Yes, Mama."

"Where on earth have you been? It's Sunday morning and you know we have breakfast as a family."

I could lie or I could tell the truth. Neither will offer a resolution to the problem at hand. "I was out, riding my bicycle. I needed some fresh air."

"At six in the morning?" she counters.

I hug my arms around my chest, feeling the remnants of the chilly wind burning my cheeks. "Herr Franco kicked them out of their home. Herr Bauer had to pay a man to take them to a village in Krumbach where each glass window of every building is in pieces. Manure lines the streets. There are no doors leading in and out of buildings or storefronts. People are napping in crevices of walls. They are all Jews, Mama."

Mama looks down at her intertwined fingers. She fidgets with her golden wedding band, spinning it in circles. "The Bauers are strong, Matilda. They will be fine, yes?"

She won't look up at me because she knows the truth. No one would be all right living in those conditions.

"I want to help them," I assert. I pull the wooden chair out from beside Mama and take a seat to face her. "How can you so quickly forget about the afternoons you spent enjoying Frau Bauer's company while sipping on tea? The two of you would be in a fit of laughter for hours almost daily. Papa and Herr Bauer traveled to and from work together every day. They went fishing once a month on Sundays. You sat by Frau Bauer's bedside for nearly six months during her pregnancy with Danya because the doctors advised her to stay put. Have you forgotten all these memories, or are you simply acting as if they never happened?"

I lean forward, forcing Mama to look at me when she responds. A mother should find difficulty staring into her daughter's face and telling fibs.

"I haven't forgotten, Matilda. What are we to do? Shall we ignore the policies set in place? Stand up to Hitler and tell him to stop what he's doing? It isn't possible. We are to abide or be seen as those who help Jews. The Nazis will stop at nothing to accomplish their goals, and if we stand in their way, we will end up living beside the Bauers. Is that what you want?"

Mama should not ask me a foolish question, knowing what I will respond with. "How can you sit back and watch this happen? What kind of woman are you?" My words are harsh with intent, but there is a frozen stare in the place of her warmth. It's been so long since she's shown compassion for others, I'm not sure she's capable anymore.

"You are not to speak to your mama in this way, do you understand, young lady?" Papa steps out of their bedroom as if he had been listening to us this whole time and was waiting to say his piece.

"In what way, Papa?" I raise a brow, testing the waters as I've never done before. As I near adulthood, my fear of Papa has lessened. I no longer feel like I must abide by his every order.

"You are not to follow or go near Hans. Do you understand me?"

I twist in my seat and loop a fallen strand of hair behind my ear. My head shakes on its own, disagreeing with his rules. Instinct is stronger than obedience, I suppose.

"Thou shalt not bear false witness against thy neighbor," I say.

The Ten Commandments are ingrained into our society and education, so I don't understand how something we have all been taught to practice can be so blatantly disregarded at the say-so of another.

It's clear by the scowl tugging at his hair-lined top lip and deepening lines on Papa's forehead that he does not appreciate my tone or proper usage of rules we should all abide by, but I will not take back what is the truth.

"Matilda Ellman, how dare you speak to your papa in that way?" Mama snaps. "If you are so keen on your knowledge of the Commandments, then you should know that honoring thy mother and father comes first on that list, doesn't it?"

I stand from the chair in one swift motion. "I see. So as long as I honor you and Papa, I may commit murder because it is less important than respect, yes?"

"Go to your room, Matilda. At once. And don't come out until you have considered the consequences of your actions and words. I will not tolerate this form of disregard, so help me God," Papa snaps, his voice echoing between the walls.

"If I'm so out of line, why are the two of you pale? Your eyes are stained red, as are Mama's. You both look ill, and it isn't because of a sickness, it's because you know that what I have said is true. I'm just the one who is brave enough to speak my thoughts out loud."

Rather than wait for another back-and-forth exchange, I make my way up to my bedroom and close myself inside. Hans has always said when we're alone, left with nothing but our thoughts, it's best to write everything we're feeling down. It helps us grow as people; learn from our mistakes and challenges. He said the thoughts he's had over the years will make for a great story someday, and he's right. His written words are the sole reason I can say without a doubt, I know every part of Hans, inside and out. He bleeds ink onto paper. That's what he tells me.

I drop to my knees next to my bed and pull out a box full of paper with my half-filled bottle of ink and a pen. The least I can do is listen to the advice Hans has given me. I will write out every thought, feeling, hope, and dream. If it's all we have left, I can't let it go.

I've sat on the edge of my bed for hours, filling page after page easier than I ever thought I could. I've watched the sun round the sky, moving toward the end of another day. The moon and stars take over and I wonder what Hans is doing, if he's watching the same scene— the only piece of beauty left in the world, or so it seems. I wonder if he still has faith that all the stars are souls watching over us and offering protection. I hope now, more than ever, he's right.

I didn't know I had so many thoughts lingering in my heavy mind, but I've filled up the front and back of ten pieces of paper. Whenever I see Hans next, I can give him what he has always given me—a doorway to my mind.

It's late when I tuck the papers beneath my mattress and place the pen and bottle of ink down on my nightstand. Sleep doesn't seem like a possibility, especially with a pit of hunger in my stomach and nerves filling the hollow space. I refuse to go downstairs and share a meal with Mama and Papa after everything they said—and failed to say—earlier. I'd rather starve.

I hope Hans isn't starving.

Hours seem to pass, and I feel just as awake as I would in the middle of the day. Ideas are running through my head about what I can do to help. I should collect food, whatever I can conceal in a bag and hide from the guards and take it to him. I'm not sure I can get close enough to even find him in the village, but I'll do everything in my power to try.

Just as the paint lines on my ceiling sway, and my eyelids become heavy, a faint scratching noise causes the lines to stop moving, and my eyes reopen as if I touched a spark. The only noise I ever hear is a faint movement from the floor below, and I heard Mama and Papa go to bed hours ago. Maybe my mind is playing tricks on me.

I try to close my eyes once again, but the scratches grow louder and I'm sure it's not my imagination. In fact, whatever is the source of the noise must be quite close for it to be as clear as it is. I throw the blankets off and sit up, waiting to hear the sound again. The hairs on the back of my neck rise this time as I realize the scratches are coming from behind me, where there is a small space between the wall and the unfinished wooden panels beneath the rooftop. I rarely poke around in the dark, uninviting, muggy confinement.

I push my bed to the side, finding the small door that blends in with the wall panels, realizing little seems to scare me now. Whatever the noise is coming from can't be as bad as witnessing a Nazi holding a weapon. I kneel in front of an old stack of books that have been collecting dust for years. I figured old schoolbooks had no better purpose than to block an attic door. As I slide them beneath the bed frame, a cloud of dust floats through the air. I pull my shirt over my nose to prevent a sneeze.

The knob is beneath a layer of dust too, and I brush it away with my hand before tugging to see if it will give easily. The wooden board seems flimsy but stuck. I run my fingers along the edges, finding it to be crooked on the left side where the hinges must be hiding. I lift the knob to ease the panel upright, straightening it to slide out from the wall. To my surprise, it works, but the darkness within the opening is nearly opaque. I cannot make out a thing.

I tiptoe across my room for my small lantern and light the candle within the glass panes. The closer I come to the opening in the wall, the more I can see by the glow of the lantern. It's nothing more than unfinished wood on four sides. I suppose I could have used this for space over the years, but I have little to store. I crawl inside, still in search of the scratching noise. It takes a moment of looking around the small space, but I finally spot a field mouse gnawing on a spare piece of lumber left behind.

"How can something so small make so much noise? Keep it down," I say, realizing I'm speaking to a mouse of all things. Although I suppose he's smart enough to find a safe place to hide, and I've certainly had conversations with worse beings.

The moment I get back in bed and replace the blankets over my body, an idea fires through me—and for the first time today, I feel a sense of hope.

CHAPTER 7
GRACE

2018

I thought I would panic over my rash decision at some point in the last several hours of the flight, but even as I depart the gate into the glass maze of Munich's airport, I still feel I've made the right choice.

It's as though I've stepped into another world. I've only traveled abroad one other time when I was in college. It was a quick trip to London with a few friends, but the signs and directions were in English, and I never felt too out of place. I know this will be quite a bit different. Just by the signs, I realize how distinct German is from English. There is nothing decipherable about any of the words.

I follow the crowd, hoping to see a hint of the baggage claim area, but the airport is much larger than I thought.

With my phone held out in front of me like a map, I scream the part of a tourist.

Sweet and savory scents fill the air; a combination of flowers and foods I'm unfamiliar with. Everything seems to blend into an aroma that offers comfort. Many of the other passengers appear to be traveling for business, dressed in suits, phones against their ears, and have a sense of direction.

My phone isn't translating much of what I see, but the farther I walk, the more open space unfurls before me, offering a view of everything, including the blue sky beyond the glass ceiling panels, wall-to-wall shops, and a dozen more signs—one of which has a baggage icon pointing toward the descending escalator.

"Fräulein, möchten sie unser neues parfüm ausprobieren?"

I glance at the person asking, feeling lost and clueless. The man is standing outside a fluorescent-lit boutique filled with expensive-looking perfumes and colognes. He's holding a bottle out to me.

"Nein, Danke."

The man nods his head and takes a step backward. At least I learnt a few words on the flight over. Yes, no, please, and thank you are at the top of the list. I've lost everything else I tried to cram into my head as the feeling of jet lag takes over.

I'm grateful to spot the baggage claim area before stepping onto the escalator. It feels like a minor accomplishment, which is unnerving seeing as I still need to find my way to Dachau.

While staring at the still conveyor belt, not yet prepared with luggage, a moment of disdain cloaks me like a dark shadow as I recall how many hours Mom spent at the computer searching for her missing family. Yet, the information fell into my lap three years after she passed away. It isn't fair that she never got the answers she was looking for. Matilda, who is supposedly her mother, doesn't strike me as the type to give up on a child. All I've learned from the written pages so far is how much she tried to help others. Even after everything I've read over the last twenty-four hours, I'm still just as confused as I was when I opened the envelope—all these pieces of information don't seem to connect.

Maybe Mom would have no trouble placing this puzzle together. I can still vividly recall how many times she skated by the fact that she was attempting the impossible, yet it never stopped her from trying. "There are over seven billion people in the world. The odds of finding any part of my family tree are as likely as being struck by lightning twice," Mom had said one evening as she clicked the mouse over every name she stumbled across. She had grown so desperate, she was trying facial-recognition software to see if anyone who could be old enough to be her parent would miraculously show up. Even if she found someone who looked exactly like she did, it could have been a coincidence. She knew this, but it gave her satisfaction to know she wasn't giving up.

After waiting weeks for the results of a new type of DNA test she had sent a sample in for, all we received were more dead ends. From what we were told, a lack of matches meant there wasn't enough data available yet, but our reports would stay on file in case one ever turned up.

"It's late, Mom. You should get some sleep," I told her.

"Oh, Grace, who is the mother here? I'll have plenty of time to sleep after I die, so let me be." Mom talked about dying as if it was the next chapter of her story rather than the end of life. It was hard to listen to, but I could see she was struggling with the thought of running out of time. Her lung cancer prognosis was poor from the start, and we had little hope of her surviving more than a year. Rather than fight it, she accepted what would be and spent her time trying to find the answer to her one outstanding question.

The buzzer on the moving belt startles me out of my hazy thoughts and the crowd tightens around me, every familiar passenger aboard my flight waiting on their luggage.

The second I spot my bags, my phone buzzes in my back pocket. I can only imagine it's Carla because I haven't sent her a text yet to tell her my plane didn't go down. While keeping my eyes on the bags swirling around the belt's loops, I pick up the call. "Hi, I'm just at baggage claim," I tell her, sounding out of breath even though I've been standing still for the last ten minutes.

"You said you would let me know when you arrived, dummy," she replies.

"I arrived," I say, forcing more enthusiasm than my exhaustion is allowing me to feel.

"Okay, don't talk to strangers. Don't make eye contact with anyone trying to sell anything and check your bags to make sure nothing is missing. Oh, and what are you wearing?"

"Why does that matter?" I ask, looking down at my torn jeans and an old Boston College hooded sweatshirt.

"Please don't tell me you're in those jeans that look like you were in a dogfight and the ratty hoodie from school?"

I don't know if it's scary or sweet how well she knows me, but I'll go with endearing. "I wanted to be comfortable traveling today. There's no cause for alarm."

"Except for the fact that your outfit is the antithesis of Euro chic, and you'll stand out like—well, like—"

I press my fingers against my forehead, imagining the look on my best friend's face as she talks in circles. "An American tourist?" I ask, matter-of-factly.

"Yes, you shouldn't draw attention to yourself when you're alone in another country," she says, lecturing me as if I missed my curfew on a school night.

"Carla, I'm fine, and I'm not here to impress anyone. Don't worry, I'll let you know when I get to the hotel, okay?"

"How are you getting there?" she continues.

I lunge for the first of my two bags, struggling to get it over the short metal barrier. "A bus," I grumble before dropping my suitcase down beside me, preparing to reach for the next bag. "Hold on." As I whip my oversized duffel bag from the belt, I accidentally hit the woman standing next to me. I drop my bag to my feet and press my hand to my temple, desperately trying to recall how to apologize in German. "Es... uh—tut—uns l ... le-i-d." I sound ridiculous.

"I'm sorry, what was that?" the woman responds in English, with a Boston accent to match mine.

"She's American, Grace. I assume she was on your flight," Carla whispers through the phone that I have almost forgotten I'm holding. "But way to go on learning German so quickly. I'm impressed."

"Carla, I'll call you back once I find my hotel. I'm fine, I'm safe, and I won't look at anyone, okay?"

"Don't forget, Grace, or I will hunt you down," she warns.

"I'm so sorry," I reply in English to the woman as I end the call. "I didn't mean to hit you with my bag."

"Oh, don't worry about it. Safe travels, girl," she says with a sympathetic smile. It's like she knows I'm doomed as much as Carla does.

I slip my phone back in my pocket and grab my bags, spotting a sign with a bus icon. Thank goodness for the universal language of stick figure cartoons.

After ninety minutes, two buses, and walking down four wrong side streets in Dachau, I find my hotel. It's dark, and it looks different to the pictures, but the area seems nice and there's a café across the street, which I'm sure I'll be grateful for tomorrow.

"Die Begrüßung," the gentleman at the front desk greets me. At least, I think he's greeting me. He's looking in my direction and I don't see anyone else around. "Welcome, miss." I must have the truth written on my face that I can't speak German.

"Hi—hallo, I'm checking in," I say, pointing to myself. I'm not sure how much English he speaks.

"Your name, miss?" he asks, smiling politely.

"Grace Laurent."

"Wonderful, I have your reservation right here. We have you staying in room 402. If you have any problems, please give us a ring at the front desk and we'll gladly help you." I guess he speaks English perfectly. The man hands me a key and my paperwork before pointing toward the elevator on the other side of the lobby. "Enjoy your stay, miss."

"Danke," I reply and set off to make my way to room 402.

The window in my room overlooks a dimly lit quaint village but the orange glow from the gas lamps highlights the mosaic of mismatched, uneven worn cobblestones that must have been traveled across millions of times throughout the years. It's a wonderful connection between the cottage-like structures with ornate plastering and gabled roofs. I've never seen the baroque style of architecture in person, and even in the middle of the night, it's more breathtaking than I imagined it would be. It's like I've stepped back in time. I don't understand how such a beautiful place could have been the backdrop to so much death and destruction.

I wonder how far away Matilda lived from here. Most of the surrounding buildings appear to be shops, or at least from what I can see from here. I circled the addresses of the law office, Matilda's property, and the hotel on a map I printed out. Supposedly, the property is only two blocks away. I might be staring directly at it for all I know. With a scan in each direction leading away from the main road, I assume it must be down one of the narrow streets. I intended to visit the law office before searching for the property, but not at this hour. I suppose I can peek into the window of the property to see what the place looks like, at least.

After freshening up for a few minutes, I see my phone lighting up on the bed. It's Carla again. She has no faith in my ability to keep myself alive, I swear. She's video-calling this time.

"I'm still alive, and you still have nothing to worry about," I tell her upon answering the call.

"Let me see the hotel room. I need to inspect it," she says, narrowing her eyes. She must be bored. I take a quick second to scan my phone around in a circle so she can see every bit of the space that's just large enough to fit a bed. "No parties for you in there."

"Who would I have a party with?" I reply.

"Me, if I was there with you. I can't believe you wouldn't wait for me."

"I know, I wish you were here too, but this is just something I need to go through on my own. I'm doing this on behalf of my mom and it's just—"

Carla taps on her screen, trying to get my attention. "Hey, I'm kidding. I totally understand. I'm just being your life proxy and making sure you're in a clean hotel," she says, tilting her head from left to right, trying to see around me. "Oh, you changed out of your sweatshirt. You look much better, but probably because that black top is mine, isn't it?"

I glance down, acknowledging her with a quick nod. "Yup. You'll get it back soon. Anyway, I'm not entirely incapable of planning a trip, so you should stop worrying so much."

"No one can plan a getaway at three in the morning and have everything turn out all right."

"Well, I was just about to go explore for a bit before I call it a night. Is that all right with you?" I raise my brows, giving her a bit of a goofy attitude.

"Isn't it the middle of the night there?" she asks, counting the time difference out with her fingers.

"Yes, but I'm still on Boston time, and I slept half of the flight." I peek out the window once more before settling on my decision. "The streets are so quiet. I'm sure I'll be fine."

"I'm coming with you," she says.

"And how would you like to do that?" I ask, taking my coat from the bed.

"Don't hang up—that's how."

"You are a pain, you know that?"

"If I know you as well as I do, you're not just exploring. You're going to find the property before you talk to anyone at the law office tomorrow. And as your best friend, I feel I should be with you when you locate this place—whatever it is."

"Fine, but be quiet until I'm outside. I don't want to be a rude American walking through a lobby with my loud friend on a video call."

"Loud?"

"Stop talking. I'm leaving the room," I tell her.

I secure my hotel room door and turn down the short hallway that leads to the elevator. Even with the carpeting along the floors, I feel like my footsteps are echoing between the walls. There isn't a peep of sound anywhere.

The silence follows me in and out of the elevator, making me feel small in such a grand and beautiful walkway that spills into the lobby.

"Wow, this place is right up your alley. The architecture is beautiful."

"It is," I reply, quietly. "There's a palace up the street that has been around since the eleventh century. Can you imagine?"

Carla doesn't respond, causing me to check my connection. She holds her finger up to her lips. "You're in the lobby," she mutters beneath her breath.

I wave at the man still standing at the front desk and smile as if I'm hiding something, or someone—on a phone. He glances down at his watch then back up at me, but his smile fades and his brows furrow. He must be wondering why I'm heading out at this hour. "Jet lag," I say with an awkward chuckle.

"Grace, maybe you really shouldn't be wandering around at this hour," Carla pipes up as soon as my feet hit the curb.

"It's fine." I pull out the map again and stop beneath a streetlight to find which direction I need to go.

"Are you navigating? Because I've driven through Boston with you too many times to know how this will end. Just take a right."

"It's actually left, but thank you," I say.

"Flip the camera around so I can see where you're going." I guess there's no such thing as traveling alone these days. "Look at those roads—the cobblestone. I can almost imagine horse-drawn carriages clomping between the buildings. It's beautiful. But, on a serious note, I hope you aren't wearing shoes with any sort of heel?"

"No, I don't think I'll be wearing anything but flat shoes while I'm here." The thought has already crossed my mind.

"Oh my gosh! Is that a tea shop? I want to have tea there with you," Carla groans.

"It's just tea and—" My thoughts trail off when I remind myself of what this town is known for. "It's hard to believe there was a concentration camp a mile away..." I say, despite the truth of the beauty.

"It's a haunting thought," Carla says.

"There's the street. It should be two buildings up on the right."

I cross the cobblestone, feeling every curved stone through the thin soles of my flat shoes. Each of the buildings on this street appears to be a different color under the little light bouncing off of each edifice, and the windows are all decorated with hanging garden beds. The well-known Bavarian timber framing and steep pitched roofing is still as the architects originally designed.

When I reach the next streetlight just in front of the second building, I stop to glance down at the map once more, confirming I'm in the correct place.

"What is it? Is it a house?" Carla asks.

I take a couple of steps closer, staring up at the wooden sign hanging from the edifice. "Runa's Wun-der-bare Bü-cher," I try to pronounce the wording on the sign. With my hand cupped over my eyes, I point the light from my phone toward the window, stealing a glimpse at the aged shop filled with walls of books sitting on wooden shelves, facing several displays lined with trinkets in straw baskets, and then some small bistro tables. "From what I can see, the inside looks like a combination of a library, museum, and a café. It's clean, but dark, and everything looks so old."

"You're inheriting a vintage bookshop café on a street that looks like it has fallen out of a fairy tale. Wow! That's better than anything I was expecting," she says.

"Why would she want me, a person she's never met—to have this shop?"

"There must be a good reason," Carla adds. "After all, you are family."

Chills run over me from head to toe. There is so much I want to understand—both good and bad—and I can't wrap my head around anything. There is much left to read of the translated papers, and I can't imagine finding out everything there is to know about this shop; why it's here, or why I should have it.

"Carla, I'm going to head back to the hotel now. I'll send you a text in a bit, okay?" I tell her.

"Are you okay? You don't sound okay."

"I'm good, I promise. I just need a minute."

"Okay, text me when you can."

"Bye." My voice trails off before disconnecting the phone. I stare up at the three levels of this narrow building, wondering what's above the shop, and if the space is Matilda's too.

When I close my eyes, I can't imagine anything. I can't create a vision of what she might have looked like, who she turned out to be, or why she would stay here, of all places, until someone found me.

CHAPTER 8
MATILDA
MAY 1940

I have never been one to skip school. In fact, for most of my life I've been a strict rule follower. To do as I'm told has been the only option, until I started questioning everything I'm being taught to think. I'm not seeing the same view as Mama and Papa, and my teacher is no better. I never imagined doubting the people we should look up to as role models, but nothing makes much sense lately. I'm left to wonder about everything.

My exchange with Mama is brief as she hands me a paper bag with my lunch in, which she assumes I'll take to school. "Come right home after class, do you understand?" Mama says, pinning her hands to her hips—asserting authority because she likely feels as though she has lost control over me and my rebellious decisions.

To avoid a lie, silence must do. I take the brown bag, keeping my gaze locked on hers. It's hard not to wonder what she's feeling, but I don't think she'll ever allow me to know the thoughts brewing behind her eyes. It's hard to tell if it's me she is truly cross with, or if the state of our lives is chipping away at her.

"Thank you for lunch," I offer.

"Have a good day, Matilda."

"Yes, you too, Mama."

I rush out the front door, hoping Mama doesn't notice the over-stuffed appearance of my book bag. The speed of my pace comes to a halt when I spot a handful of soldiers moving into Hans's flat.

It's only been a day.

One soldier tips his head in my direction as if it is appropriate to be greeting me after stealing my best friend's home. Does he know? He must. They have been at this for months. The landlords are being rewarded by the Nazis for creating habitable spaces for soldiers to billet. All Jewish tenants are being sent to select areas where they must live with either someone they know or someone willing to share what they have.

I force myself to continue down the stairs, trying to clear my mind of the strangers moving into the building.

The air is colder than usual this morning. The wind will bite at my face throughout the long ride to Krumbach. I settle my book bag on my back and tie my scarf over my head and around my neck.

With nothing but the freedom to think as I keep my eyes on the never-ending green pastures, I devise ways to convince Hans that I can help him. He isn't one to accept a handout from anyone, and it will be my biggest hurdle. Surely, his mama will take the food I've brought and a few other items they can use.

As I approach the outskirts of Krumbach, I notice an abundance of German flags dominating neighborhoods. I didn't notice the sights yesterday as I followed the vehicle that was transporting Hans's family, my heart in my throat. As of last year, Hitler's laws forbid Jews from owning the German flag, which means every one of these people is afraid of being labeled as a Jewish person or they are proudly stating they are not of Jewish descent. Daily, I wonder how many people are living in fear versus how many people believe our country is doing what's right.

I'm thankful that I remember the streets I rode yesterday, recalling where Hans went. It's hard to predict if there will be soldiers guarding the area again or if today will be different. I take precautions before traveling down each street leading to the tiny village, and I'm relieved to find people walking around, working, and going about their business. There aren't any soldiers in the nearby vicinity, and I have my sights set on the building Hans walked into.

I hide my bicycle behind a reeking dumpster. Though I'm cold to the bone, sweat beads on the back of my neck beneath the collar of my coat as I cross the open area of cobblestone between two rows of buildings. I fear being asked to show my identification. I should know better than to associate with any Jewish person. We are not to mix with their kind.

The street smells of sewage and rotten food. Rats are scurrying between buildings, searching for trash, and the puddles left behind from last night's rain contain no reflection. It's as if the sun doesn't shine in this small area.

I see the entrance Hans walked through yesterday and I find there to be no door, just a short hallway with a set of stairs leading both up and down beneath the street level. People are sitting in the hallway on the second floor, staring at me with a questioning look in their eyes.

"I'm—" I clear my throat, finding it hard to talk through the tight feeling around my neck. "I'm looking for the Bauer family," I announce to anyone sitting within a few feet of me.

"They are up there on the fourth floor," a young girl says, peeking around the stairwell leading up. She has soot on her cheeks, but her long dark braids are neat and the whites of her eyes glow with innocence. "I'll show you." She races up the stairs ahead of me. "They just moved in yesterday and now I have a new friend, Danya. We're the same age."

"How wonderful," I reply. My stomach aches saying anything within these walls could be wonderful.

The little girl points to an open door from the top step. "Right in there," she says.

"Thank you—"

"Cilla. That's my name."

"Thank you, Cilla. You've been a big help to me."

I knock on the open door, lightly tapping my knuckles for fear of startling anyone.

Frau Bauer pokes her head from around a wall just a few feet from where I'm standing. Her eyes widen upon spotting me in the doorway. "Matilda, what are you doing here?" She rushes toward me and takes me by the hand, pulling me inside a small, empty room with four barren walls, a sheet-covered window, and a narrow archway in the corner that must lead to another room or two. She presses on the main door but doesn't close it the entire way—just enough to hide my existence, I assume. "You shouldn't be in this town."

Her hands are as cold as ice. There is no heat in the corridors or this empty space, and as I take a closer look around, I see there is no furniture. "I have an idea," I tell her.

"Let me fetch Hans, dear. He's in the—the room where we're sleeping, with Danya."

"Frau Bauer," I interrupt, stopping her before she steps away. "There is a crawl space behind my bedroom wall. I know it isn't much, but I also know you and Herr Bauer have little at the moment. If you were closer, I could help."

Frau Bauer presses her palms together and rests them over her lips before releasing a long sigh. "It is so sweet of you to offer, but I don't see how it could ever work without causing trouble."

My gaze drops to her hands that are now encompassing mine. "The space is very small. Two of you might fit comfortably, but I'm sure we can fit all four of you. There must be a way."

Frau Bauer leans her head back, staring up at the ceiling. She cups her hands around her throat as if she feels strangled. "It will never work, Matilda. We would be putting you and ourselves in danger and—"

I shake my head before she completes her sentence. "You can't worry about me, Frau Bauer. I'm safe in comparison to you, and I'll do whatever it takes to protect you. You are all like a second family to me."

Frau Bauer glances over her shoulder, toward the small hallway with closed doors. "Herr Bauer won't know where to find me when he returns."

"Couldn't you tell your aunt? I'm sure she could let him know. Then we can make room for him too."

She places her hands on my shoulders and lowers her head a couple of inches to look me in the eye. "Matilda, you have a heart made of gold, and I love that you want to help, but I can't—"

"You can," I argue.

The moment of silence between us feels like hours passing during a sleepless night.

"Hans should go with you," she says softly, wrapping her arms around her waist.

"Oh, I know he wouldn't dream of leaving you behind."

Frau Bauer shakes her head, then reopens her eyes. "They have already sent Herr Bauer to a type of prison where he will work for the time being. It's temporary, but all men between the ages of eighteen and forty-five are being sent there. Hans will be eighteen soon and the soldiers will send him away, too." She places the back of her hand to her mouth, trying to hold in the pain. "Danya and I will be fine here for the time being. She's already made a friend. It's good for her, and my aunt—she's old and has taken us in, so I must stay and help her."

"Matilda?" Hans's voice is full of surprise when he ducks beneath the low-arched opening. "Why are you here?" His brows knit together as the sound of shock in his voice turns bitter. I think he's angry with me for coming all this way. The sight of him is heartbreaking. This isn't the boy I've always known. His white shirt is soiled with dirt and the bottom cuffs of his gray trousers are damp as if he's been trudging through mud and puddles. I've never seen my friend look so worn. Even his hair is a mess, and the whites of his eyes are stained red.

"I've brought you food, writing supplies, and an idea to help you out of here."

Hans is shaking his head before I finish speaking. "No, no, Matilda, you must not come here again. If you're caught, they'll know you are up to no good. I can't let anything happen to you. Do you understand?"

"Hans," Frau Bauer interrupts, "you are to go back with Matilda. She'll keep you safe."

"Mama, no. I cannot leave you and Danya. The Nazis already forced Papa away, and we don't know when he'll be back. I'm all you have."

Frau Bauer turns around, placing her hands on Hans's cheeks. "You cannot take care of us if they take you away to work. They won't let you."

"I can't just leave you here, Mama."

A lump rises in my throat, threatening to become tears that I have to squeeze away. I tighten my jaw so hard that a pain sears down the sides of my neck. Maybe I was wrong to come here. I shouldn't be breaking up their family. It wasn't my intention. I clench my fists by my side, debating whether I should tell him to stay and forget my visit. I don't know what's best for him.

"Your sister and I will be safe here with your aunt. I must take care of her after she has offered to share this space with us. It's the least I can do. Danya is only six. She doesn't understand what's happening but has made a friend and she's happy."

"Mama, has someone come to visit?" Danya sings out from the room on the other side of the wall then she skips into the tight space we're standing in. Her innocence is still prevalent, and I pray it always stays that way. "Matilda!" She runs to me and wraps her hands around my waist, pressing her cheek against my stomach.

"How is the most beautiful little girl in the world doing today?" I ask her.

Danya doesn't release her grip around me. She continues to hold on as if I'm a safety net she unknowingly desires.

When I pull my attention away from Danya, I notice Hans's face is pale, his freckles nearly blending into his natural skin color. "We will all be apart," he says.

"It's the best way to keep us all safe, son," his mother says, her voice hitching in her throat as tears well in her eyes.

"No, Mama. I can't—"

"What's happening?" Danya asks.

"You will do as I say and there will be no further questions. Do I make myself clear?" I've never heard Frau Bauer speak so sternly and yet sound so weak at the same time. By the reaction on Hans's face, it seems he agrees.

I drop my book bag to the ground and unpack the food I have brought. It's mostly canned items from our cupboard that have been sitting awhile. It's not much, but it's something. I also hand over the bagged food Mama made for my lunch. "These are leftovers from our supper last night," I say, giving them to Frau Bauer, avoiding the distraught look on Hans's face.

"I will never forget your kindness, Matilda. Please know this." Hans is still quiet, standing with a look of puzzlement brewing behind his big tell-all eyes. "Son, get your bag. You two need to leave right away before someone spots you." Hans doesn't move an inch. "Now. Go now." Frau Bauer shakes her son's arm, pulling him out of his deep thoughts. "Go."

He does as she says and turns back toward the arched opening. His footsteps stop only a few seconds after he's out of sight. I imagine the other room must be just as small as this one.

"Where is Hans going?" Danya asks in a whisper. No one answered her last question.

Frau Bauer wraps her arms around my neck and holds me tightly. "Your brother is going to stay with Matilda for a bit until your papa comes home. Everything will be okay, sweetheart," she tells Danya.

"I want to go too," Danya replies.

"You're just not old enough, darling," Frau Bauer says, running her shaking fingers through Danya's short auburn curls.

Hans returns within a minute with his satchel, but a look of shame is tugging at his shoulders.

Danya runs to him and takes his hand, holding it against her cheek like a favorite toy. "I don't want you to leave," she says.

Hans kneels in front of her and wraps his arms tightly around his sister. "I need you to take care of Mama. Can you do that for me?" he asks her quietly.

Danya takes a step back and stares into Hans's eyes. She takes a deep breath and shoves her chest out in a gesture of bravery. "You taught me how. I can be brave. I can take care of Mama too."

Hans grits his teeth and pulls his sister in for one more embrace. "I love you. I'll see you soon." With a kiss on her head, he stands up and clears his throat, prepared to face his mother.

Frau Bauer says, "Please be careful. I don't want to upset Matilda's parents and I—"

"Are you sure this is what's best, Mama?"

Frau Bauer pinches her lips together and her chin dimples as she silently agrees. "Yes, son. I love you very much."

I can hardly find a way to speak without losing control of my emotions, but I manage to offer my promise at the very least. "We'll be careful, and no one will know where he is. I'll keep him safe."

"May God bless you, sweet girl." She turns to Hans. "We need you to be kept safe. Men are not safe here, son."

Hans offers a slight nod of understanding and kisses his mother on the cheek.

She embraces him so tightly, her arms become pale, and her knuckles burn red. "I love you so much. God will keep us safe. Don't forget this, yes?"

"I love you, Mama."

As if the words sting Danya, she runs off to whatever room she came from. Upon hearing an object hitting a wall, we all face the direction she ran to.

"I'll go tend to her. You two need to go," Frau Bauer says.

"I'll continue to bring you food," I reply. "Anything I can bring, I will."

With a shuddered inhale, she lowers her head. "No, dear. We'll be okay. It's a long way to travel and dangerous for us all."

I wasn't thinking this would be a goodbye. I want to believe all of this is temporary, but the wrenching pain in my stomach tells me otherwise. I won't know how much heartache I might be causing until there is nothing left but a family full of broken hearts.

I take Hans's hand and lead him out into the dingy corridor. There's a slight resistance, but he follows. Once we are downstairs and outside, we find our way around the buildings, staying out of sight until we reach the dumpster.

Hans stops suddenly as if he forgot something important. "My heart hurts, Matilda," he says in a low voice. "This isn't right. I can't just abandon my family. How can I choose between my safety and theirs?"

Was it selfish of me to come here, thinking I could do something to help them? "I'm sorry for forcing you to make an impossible decision. If you want to stay, I understand. There is no question of how much you love your family, and this isn't a choice anyone should have to make," I say.

Hans seems to be lost in thought for a long minute. "Mama is probably right. I will be sent to a work camp like Papa. I would be of no use to them anyway, but this guilt—" Hans's voice crackles through every word, and by the heavy heaves of his chest and the sweat beading on his forehead, he looks like he's just run for miles as he tries to slow his breaths. "It hurts terribly." The narrow, strained tilt to his eyes proves the meaning of every one of his words.

"I can't imagine," I say, dropping my gaze to the cobblestone.

Hans inhales sharply. "Well, let's get on with it. I'm sure there will be plenty of time to feel remorse later."

I feel terrible. I was only trying to help. "Of course," I reply.

"Your parents hate me," he says. "Where will I stay?"

"There is space behind my bedroom wall. It's small, but we can make it livable. No one will find you there."

"What if they do? Do you know what could happen to you?" he asks, backing away from me.

I grab ahold of Hans's hand, forcing him to stop again. He looks like he has something more to say, but instead seems to lose his train of thought when his eyes meet mine. "You are worth the risk to me."

CHAPTER 9
MATILDA
MAY 1940

There is only one bicycle between the two of us, we have to walk through the uncut paths parallel to the roads that lead back home. With so many soldiers lining the streets, searching for innocent lives to destroy, we must do what we can to stay out of sight. School will be letting out just as we cross the border into town, but I need to keep Hans hidden until nightfall when I can sneak him into the flat.

"You are very quiet," Hans says. "A quiet Tilly is never a good sign, yes?"

It's the first hint of a joke Hans has made in the hours we have been walking.

We cut into the woods to make our way around town without being spotted by anyone we know. Most don't travel this way, as the paths aren't maintained. The shrubbery is overgrown with dried-up thorns and rocks hiding beneath piles of dead leaves. Hans has found a thick branch to poke around in search of ditches or rocks hiding beneath all the brush. It reminds me of the days when we would search through these woods for the perfect spot to build a fort out of the trees that had fallen in prior winters.

"Do you ever find yourself lost in an infinite circle of a question that doesn't have an answer?" I ask.

"I like to think there are answers for every question, even ones that are hard to believe," he replies. "What question are you stuck pondering?"

I think for a moment, wondering how to explain myself without inviting him into the worst fears I have for the future—*his* future.

"I just mean... sometimes when I lay in bed at night, I wonder what comes after death and I can't come up with an answer. A person doesn't come back to life, or not that we know of, and yet, there's nothing else after we die, and it's forever."

Hans stops walking and turns to face me, forcing me to halt with my bicycle. "Are you afraid of dying?"

"No, but it's hard to wrap my head around..."

"What else are you wondering about, Matilda?"

I lean my bicycle up against a nearby tree and find a rock to sit on. "Well, I listen to everything going on around me. I tune into the radio and hear every word Hitler says to our country, but I can't figure out what he is trying to fix, or why he thinks punishing the Jewish people of our country will solve any economic issues. It's as if we only know part of the story... Everyone follows his directions blindly and on a promise that he will make things better for everyone—everyone except the Jews. To me, it doesn't make sense. To me, it's hurting one to help another and nothing about the way our lives are evolving. There are no answers, no matter how many questions we ask."

Hans takes a seat next to me on a pile of pine needles. "This is true, but we may also choose to believe everything will get better with time. Before he was forced to leave this morning, Papa told us that this is temporary, and we need to play along to find our way to the other side. He said the work he was being sent to do was one step closer to ending this madness. I can only pray that by some miracle he's right."

I can't take away the hope Hans has. It wouldn't be fair to him. But there hasn't been a hint of improvement. There only seems to be more rules that come without warning. Hitler has the country in the palm of his hand, and he could tighten his grip on all of us at any minute. I'm not Jewish, but it's only a matter of time before he finds another group of people to hate.

"I'm sure your papa is right," I finally say. "He is a very smart man."

"Maybe we should be honest with your parents, Matilda. It might be easier on you, rather than being forced to hide me at all hours of the day."

I don't know how to tell him that Mama and Papa seem to have understanding for Hitler's outrageous rules and laws. If he knew how much they wanted me to stay away from him, he would be even more hurt. "On the chance they don't agree, you heard your mama. The soldiers will send you somewhere to do labor like your papa. She doesn't want that for you. I don't want that for you. Isn't it better to know you can stay somewhere safe and I can bring you food?"

"How long can I go on hiding? What if this doesn't end soon like we hope? I will be living like a mouse in the attic."

I almost forgot about the mouse that led me to this idea. "We can take it one day at a time. Let's not look at this as hiding, but instead that we're keeping you safe. My parents never come up to my bedroom. Think of this time as your opportunity to write to your heart's content. You have books to write, Hans."

He snickers at my statement. "Jews cannot write books, Tilly. A person needs an education and skills to do such a thing, and even then, no one wants a book that a Jew has written. My stories are for me, and you."

I stand from the rock and dig my hands into my hips. "What on earth are you blabbering about? You're the most talented writer I've ever known. Of course you can write a book—one that should be bound, published, and placed on shelves for the world to read."

Hans stands up in front of me, brushing the pine needles off his backside. He stares down at me as a small smirk tugs at the corner of his lips. "With all due respect, Tilly, you don't know too many writers, more so, ones who are Jewish. We shouldn't exist, remember?"

I huff out a lungful of exasperation. "Well, I know good writing when I read it. You'll see. Someday you will have a book with your name on it."

"If you say so," he replies, running his knuckles down the side of my cheek.

Hans and I could argue about nothing for hours, and we have done so many times before, but his touch—it's as if I can't remember how to speak.

"Oh, cat got your tongue?" he jests. "Who would have known how simple it is to keep you quiet for a few seconds?"

I slap his hand off my cheek. "Here I am trying to save you and you're spouting off about me talking too much."

Hans leans down and presses his lips against the tip of my nose, then my lips, stealing my every breath. "I love listening to you. I've spent nights worrying about the words I might not hear you say, and it would be a tragedy to the story that might take me a lifetime to write," he mutters against my mouth.

"My words aren't worthy of a story," I argue as the heavy beats of my heart thump against my chest.

"I disagree."

This conversation is going nowhere, and I need to regain my bearings to figure out how to keep him hidden until tonight. "I think we should find a spot in the woods near home and build one of our famous forts for you to stay in until tonight when it's safe to bring you upstairs."

"I'll take care of keeping myself out of sight. You should go home before your parents become suspicious. If we don't cause a need for questions, you won't have to come up with answers."

"They are both in bed by nine. Will you be okay until then?"

Hans takes my hands within his. "I will be fine. You mustn't worry so much. There is a way up the fire escape through the back of the building. If you open the rooftop door at nine thirty, I'll be there," he says.

"How will you know what time it is?"

"The clock tower downtown."

Of course. I should have thought of that, but my nerves are catching up on me.

"All right then, I'll see you tonight?" I feel the need to ask rather than confirm. It isn't hard to see he's being pulled in two different directions.

"You will see me tonight, I promise."

Hans leaves me with one last kiss on my cheek before he lifts my bicycle away from the tree. As if hyperaware of all sensations, my fingertips sweep across the spot his lips touched. I wish some moments could last forever. I don't want to forget this feeling and there isn't a way to keep it locked away and safe.

As I take a few steps away, I remember packing some paper and a pencil for him in case I was forced to leave him behind in Krumbach; I wanted him to continue writing.

The zipper on my bag screams louder than I'd like as I drop my hand in my bag. I glance around the woods, feeling as though someone is watching us, even though I'm sure we're alone. "I brought this for you."

He reaches for the paper as if it's gold. "You are the most thoughtful person I've ever known, Matilda."

"It's only paper and a pencil."

He shakes his head. "This paper is my door to someplace better. You know this."

"How was school today, Matilda?" Mama asks as I walk through the front door, feeling hungry and sore from walking and riding my bicycle so far today.

"It was fine." The scent from a fresh apple strudel wafts into the foyer as I close the door behind me. "Who are you baking for?" Mama doesn't typically bake sweets during the week. Often, she will prepare dessert to go along with our supper on Sunday night, but on any other day of the week, it must be for someone else.

"I'm making strudel for the gentlemen who moved in downstairs."

"The Nazis who have taken the Bauers' home?" I do little to hide the fury I'm feeling.

"It's best to keep the soldiers on our good side, Matilda."

I can't look at Mama. The anger firing through me is something I have never felt for either of my parents before. "Those men watched a family leave their home—the home they have lived in for fifteen years—and you are making them a treat. I would feel a great deal of shame if I were you."

She can't look at me. A blonde curl falls from her pinned hairdo, and she stares down at the strudel as if she made it with poison. To feed the enemy as the innocent starve is not something we, as bystanders, must take part in. For us, it is a choice.

Mama's jaw grinds as if she's contemplating what to say or maybe what she should think, but whatever it is, I don't have the stomach to hear any more.

I take my belongings upstairs and close the door before sliding down against the wall until I'm sitting on the cold wooden floor panels. I pull my knees into my chest and hold myself so tightly I can hardly breathe. It's impossible to be the only one who sees through the madness, yet it seems as if I'm alone in every way. There is nowhere to hide from the truth, no attic, crawl space, story, or dream. We are living in a nightmare, but some see this as just a bad dream— one, we will someday wake up from.

CHAPTER 10
MATILDA
MAY 1940

The thought of enduring a meal with Mama and Papa was enough to leave me without an appetite, but I needed to save an extra portion for Hans's supper. I offered to clean up the dishes on my own after we ate and scraped out the remnants from the casserole dish into a can. Then, I hid it beneath the sink behind bottles of cleaner Mama hasn't touched in years.

Just after Mama and Papa turned in for bed, I brought a small canvas tote downstairs, retrieved the can, a set of silverware, a couple of sweet oranges, and a bottle of root beer for a treat.

Hans has probably eaten even less these past couple of days than what he had already become used to over the last year.

I've been watching the clock tick closer to nine thirty, but in the meantime, I have been pulling blankets out of closets, unpacking old pillows, and collecting candles to keep a lantern burning in the crawl space for as long as he needs light at night. During the day, we can crack open the wall panel door to allow the sunlight to illuminate part of the space.

I've pinned some of his handwritten quotes that he has given me over the years to the walls inside the small space, trying to make it feel warm and comforting. It isn't much, but whatever I have, I will gladly share. I don't want him to feel like he's a prisoner here.

It's a few minutes before we are supposed to meet, so I make my way up to the roof. I shove open the door to the outside, and a burst of cold air slaps against my face. This spring is struggling to fight off the frigid temperatures. It just seems to be getting colder and colder. Hans must be freezing.

After a few minutes of standing on the rooftop, staring out into the dark sky, I hear a metal clink coming from the right side. I run to the edge and peer down, finding Hans scaling the rusty ladder with sluggish steps. "Are you all right?" I whisper down to him.

"Yes, yes, I'm just cold and tired. Everything is fine."

"My parents are asleep, and I've prepared the space for you."

He reaches the top and I notice how pale he is, even in the orange glow from surrounding lights. I take his hand, feeling his icy grip. The cold is emanating from his body.

"You can sit beside the radiator for a while until you warm up. Come on, let's get inside," I say, urging him to go faster than he might be capable of. "I'm going to walk in first to make sure the coast is clear, and when I see it is, you can follow me up to my bedroom. Do you remember which floor panels creak?"

A small smile struggles against his lips. "You numbered the floor panels when you were ten. You even made up a rhyme so we wouldn't forget. I think it went something like, 'Three, five, eight... skip a few, then skate. Fifteen, sixteen, and lean. Left, one, three, six, then scoot over to the bricks.'"

My gaze broadens with amazement that he remembered the silly jingle I came up with so we could sneak out of our flats at night to stargaze on the rooftop. "I can't believe you remember."

"I forget very little, Tilly," he utters.

Once I open the small door that leads into the building, we stop talking. We move down the one set of stairs without making a peep, and I lift the front door a smidge to avoid a squeak from the hinges. After a few steps into the flat, I find the coast is clear. Not even a faint glow from the bedside lamps in Mama and Papa's bedroom is filtrating through the crack beneath the door.

I wave Hans along, skipping the inches of moaning floor panels until I reach the steps that lead up to the attic. By the time I'm halfway up, Hans has made his way to the first step.

My heart is racing with panic and fear, hoping against all hope that neither Mama nor Papa open their bedroom door in the next fifteen long seconds it will take us to secure ourselves upstairs.

It isn't until my door is closed that I can take in the deep breath I feel I've been holding onto for hours. "You're safe now," I whisper.

I reach for his bag, helping him through the stiffness of his limbs. I place it to the right side of my bed, out of sight from the door.

"Over here," I say, waving him toward the side wall and the radiator.

He carefully slides down the smooth wallpaper until he's resting on the floor and stretches his legs out in front of him, then leans his head back with what looks like a sigh of relief. I tear my blanket off my bed and wrap it around his shoulders. All the while, he's staring at me with his big eyes that sparkle with the flickering glow of the candles I have lit. "Why do you care about me this much?"

"Why would you ask something so stupid?" I reply.

From beneath my bed, I pull out the tote bag and carefully remove the top of the can from tonight's supper. The aroma spills out and I'm thankful it still smells as good as when it was served. I place it down on his lap and hand him the silverware.

"Some supper will warm you up too," I tell him.

"Matilda, how did you manage—"

"Shh, just eat." I place the two oranges down beside him and press my palm onto the bottlecap of the root beer, twist, and wait while quietly letting out the bubbling fizz before releasing the pressure to avoid any unnecessary sound.

"Root beer," he mutters. "I haven't had one in ages. You're going to spoil me rotten, Tilly."

My heart breaks as he struggles to pace himself eating every morsel of food. I know they've been living off so little.

"Tomorrow, Mama will go to the butcher just after Papa leaves for work. You can use the shower and freshen up then. Aside from that, I've left you a bucket of water and other supplies you may need in the crawl space."

Hans's gaze drops and his head falls with a sense of disdain. I didn't mean to embarrass him, but we aren't left with many choices at the moment.

It takes Hans less than a few minutes to finish everything. His cheeks are slowly refilling with his natural pink hue and his eyelids appear less heavy than they were before.

"Are you warming up?" I ask.

"Oh yes, I feel much better. In fact, I might have overeaten, but the feeling is wonderful."

When I look at his face, I feel so much inside—love, compassion, endearment, sympathy. The last part hurts. All humankind should have empathy for one another, but I'm afraid that will no longer be the case now.

"I will do whatever it takes, Hans. I promise."

"How could I doubt it by what you have done for me today?" he asks, placing his hand down on top of mine. "I can't possibly tell you how much this means to me."

"There's no need for that."

"You know, the last time I peeked inside of this crawl space was when you had me searching for the monster you were certain was living behind your wall."

I can't help the small smile stretching into my cheeks. "The monster is gone. If I remember correctly, you banished it from this building *for all eternity*," I say with laughter while twisting around to move the bed from its place against the wall.

"Tilly, wait, that will make a lot of noise," Hans frets.

"You don't give me much credit, you know that? For your information, I cut up four pieces of felt earlier and stuck them to the bottom of the bed's legs. Now it can skate across the creaking wooden panels."

He smiles. "My goodness... You never cease to amaze me. I should never question a thing you do."

"You shouldn't," I agree.

I push the bed to the side several feet, unveiling the stacks of dusty books. I layered them on top of a small piece of linen so they can all move together at once. With a slight lift of the wall panel, it slides out seamlessly, creating an entrance I've prepared for Hans.

"You've thought of everything, haven't you?"

"I hope so."

Hans places my blanket neatly on top of my bed and squats down before the opening to poke his head inside.

"Oh, here, a lantern." I hand him one of the two I have lit, and he puts it on the inside of the wall, lighting up the space.

He crawls inside and I follow. "Tilly, you decorated the space. Are these my words?" he asks, running his fingers across the hanging papers.

"They are my favorite words."

"It looks like a regal fort made for a king. I'm not deserving of this. Surely, your mama will notice these blankets and pillows missing?"

"Not when I tell her I donated them to the 'lovely soldiers' downstairs." I grit my teeth at the statement, enhancing each word with bitterness.

Hans looks at me the way he always has, like I'm full of silly jokes and ridiculous ideas. "No one could ever wonder why I love you."

I wrap my hand around his arm and squeeze gently. "And you shall never have to wonder about me feeling the same for you." I pinch my lip between my teeth.

"What is in that little crate over there with holes?" he asks, scooting toward the corner it's resting in.

"Oh, how could I forget? I thought there may be times during the day where you might find yourself lonely, so what better way to solve that problem than giving you a pet?"

"A pet?" he questions.

"Yes, in fact, Georgie is the one who reminded me of this space."

Hans removes the top of the old crate. He's hesitant to look beneath the lid, but when he sets his eyes on Georgie, he looks elated. "A field mouse—Georgie."

"I named him myself, of course," I say. "I couldn't bear the thought of kicking him out after the help he gave me."

Hans cups his hands into the box and lifts Georgie up to his chest. "We're going to be old chums, you and I," he tells the mouse. "He's just a baby, isn't he?"

"I'm not sure, but he sure is cute."

"He is," Hans says, placing him back in the box. "Matilda, thank you again. For all of this. I'm not sure I'll ever be able to repay you, but I need you to know how grateful I am."

"There's no need to keep saying so, really."

"I know. I'm just trying to keep myself focused on the good rather than whatever else is happening outside of this building right now."

"That reminds me of something." I crawl out of the opening for a moment and return with more paper and a pen with a couple bottles of ink. "This should keep your mind busy too."

"I spent the afternoon writing. It was quite helpful to pass the time."

"To find out there are more pages to your story is always good news to me."

Hans leans forward on his knees and slips my hair behind my ears, kissing my cheek. "You should get some rest. You must still go to school in the morning. We can't have anyone getting suspicious, can we?"

"Of course," I tell him. "Is there anything else you need before I go?"

"A smile. That's all."

His request sends a smile straight to my lips. "Goodnight."

"Goodnight, sweet Tilly."

CHAPTER 11
GRACE
2018

I slept hard for a solid four hours after I finally fell asleep, but jet lag has set in, and I woke up feeling confused about where I was for a moment. The hotel room is unlike any I've seen before. It's not quite eclectic, but almost gothic with a splash of color. The ceiling is dormered in several spots and finished with mahogany hardwood and decorative trim, a bronze candelabra chandelier in the middle. I assume the look mimics the centuries when the glow of lights was from flames rather than electricity. The lower my gaze drifts along the walls, the more modern the space appears.

The overwhelming feeling of what I should or shouldn't expect today is encouraging me to get up and push forward. I have a meeting at the law office set up for ten this morning, which leaves me just enough time to find something for breakfast. Although I feel like breakfast won't be enough to fill my raging hunger at this point. I don't know what meals I missed yesterday, but I went to bed on an empty stomach. Now, the jet lag and time difference are hitting me like a ton of bricks.

I pull the sheer linen curtain away from the window to peek outside, finding blue skies and just a few clouds. It's certainly colder here than it was at home, but I imagine it will warm up throughout the day.

Once I've showered and dried my hair, I feel a little less out of sorts. I grab my phone and head down toward the lobby. Multiple scents from a variety of foods hit me at once and I'm not sure which direction they're coming from, but there must be a restaurant or café in the hotel serving breakfast.

As I see more visitors, I feel a bit more out of place than I did last night. Most people appear to be from Europe. Until Carla mentioned it, I didn't realize there was such a different clothing trend here, and I stick out like I have a label stuck to my forehead because of my denim coat over a zip-up sweatshirt, along with leggings and sneakers. I packed mostly casual clothes and a couple of nice shirts. Everything else I own is business formal and it's the last thing I want to wear this week. But everyone else looks as if they're prepared to walk down the catwalk of a fashion show with their fitted clothes and chic footwear.

Maybe coffee and a pastry might be the best way to ease into today.

The longer I walk around the maze of the hotel, the more hallways I pass that may or may not lead to a café or restaurant. Once I end up back in the lobby again, I decide to visit the café across the street—the one I noticed yesterday.

The café is empty, and the young woman behind the counter has her eyes set on me, waiting for my order. I gaze up at the menu above her head on the wall, grateful for the ability to detect the word *kaffee*.

"Guten Morgen, Fräulein. Womit kann ich Ihnen behilflich sein?" she asks. I can only hope she's asking me what I would like because I didn't pick up much more than "good morning".

"Uh, uh—da, ah—kaffee and..." I scan the glass window in front of a line of pastries and cakes, spotting a row of croissants. I point to the croissant. "A croissant too—Danke."

"I speak English," the girl says with a friendly smile. "How would you like your coffee?"

I place my hand on my chest, feeling relieved for a moment. "Oh, thank you. Milk and sugar would be nice, please."

"And would you like the croissant toasted, or anything added?"

"No, thank you. It looks delicious as is."

"Where in the United States are you from? I—ah—I want to guess New York or Boston by your accent, yes?"

My face burns with embarrassment. I can't imagine what I must sound like here. They speak so beautifully, and it must make my Boston accent sound lazier than other states in the US joke about. "Boston, yes. Born and raised there," I say with a mortifying chuckle.

"Oh, wonderful. I have an uncle who lives in Seattle. I have visited twice. America is quite beautiful."

I want to disagree, with the sights I have spotted over just a few hours here, but I suppose everyone across the world believes that the grass always seems greener somewhere else. "Seattle is a great place. It's very rainy, but there's lots to do there."

"The weather is much the same here half the year, so it didn't feel too different." She's got her hands moving in different directions, talking and working as if she can manage ten things at once. Within a matter of seconds, she sets my coffee down in front of me with steam pouring from the spout, and wraps the croissant in a piece of brown parchment paper. "That will be five-seventy-eight euros, please."

I reach into my purse and pull out a five-euro note and a handful of coins, studying them for a moment. I hand her the note and two coins, hoping I added up the money correctly. "Here you go," I offer.

She returns one of the coins, but I was trying to leave her extra for a tip.

"For you," I say.

"Danke, Fräulein. Are you here for business or pleasure?"

My first thought is wondering who would come to an area that was home to a concentration camp as a trip for pleasure, but I tell myself not to assume anything.

"It's complicated. I have a long-lost relative who has left me property in the area, but I don't know too much about her or the shop, honestly. I have a meeting with a lawyer soon."

"Oh, wow, what property? If you don't mind me asking."

Maybe I shouldn't be talking about this until I sign the papers, but it all seems pretty set in stone according to the forms I was reading. "It's a bookshop up the street."

Her head tilts to the side and a small smile presses into her lips. "That's wonderful. Runa's Wunderbare Bücher?" she asks. The way she pronounces the name of the shop is nothing like the way I sounded out the words. She makes it sound like a beautiful lyric.

"Oh, yes, you know the shop?" I ask.

"Many of us call it the heart of this town. It's a very special and unique spot. It's a place to go when feeling lost—or that's how it has always made me feel. I think it makes everyone feel differently, but in a wonderful way." I've never heard of a shop spoken about in such a way. "Anyway, I wish you luck."

"Thank you. Danke," I correct myself.

"Come back again," she replies as I walk out into the brisk morning air.

I'm not sure which direction the law office is in, but instinctively, I walk in the bookshop's direction again, taking a few minutes to eat the croissant that tastes like sweet butter. The dough melts in my mouth. I must look like a savage, eating the whole thing in less than thirty seconds, but between the incredible taste and my hunger, I can't stop myself. I chase the warmth traveling through my body with a sip of the coffee that puts all coffee in the United States to shame. It's clear I've been missing out on a lot over the last ten years.

People seem friendly in this area. The shop owners are sweeping their front steps or watering flower beds. Walkers and joggers wave with a smile, but the feeling of this being a friendly place is making my mind dizzy with questions.

I pull out my notes and map from my purse, finding the address on the business card. The law office is only two blocks away from the hotel, but I think it's in the opposite direction from where I'm walking.

I retrace my steps, unexpectedly spotting a sign with German writing. In smaller print beneath the large letters is Brigitte Cora, the attorney's name on the card. That was easier than I expected it to be.

The door looks welcoming and leads into a well-lit lobby area with chairs scattered about and a front desk toward the back.

"Good morning. You must be Grace Laurent," a woman sitting behind the front desk greets me.

"I must look like I'm lost," I respond with a grin.

"To be fair, we only have one appointment at this hour. It was safe to assume," the woman says, standing from her seat. "Attorney Cora is all ready for you. I'm happy to take your coat and show you to her office."

I slip my coat off my shoulders and fold it over my arm to hand over. "Thank you very much. That's so kind. Is it okay to take my coffee back there?"

"Of course," the woman says. "Follow me."

The building is beautiful, covered with updated hardwood floors and white pristine walls decorated with unique trim work. Glass walls surround Attorney Cora's office.

The woman opens the door and invites me inside. "Attorney Cora, this is Fräulein Laurent. Please let me know if you need anything."

The door swooshes closed behind me, hardly making a sound, and Attorney Cora stands from her desk to greet me with a handshake. She's stunning, in a fitted suit, not a blonde hair out of place, and bright green eyes that glimmer beneath the fluorescent lighting. "It is such a pleasure to meet you, Fräulein Laurent."

"It's so nice to meet you and, please, call me Grace."

"Of course, and you may call me Brigitte." She returns to her chair but waits until I take a seat across from her desk first before sitting back down. "How were your travels? Did everything go smoothly for you?"

"Oh yes, I didn't have any issues at all, which is surprising considering how quickly I planned the trip out here." I shift around on the chair, trying to find a comfortable position, but I'm not sure there is any way to calm my nerves at the moment.

Brigitte pulls out a folder. "You seem nervous. Can I do anything to ease your apprehension?"

I cross my legs, feeling more than uneasy. My heart is racing. My chest is tight, and I'm suddenly burning up. "I have quite a few questions, as you can imagine."

"Of course," she says.

It was wishful thinking that she would offer up the full story before I began asking questions, but it appears she's waiting on me. "I'm not sure how much you know about my family's history, but I never knew Matilda Ellman. My mother arrived in the United States as an orphan when she was just a couple of months old, and we had no family records to track down. Unfortunately, she passed away a few years ago, but I know she would want me to know every detail about Matilda."

"Yes, I'm aware. I'm very sorry about you losing your mother. I wish we could have answered the questions she must have lived with her entire life, but the 1940s were not a very forgiving time, and unfortunately, we are still picking up many of the pieces seventy years later."

"I figured as much by the DNA report. My mother went down that route several times, but we had no records returned to us as a close match. Well, not until last week."

"I'm sure it was a frustrating experience for both of you," Brigitte says with a genuine look of empathy tugging at her eyes. I wonder if she knew Matilda. She pulls out a stapled packet of legal documents from the folder. "As you know, Matilda stated in her will that she wanted her next of kin to be the recipient of the property she has held the title for since 1945."

I want to ask about Hans, but I'm not sure if Brigitte has read the private pages sent to me. I don't know how their story ended.

"I'm feeling quite overwhelmed by all of this. When did Matilda pass away?"

Brigitte's gaze drops to the folder she has gripped between her polished fingers. "I would love to offer you more information about Matilda, but I have only been retained to handle the transfer of property. However, I'm more than happy to offer you any information about the location and point you in the direction of someone who will have more knowledge regarding your questions."

"Of course. I completely understand. I've been searching all over for information, but there doesn't seem to be much of anything online."

"This must be frustrating." Brigitte sets the folder down to the right of the stapled stack of papers. She settles her hands on top of the documents and taps her fingernails for a quick second. "If you would like, I can walk up to the bookshop and introduce you to the gentleman who has been tending to the store. He is a family friend of Matilda's, and I believe he may be able to help you more than I can."

"Is there a deadline for the decision about the property?"

"You are welcome to take some time, but regardless of your decision, the property will either become yours to sell or yours to keep."

"OK, I just don't want to rush into any decisions."

"Let's take a walk to the bookshop, yes?" she offers again.

CHAPTER 12
GRACE
2018

"I must admit, it surprised me to find out you were flying all the way here," Brigitte says as we walk out the front door of the law office.

I wrap my arms around my chest, fending off the cool wind funneling down the street. "Believe me, I surprised myself. I usually plan everything out weeks or months in advance, but my mother and I had been searching for answers for years and I couldn't bear to wait any longer."

Brigitte straightens her royal blue coat, pulling at the collar to shield her neck from the wind. "Well, you've come to the area at a good time. It's beautiful this time of the year. I'm not sure how long you plan to stay, but you must visit the Dachau Palace up the hill. It was built in the year 1100 and rebuilt in the 1500s. Aside from the beautiful structure, the gardens are blooming just about now, and you can see all the way to Munich and the Bavarian Alps on a clear day like today. It's quite breathtaking."

"As an architect, it sounds like a must-see for me. Thank you for the tip," I say, while another part of me wonders if the locals skip the part about this city housing the remnants of a concentration camp.

"You will love the palace. There's no one better to appreciate the renaissance design than an architect," she says. "And, of course, you should squeeze in a tour of the Dachau concentration camp if you are interested in the history of this area. Most visitors come to see one sight or the other and miss out on learning about how this city has come together over the years."

"To be truthful, I was a bit thrown to find out the property is here in Dachau. I suppose I think of the areas that held concentration camps as memorial grounds."

We turn around the corner onto the street I strolled down late last night. The shops all appear to be open, with people coming and going from the various colored buildings. It's busier than I would have thought.

"I hear that a lot from people who don't live around this area. It can be a controversial topic of conversation for many, but I think you'll come to see that most people who live here, especially in this city, have a personal reason," she says, stopping just in front of Runa's *Wunderbare Bücher*.

"Are you ready?"

I dip my hands into my pockets and take in a deep breath. "I'm not sure, but it's long overdue," I reply.

Brigitte wraps her hand around an intricately designed rusty door-knob and tugs at the painted wooden door. The sound of an old running shoe peeling away from a sticky floor is the first experience of what I could only imagine by peeking through the dark window last night.

The interior is dimly lit, aside from the sunlight trickling in through the one glass windowpane. By the sound of the door opening, I expected a musty scent to follow, but I'm greeted with old pine and aging books. The books are organized by color and size on each shelf, offering an esthetic feel to the enclosed area. The floors look to be original, yet shiny, even with all the wear and tear from footsteps. Antique chandeliers hang from the exposed wooden beams along the ceiling, and there is a hum of calming piano music permeating the space. There's a sense of serenity here—something I wasn't expecting. "It's beautiful," is all I can think to say. There is so much to look at and I wish I could take it all in at once.

"It is," Brigitte follows. "There is a living quarter upstairs, and a small basement as well."

I'm forcing myself to pay attention to every word she's saying, but I'm overwhelmed.

"Guten Morgen." We're greeted by a man walking in from a back area we can't see from where we are standing.

"Herr Alesky, Guten Morgen," Brigitte responds. "I would like you to meet Grace Laurent. Grace, this is Archie Alesky, the gentleman who has been caring for the shop."

Archie is a young man, possibly close in age to me. He appears prim and proper, dressed in what looks like a tailor-made gray sweater, a white dress shirt, and navy-blue trousers, complete with shined cognac Oxfords.

I think he might feel caught off guard as he sweeps his dark golden hair up and away from his forehead. There's a long moment of silence, making me wonder what he's thinking or what he might already know about me. Maybe he isn't aware of who I am at all. As his brows lift, the tawny-olive hue of his eyes reflects the chandelier hanging just above him and his shoulders fall along with a quiet exhale.

"I—" He clears his throat and runs his hands down the side of his pantleg. "I apologize, Miss Laurent, I can't believe you are here in Dachau." He takes a few steps in my direction, almost tentative, like I might disappear if he moves too fast. "You're a spitting image. It's unbelievable," he says.

His words are like a stake through my heart. I read the DNA report so many times, trying to convince myself this wasn't an error of some sort, but his response makes this much more real.

"You and your mother—your family—we have been searching for you for such a long time, but I suppose we had to wait for the innovative ways of science to catch up with us."

Family. "Are we related?" I ask, curious of how Archie fits into this story.

"Oh, no, I'm a family friend. Well, my grandfather was a family friend. The friendship survived the generations, as did the search for your mother, then you, it's all I've ever known."

A rush of emotions quake through me like the rumble of an avalanche just before everything crumbles to the ground. "My mother, then I, spent our lives looking for our family too. I've been reading handwritten papers with bits and pieces of Matilda's story, but it seems I'm missing most of whatever happened."

"Grace, would it be okay if I let you spend some time here with Herr Alesky?" Brigitte asks. "Whenever you are ready to continue discussing the acquisition process of the property, I'll make myself available."

I almost forgot Brigitte was standing behind me. I spin around on my heels, placing my hands on my chest. "I'm so sorry for taking up so much of your time. Yes, of course. I would like to spend some time here and that will make my decision easier, I'm sure. I appreciate you bringing me here."

"It is my pleasure," Brigitte says. "Runa's Wunderbare Bücher is a favorite location in this village, and I'm so pleased you can experience the beauty of this property."

"Danke, Fräulein Cora. Es war mir eine Freude, Sie zu sehen. Auf Wiedersehen. Goodbye."

"You're welcome. It was a pleasure to see you too, Herr Alesky. See you soon," Brigitte replies before turning to leave.

Once Archie and I are alone in the bookshop, another wave of silence grows between us. He's a stranger to me and I'm not sure what to say, ask, or where I should start at all.

"Would you like me to show you around the property?" he asks.

"Yes, I would appreciate that. It's like nothing I've seen before. The shop feels like it's from another century, untouched since whenever it opened."

"There have been very few updates, aside from the electricity, plumbing, and some fixtures. The intention has always been to keep the original setting as is."

I glance along the nearest shelf of books, squinting at the titles embroidered onto the spines. "I don't recognize any of the titles or authors." Of course, I'm in Germany and I'm sure they have an additional selection of classics here to those we have in the United States.

"There's a reason for that, and it isn't what you might assume."

Archie steps over to the next shelf along and slides a red book out from the center. He opens it to the first page, scanning the words. A strand of his styled hair falls to the side of his eye, and he smiles at what he is reading.

"Asher Solomon's book of poetry, *For Love of All Humanity*, written in 1930. You won't find this book in any other shop or home in the world, or the likelihood is very slim, at least. He was an up-and-coming poet, talented beyond recognition, but after the book became available to the public, the Nazis burned every copy they found, except for this one, which was signed and gifted to your grandmother when she was a young girl. To be Jewish and have love for all was a sin in Hitler's eyes, and he began a practice of burning all books by all Jewish authors and non-German authors who voiced opposing opinions. They burned twenty-five thousand books throughout 1933."

I'm quickly realizing how little I know about World War Two in Europe. I learned about the Holocaust and Hitler in school, but beyond the act of genocide and how the Nazis got from point A to B, I don't know much else. "They burned books?" I question.

"Oh yes, it was a big event throughout thirty-four universities in Germany."

"Are these—" I can't help but look in every direction of the shop, spotting the number of books the shelves hold.

"These are all books that were spared from the burnings—literature by Jewish authors. We have a couple of copies from Albert Einstein and Helen Keller too."

"They are collectables," I state.

"Sort of. The shop is unique. When a customer would like to purchase one of these books, we have a custom copy created for them so that we can use this space as a museum for lost items. Matilda didn't want any of the copies to be sold because there isn't a price tag worthy of the literature we have. Many of the locals come by and settle into a chair to read, then return the book to its spot before leaving. We have a lot of friendly locals who are frequent visitors."

I'm at a loss for words. How can I think of anything worthy to say when I'm surrounded by pages that will probably never be seen by most of the world's population? "There must be so many souls living in this store."

"We like to think so," he replies.

"Do you mind if I take a minute to sit down? The jet lag must be catching up to me. I'm a bit dizzy."

"Of course," Archie says, taking me by the elbow and leading me over to an area with empty reading chairs, each different, with contrasting regal patterns.

I take a seat and sip the lukewarm coffee I got at the café. I almost forgot I still had the cup in my hand. "It's been a lot to take in over the last couple of days. I'm not even sure what I've been reading in the packet of information and notes I received. Everything feels like pieces of a puzzle, and I can't find the edges to know where to begin."

"That may be my fault," he admits. "I didn't want to overwhelm you. I was trying to avoid doing so at all costs, but there's a lot to explain and it is hard to do so through a phone call, email, or letter, especially since we have never met, and you didn't know I existed until today."

"You sent me the envelope?" I question, taking another quick sip of my coffee.

"No, Fräulein Cora sent you the envelope, but I asked her to include the handwritten story. Of course, it wasn't until after Fräulein Cora mailed the information that I realized the slim likelihood that you speak German. I wasn't sure you'd be able to read any of the papers."

"Well, I don't speak German, but I was able to scan and translate them online. I didn't think it would be so easy, but it worked fairly well—better than my phone translator in the airport worked out," I add with a chuckle.

Archie takes a seat across from me and leans forward, resting his elbows on his knees. "I can tell you everything you need to know, but someone else preferred that you read all the details for yourself because it's the only way to fully understand where you came from."

"Someone else?" I question.

"Here," he says, standing from his seat. He walks toward the back counter, and I try not to notice his handsome physique, and how nicely dressed he is. He's not the type of man I'm used to crossing paths with. "I translated the pages as well in case you weren't able to, and of course there is more here for you to read than what I sent. I didn't want to mail too much in case it ended up in the wrong hands."

He hands me a bound stack of papers with three brass fasteners aligned on the left side, just how the first pages arrived.

"Archie, if we're not related, how did you end up being responsible for locating me?" I ask.

Archie slips his hands into his pockets and rolls back onto his heels. "Sometimes, friends can be closer than family members, and it was never a question in my mind that I would continue what your family had started. Your family would have done the same for mine, believe me."

I flip through the pages, trying to pick up where I had left off. "Oh yes, the pages ran out just as Matilda made a space for Hans in the crawl space of her attic."

Archie wrings his hand around his opposite wrist. "The story has a lot to take in. You should take your time while reading."

I had already assumed there was more, but I also wondered how much more I would want to know. Now that I'm here, there isn't a question in my mind that I need to know everything there is to know about Matilda and Hans.

CHAPTER 13
MATILDA
JANUARY 1941

Routines have never been my favorite part of life, but without one today, a life could be at stake. I have managed to keep Hans safe for nearly eight months, but it has been anything but easy. To try to act as usual while pulling off the unthinkable has my heart racing from the minute I wake up until I fall asleep at night. School seems to stretch for days as my fears of what might happen when I'm not in my bedroom play through my head like a reel of pictures, repeating in a never-ending loop.

What if Mama or Papa find Hans, hear him, or go searching through my room? My stories are becoming too complicated to keep up with some days, and my excuses for noises and missing food have been hard to cover up, but I don't have a choice.

I listen to the radio far too often. My mind has trouble digesting Hitler's daily speeches regarding his plans to fix the country. Classmates follow his words blindly, believing everything he says, which includes the adverse remarks about Jewish people and how they are the biggest misfortune of our country. He has been working diligently to deport all German Jews to Poland as a part of his revolving plan. With this being put into motion over the past few weeks, Hans and I have been worrying about his mama and Danya. His papa too.

There are very few forms of communication available to us, so we haven't been able to check in with his family. The unknown toys with Hans's mind, making him sick with worry. I want to tell him the worst is behind us, but there is no end in sight, especially with us being in the center of this war. We should have faith in our country's military, but for me to have hope that Germany will come out on top is as good as giving in to Hitler's plans.

"Fräulein Ellman, have you listened to a word of today's lesson on the neo-Darwinian evolutionary theory? I can't express how important this matter is, and yet you are staring out the window like a lovesick fool," Frau Welling chides, pulling my attention from the aforementioned window.

"Of course," I reply. "However, I don't agree with the idealism of Darwin's theory of natural selection being used for the purpose of growing one race that shares genetic similarities. Forgive me, but the result of forcing life to evolve in a particular path is discrediting all other opinions in the world—ones I have yet to hear."

Normally, I wouldn't dare speak out of turn in class, but I have just a few months left of school and I'm tired of the hyper-focused education that is being funded by an uneducated man who would like this country to consist of people with only blonde hair and blue eyes.

"Fräulein Ellman," Frau Welling replies with a sharp tongue, then slaps her ruler against the chalkboard in the hope of shocking everyone into paying closer attention, "I will not tolerate this nonsense."

"Am I not allowed an opinion?" I question, placing my notebook in my bag. I assume she's seconds away from dismissing me for the day, hoping to continue her hypnotic lecture without a source of interruption.

"By all means, please feel free to use your opinion in the next exam, and we will see how your grade fares. This subject is non-negotiable, and the curriculum is standard for all students. If you cannot keep your opinions to yourself, I will have to expel you from this class. Do I make myself clear?"

I rest my hands on top of my desk and interlace my fingers, trying my best to appear unaffected at being told I'm not supposed to voice my personal beliefs. "Yes, Frau Welling."

For the rest of the lesson, I watch the minute hand on the clock ticking like a leaky sink. There isn't much that can make a day go by any quicker, but seconds before the bell rings, I gather my belongings and stand promptly at the hour, ready to make my way home, where my burning opinions are overshadowed by the life we are being forced to live. To lose my freedom of speech is nothing compared to losing my right as a human being to live without cruelty.

Winter has settled over us, an unrelenting gray sky that engulfs the country like a snow globe full of Arctic air and pellets of ice rather than the delicacy of beautiful snowflakes. There isn't an item of clothing I own that will keep the damp air from numbing my limbs as I make my way home. The days when I used to head home with Hans, the weather never bothered me much because our conversations would carry our minds to a faraway land. One of my favorite quotes from Hans is, "To dream of a better reality is a peephole into a future we have yet to see. It's our hope and answers to prayers, waiting for us to complete the challenges standing in our way." That is one of the few handwritten notes of his I keep hanging on my wall rather than in the crawl space.

As I place my bicycle along the brick wall of our building, I spot Papa's car parked along the street. He shouldn't be home for another couple of hours. Maybe he isn't feeling well. His mood has certainly not improved over the last few months. It wouldn't come as a surprise if he fell to his knees in the plea for a break from work, or life in general.

I make my way up the stairwell, ignoring the ache behind my stiff knees from pedaling against the freezing temperatures. But the pain in my body is about to be the least of my concerns as I step into our flat. Unwanted answers are written across Papa's face as he rests in his salmon-pink velour-covered armchair. He crosses one leg over the other, then lowers the daily newspaper down to his lap.

Before I'm able to remove my coat, Papa is pointing to the empty matching chair across from him, not where it usually resides on the other side of the small side table where he keeps his fine liquors.

"Where is Mama? And why are you home so early?" I question.

"Your mother is at the farmers' market. She forgot to pick something up this morning. I'm home early to handle a situation with the flat."

By the time he completes his explanation, I'm sitting stiff as a board on the chair across from him. "A situation, here?" I ask.

"Yes, I'm waiting for the pest exterminator to arrive. There have been some odd noises coming from within the walls above our bedroom. We think there might be a family of mice. I would hate for one of them to find a way into your bedroom, yes?"

I stand up from the chair. "Well, that's absurd. Certainly, I would hear such a noise, seeing as I'm up there as well. We don't need a professional, Papa. I can look around, and if there is a mouse or two, I'll find them a new home outside. However, you might consider the tree branch that has been rattling against the rooftop for the last year. Every time the wind blows, the branches rake along the outside wall."

Papa leans forward, crushing the newspaper beneath his elbows. "You've never cared for mice before. In fact, I believe you've called them pesky creatures in the past. What's changed?"

I ball my hands into fists, straightening them by my sides, and turn away from him as I hold back the need to scream at the top of my lungs. "I've seen people being treated worse than a mouse and I have a newfound appreciation for all living beings."

Papa clears his throat, likely because he can't come up with a response quickly enough. He's seen the same things I have. None of it is fair.

"Did you hear about the proclamation the Führer made today?"

"No, I haven't listened to the radio in a couple of days," I respond curtly.

"Yes, well, he made a proclamation to isolate all Jews. If they catch any citizen taking part in the growing German resistance, persecution —or worse, execution—will follow. You should know the gravity of the current situation here."

I open my mouth without thought or concern. "He's a crooked monster who deserves all that he has served." I hide my clenching fists behind my back, so Papa doesn't notice my tension.

He runs his fingers along his bottom lip, appearing to be lost in contemplation. "Think as you must, but our only job right now is to lie low beneath the radar, avoid trouble, and do as we are told. Those who are not cooperating are found far too easily, and it isn't ending well for them."

"Did Frau Welling telephone you about me speaking out of turn in class?" To put the spotlight on another unwanted action will hopefully distract him from whatever assumption he has about what's happening under his roof.

"No, Matilda. Why were you speaking out of turn?"

"Frau Welling seems to dislike me for whatever reason. She doesn't welcome opinions. She asked me to stop talking today."

Papa grumbles through an exhale. It's almost like it's his version of a scene break in a book. "Matilda, again, we are to fly beneath the radar. This world is at war, and this is not the time to test your boundaries as a coming-of-age adult. You must understand."

"Yes, Papa. I understand very well. I will stop taking part in class discussions unless I have something agreeable to speak about." Isn't that what every father wants for his daughter?

"If you need help removing the rodents from the attic, let me know and I will put in an emergency request to the exterminator."

"Yes, Papa."

"Good. Now then, go on and do your schoolwork before supper time."

My heart feels as though it's beating within my throat as I make my way into the bedroom and close the door. I turn on the old radio I claimed as my own when Papa brought home a newer, larger one for the family. I take a minute to settle the tuner to a channel without static, but no sooner than I become frustrated with the lack of tension in the knob, I hear the Führer ranting about his daily agenda. With the volume turned up a few notches, I feel safer sliding the bed and books away from the crawl space wall panel, eager to find Hans.

He's resting on the makeshift bed made of old blankets. The lantern I left lit this morning has burnt out.

"I'm home," I whisper with just half a breath.

It takes a long second for Hans to respond, but with slow movements, he sits up straight as if he is being lifted by a string—weightless, like a feather. "I have a terrible feeling your papa might know I'm up here, Matilda. He was yelling through the vents earlier, threatening to call an exterminator. He must be irate to think I'm here."

I shake my head furiously before he finishes his breathy statement. "He thinks he heard a family of mice. That's all. I told him I can handle it so he has nothing to worry about. I promise, he doesn't know you're here. Papa would have been more direct with me if he did."

I feel around for the box of matches that should be near the lantern. With the sun hiding deep within the clouds today, there is little light leaking into the space. Once I find the matches and light the short stub of the candle, I see a sickly look draining Hans's face.

"I can't allow anything to happen to you, Tilly. You were not born as a Jew, and you should not have to pay a consequence as if you were."

The shadows protruding from the lantern are not painting Hans in a wonderful light. The change in his appearance is becoming more prominent. His cheeks look concave, and the dark circles under his eyes are growing larger by the day. I'm not supplying him with enough food. That must be it. "Are you hungry?"

"You cannot avoid my statements forever, Matilda," he utters.

I pull my bag up behind me and retrieve the rolled-up brown paper bag containing my lunch. "Here, you need to eat," I whisper as I unroll the bag and release the items onto the blanket.

"I told you not to skip any more meals. What good is it if we both starve? There's no sense in trying to feed us both one portion. I will be okay, Tilly, but we are running out of time. You're going to need to find a family of mice if we want any hope of holding your papa off for a bit. I'm not sure what he even heard up here. I hadn't moved. Your mama was home until he returned from work early."

"Papa said she was at the market this morning."

"No, she was home," he responds.

"I'll figure something out, Hans. I will. Don't worry, okay?" I curl into his side and wrap my arm around his torso. "I'll keep you safe."

"You're freezing, Matilda."

"It doesn't matter. Because you're warm," I tell him.

School isn't an option this morning. I'm walking such a fine line between landing myself in trouble or someone finding Hans. I'm fighting to keep him safe by ensuring the attention is on myself. If I must choose one of two outcomes, I will take the wrath for skipping school. After a few weeks of ensuring Hans doesn't move so much as a hair during the hours Mama and Papa are home, I haven't been able to scrounge enough food for him because Mama has donated whatever we don't eat to the soldiers living downstairs. I give Hans as much of my meals as I am able to sneak away, without being noticed. It isn't enough. He's starving.

I've collected the gold jewelry I keep safe in a box on my nightstand. It isn't often we get dressed up anymore and I haven't needed to wear earrings, a necklace or bracelets lately. The jewelry is all family heirlooms, but it means they are worth something in exchange. With enough marks, I can gather more food for Hans and store the essentials away.

I heard Mama telling Papa she has plans to visit a friend for tea today, which means she will be out of the flat for at least a few hours. I need to plan my time accordingly.

My hands are shaking as I unfold my fingers and drop the jewelry onto the counter of the shop known to exchange goods for money. The man standing on the other side is staring at me as if I will eventually break and admit to what I'm doing here, but my guess is he is wondering about the value of gold a girl my age could be offering. I'm sure he doesn't often see many young women here.

He pulls out a magnifying glass to inspect each piece of jewelry, taking at least a minute with each item. His expression doesn't change, but a million thoughts are running through my head. He might take me for a fool and offer me less than what the jewelry is worth. I know little about trading gold for marks, but Hans mentioned the worth of gold per gram because his papa had to figure it out when the Nazis forced them to turn in all their valuables.

"My papa is a soldier, and his birthday is next week. I want to buy him something special to show him how much I love and appreciate everything he is doing for our family and our country," I tell the man. If I were to tell him the truth as to why I'm here, he would hand me back the items and tell me to go somewhere else, or worse. "It isn't easy. He's been working so many hours and he's so exhausted when he comes home late every night. I just want to make him smile again."

The man places the magnifying glass back onto the counter and leans toward me. "I could only wish my daughter would think so highly of me. Your papa is a lucky man," he says. "I'm going to give you ninety marks for all of this." The man stares me in the eyes as if he's being serious. From the math I did, the amount of gold I have is worth closer to five hundred.

"No, you can't be serious. There are at least nine grams of gold here." I placed it all on a scale the other day at school in the science lab. I'm sure the scale could have been off a bit, but not by as much as he's claiming.

The man chuckles and yanks on his suspenders. "Have you looked around, young lady? Gold isn't worth what it used to be around here."

"One hundred and ten marks or I will find another goldsmith." I raise my brow, proving the seriousness of my statement.

The man grinds his teeth, his jaw muscles flexing the sides of his cheeks. "One hundred and five or no deal."

"Is this how you would treat your daughter? If so, maybe I understand why she doesn't surprise you with gifts." I regret my words the moment they slip off my tongue, but the truth has a magical way of working from time to time.

The man slams his hands down on the counter and I do my best not to jolt. He pulls the drawer to his register open and counts out the marks. I watch as he makes his way to one hundred and ten before pushing the pile of money over to me.

"You better watch yourself, young lady. We are not living in a friendly world at the moment, and if you think you're going to work people over with quick-witted words, you might run into the wrong person one of these days."

I'll take his remark as a warning not to return to this shop, which is fine by me.

"Have a good day," I say with a slight curtsey before walking out the door.

I pick up my pace while making my way over to the village market, hoping they have enough canned goods. I need foods that won't perish quickly.

The shop is busy, as I expected for this time of day. While there is a higher chance of running into someone who might recognize me, I have to hope there's less of a chance that anyone will have long enough to put a name to my face. I've lived here long enough to know how quickly gossip travels.

I keep my scarf covering my head as I stand in the long line looping out of the store and around the corner of the block. The queues keep growing longer and longer by the day, and there are rumors of food rationing. It seems we're already at that point, but I'm not sure I want to know how much stricter they can be.

It takes nearly an hour to make my way to the entrance of the store and I can already see the selection isn't great, but there should be enough to fill up my bag with foods that will sustain Hans. This could be enough to last a couple of weeks at least. My rations allow for a small quantity of canned peas, beans, jam, salmon, and two units of sardines. I'm not sure these food items are very desirable, but it can't be much worse than the stale bread and cabbage he has become accustomed to, but food is survival at this point.

Once I place my bag on the counter and the clerk tallies my items, I'm rushed through the checkout process so the next customer in line can step forward. I'm happy to comply after waiting so long to collect what I need.

The clock tower in the center of town makes my heart skip a few beats when I see the time. I'm not sure when Mama will be home from tea, but it's close to one. I'm only a couple of blocks away and I walk as quickly as my feet will carry me through the ankle-deep snow left behind from the storm we had a few days ago.

The front of my building is within sight, but I'm forced to stop dead in my tracks when I find Papa home early again, this time having what looks like a friendly conversation with the two soldiers who are taking up residence below our flat. I don't know what to think, but it's hard not to jump to the worst-case scenario. Papa could have found Hans. Maybe he's telling the soldiers he has a stowaway.

I race around to the back of the building, taking the steps two at a time. The cans in my tote are crashing together, and the marks in my pocket are clinking like pieces of glass. Our front door is unlocked, Papa's coat is hanging from the hook on the wall, and the stairs leading to my bedroom look like they are a mile away. I fear every worst potential outcome with each step.

The lock on my door is rarely something I touch, but I need the extra seconds so I ease it closed behind me. I drop the bag down to the left side of my bed and throw myself toward the window overlooking the front entrance to the building. Papa is still talking to the men. I wish I could hear what they are saying.

They are all laughing, and the conversation looks more casual than I can stand to believe. Who would want to talk to those soldiers? Mama and Papa must somehow block out the thoughts of what these men and their counterparts do on a day-to-day basis. We hear the orders given on the radio. It isn't a secret, they are under the Führer's command.

I hide the bag behind my bureau and continue to watch the conversation outside. I wonder what Hans is thinking, if he knows Papa was here or if he's talking to the soldiers. What if they were all in our flat?

The moment I spot their conversation end, I unlock my door and jump into bed, pulling the covers up to my neck. For minutes on end, my heart races, my body sweats within my winter clothes beneath my blanket, and my mind darts with worry.

The door to our flat doesn't open. Papa doesn't come inside. Unless he's figured out which wooden floor panels don't make a sound versus the ones that do, he's not here. He has never had a reason to know how to avoid noises in our home. I doubt he even notices the creaks like I do. Yet, he can apparently hear a family of mice walking around the attic.

It's been almost four hours since I left Hans with a quick goodbye this morning and I'm eager to see him. I climb out of my bed and push it to the side. The books are next, and then I lift the wall panel away from the opening. I push in the tote bag first and follow. This time I replace the books and the bed to its proper position, leaving just enough space to open the panel a few inches to make my way back out later. The lantern is still lit, and Hans is asleep on his side. Ink-covered papers are lying all around the area, and I'm relieved to see that he's writing again. It has been over a week since he last wrote, and I was hoping he would pick up the pen once more. Starvation is bad enough, but keeping all of his words inside when he needs to release them is like suffocation.

He rolls onto his back and props himself up on his elbows. "You're home already."

"Yes, I didn't make it to school today. I went somewhere better, though."

"Tilly, what are you talking about? If they catch you skipping school, your papa is going to go mad."

"I don't care, Hans. Look in the bag. It's all for you."

I lift the tote and place it down gently on his lap.

He peeks inside and his eyes bulge with surprise. "Where did you get all of this?"

"It doesn't matter," I tell him.

His head falls to the side, giving me a long, hard stare. "You're lying, hiding things, and skipping school. You're not stealing now too, are you?"

"Stealing? You mean like the Nazis? What they're doing to every civilian? No, I'm not capable of that kind of despicable behavior."

"Then how, Tilly?"

"If I promise you that I did not steal, will you accept my request not to ask any more questions?" The last thing he needs is guilt attached to each tin can, every morsel of food that he eats.

He holds his stare against mine for another long minute before peering back into the bag. His stomach grumbles, echoing against the walls that surround us. He grabs his waist and curls over to mute the crying pang of hunger.

"No one is home," I say.

"Your papa was here. He was doing something around the house. I could hear his footsteps after your mama left this morning."

"Well, now you can eat," I tell him.

He twists toward me and places his hands on my cheeks, gazing at me with so much love, it's hard to understand how anyone being treated like a caged animal could love another being at all. Hans shifts his glance to my lips just before he leans down, touching his nose to mine. The kiss is soft as he scoops me up onto his lap. The intimate moment lingers much longer than it has before, and it's clear neither of us wants to move away from this point in time. "Whatever our future brings, please know you have given me everything and more."

"Don't speak that way. Everything is okay. You're safe. I'm safe. Okay?"

He shakes his head slowly and kisses me again. "Will you lay with me for a bit?"

"Forever, if I could."

At some point, we must shut off our feelings and stop asking the questions about a tomorrow we cannot predict. For the last few weeks, I have spent almost every night curled up in Hans's arms, staying by his side in the crawl space. Each night I fall asleep listening to the whispers of pages he has written during the day. Most of his thoughts are about me, imagining what life was like through the view of my eyes. I don't have to wonder what he thinks I see when I look at him. He knows I still stare into the eyes of my best friend, the man I love, and the one person in this world I would do anything for. Nothing else matters.

"You need to go to school, Tilly," Hans whispers in my ear.

I run my fingers through his hair and sweep my knuckles down the side of his face. His cheeks have filled out a bit since I brought in the canned food. I wasn't sure how much it would help, but it seems to have done enough to bring a glow to his skin and to brighten the whites of his eyes. He smiles at me each morning as if this is normal, the two of us waking up together side-by-side in a small attic space we share with a field mouse.

When I allow myself to forget about life outside, there is nothing abnormal about us. When we close our eyes, we can be anywhere we want to be. We take turns describing scenes of endless fields of green grass and wildflowers that smell like the sweet morning dew. Sometimes we imagine a day at a beach where the sand is gold and the water a perfect distribution of blue and green hues. A light breeze blows through our hair with the sun gently warming our skin, as a flock of seagulls sing perfectly out of sync over the mellow waves. Our lungs pull in an abundance of fresh air, and we are worry-free, anchored from the gravitational pull of darkness on the other side of our eyelids.

"Frau Welling is the very last person I want to see today," I mutter.

"I will be the last person you see today," Hans says, pinching my cheek.

"I suppose there could be worse things in life than waking up next to you every morning," I tease.

He cups his hand around the back of my head and kisses me with a fervent heat. "I'm lucky. That's all I can say, Tilly."

"Me too," I reply, touching my forehead to his. "The luckiest."

"The quicker you go to school, the faster you can return, yes?" he says.

"I suppose if you want to look at it that way, I'll get moving." I give him one last kiss and wrap a spare blanket around my body, preparing to crawl out of the tight space. "When I come home from school today, there's something I want to talk to you about—something wonderful."

"How can you tease me like that, Tilly?"

"Some things in life are worth waiting for," I whisper, leaving him with a kiss on the cheek. "Perhaps, it will make the day go by quicker."

"I'll dream about whatever it is all day then," he says. "Be safe, love."

Once I've secured the wall panel and replaced my bed and books, I find a fresh set of clothes and get ready for school.

Mama and Papa have been quiet toward me lately. They haven't been asking me hundreds of questions or giving me looks of curiosity. It's as if they've lost the energy to fight for the answers I refuse to offer. At least, I hope that's the case.

There have been a few occasions where I have heard them arguing in their bedroom late at night, but I can't make out what they're in a disagreement about. It's been a few days since the last outburst, so maybe they have settled their differences. One can only hope.

By the time I make my way downstairs, Mama appears to have been up for hours, baking and cooking.

"It looks like you're preparing a feast for more than three," I say, taking a seat at the table with a bowl of oatmeal.

"I got to the butcher early enough this morning that they had larger portions of pork available. So, I'm making a nice dinner for our family tonight, and I thought it would be a kind gesture to invite the young gentlemen from downstairs up for a home-cooked meal. Food always helps people feel better. At least that's what my mother used to tell me," Mama says.

"The gentlemen downstairs?" I question. "The Nazis?" My brow rises with a question, hoping she will understand the difference between a gentleman and a Nazi.

"Yes, Matilda, the soldiers have been away from their homes for almost a year, and they deserve a home-cooked meal."

My stomach feels hollower than it did a moment ago. We're bringing these men into our house, just feet away from where a Jewish man is hiding?

"Mama, I'm sure they are being taken care of just fine. After all, they were so nicely given a family's home instead of them going to live in a building without windows and doors."

"Matilda, I cannot endure this argument with you any longer. Can't you see what problems it is causing here?"

"Is everything all right between you and Papa? Is that what this is about?"

Mama dries her hands on a dishrag and turns around to face me, leaning against the kitchen sink. "I'm not sure." I notice the red stains in the whites of her eyes and her blotchy cheeks.

"I don't understand," I say.

"I assume you have overheard the disagreements between your father and I over the last few weeks?"

Rather than respond right away, I drop my spoon into the oatmeal, watching the mush spill into the small metal basin. "Nothing specific, just the volume of your voices," I reply.

"Papa constantly worries about our well-being."

I'm sure everyone feels the same. We're at war with France and Great Britain. There is more to worry about than I want to wrap my head around.

"Therefore, we should invite the Nazis over for dinner?" I reply. "What sense does that make?"

Mama takes a step forward and pulls out the chair beside me to sit down. "Matilda, I have told you time and time again that we must keep our friends close and our enemies closer."

"Of course, except you watched as they kicked your friends out of their home and did nothing about it, right?"

Mama's mouth droops at the corners as she pinches her lips together tightly, trying to hide the truth she must feel inside. "Matilda, please."

"Or are they the enemy now? Because, if so, we certainly aren't keeping them close either. So, forgive me, Mama, but I'm very confused."

She folds her chapped hands together on top of the table. It looks as if she's been doing extra loads of dishes by the red, dry scales covering her fingertips.

"Your papa knows."

Her three words force the one bite of oatmeal I have consumed to catch in my throat, making me cough.

Mama hands me a glass of orange juice. "Drink, drink."

After I clear my throat, I place the back of my hand over my mouth. "What are you talking about? What does Papa know?"

"How long do you think you can keep him up there, Matilda?"

"The mouse?" I'm up against a wall with nowhere else to turn.

"Matilda, I am not talking about a mouse." Mama hasn't spoken so sweetly to me in years. The softness of her voice is causing me more concern than contentment. "We know Hans is upstairs."

Without wanting to confirm or deny the accusation, I take a long moment to stare directly into her eyes, wondering where I got my heart from when theirs seems to be frozen solid with ice.

"Jewish people are humans like us, Mama. Surely, you know what Hitler is doing to them," I whisper through my gritted teeth.

Mama inhales a sharp breath of air through her nose. "Who are we to fight against the Führer? We don't have a chance of overturning direct orders, and by trying, we are putting our lives in jeopardy. Your papa wants to keep us safe, and you make that impossible. Why must it be this way?" she pleads, holding her hands up in prayer.

"Ask Hitler," I say, lifting my bowl from the table to take my half-eaten breakfast to the sink. The thought of pouring any remnants out when Hans would do anything for a hot breakfast makes my stomach hurt.

"Matilda, I can't be responsible for your papa's actions," she says.

"What does that mean?" I ask, turning away from the bowl I have placed on the counter.

She presses her lips into a straight line and shakes her head. "I'm so sorry, darling."

My feet feel as if they are sticking to the floor. I can't figure out how to move, even though shivers are trailing up my spine. My stomach lurches and a wave of sickness washes over me. I lean forward, clutching my stomach, waiting for my legs to regain control so I can race to the washroom, hearing Mama follow closely behind.

I thankfully make it to the toilet before the bit of breakfast I ate travels back up my throat.

"I'm sorry, Matilda. I am. I didn't mean to make you ill."

"What's going to happen, Mama?" I ask through a rasp in my throat.

Mama hands me a glass of water and sweeps a fallen strand of hair away from my face. "Your papa wouldn't tell me. He doesn't trust me to keep this information from you."

I need to get Hans away from this building.

"Well, where is he now?"

"He said he was going to work, but I'm not sure what to believe. He has not been at work when he says he is lately. I don't know what else he is hiding, Matilda. All I know is he is trying to keep us safe."

"From what? The men you have invited into our home tonight?" I groan through the burning pain in my throat.

"I'll let the school know that you're ill and won't be attending today," she says. She pats my back and stands up. "Come on, sit down."

"Why, so I can sip on some tea while we wait for more atrocities to happen in this world? No, Mama. I can't play along with these charades."

"Matilda, if anyone thinks you are intentionally hiding a man in our attic, they will—" She folds her hand over her mouth as tears bubble in the corners of her eyes. "You have a heart made of gold, but that isn't a quality anyone admires right now. It will get you killed."

"I'm not sure I care, Mama."

She combs her fingers through her hair like she does when she's upset and clenches her eyes as if she is fighting an internal battle she cannot win. "Okay," she sighs. "Maybe there's something we can do to help. He must be hungry, so let's get him a proper meal—something warm and fresh. I'll give you some marks to go and see if there's anything left at the store today. Then we'll come up with a plan together."

If I take the money, it is a confession that he is upstairs, but if I don't take it, I will end up denying him a warm meal. "Do you promise, Mama?"

"I will do whatever I can to help you, Matilda."

I'm not sure if I would know if she was lying. I should be able to look into my mother's eyes and know whether she is telling the truth.

She walks over to the coat hook and pulls a handful of marks out of her purse. "Here you are. I will stay here and make sure nothing happens if your papa returns. I don't think he will listen to you if you are here alone."

"How are you so sure he will listen to you?"

"Matilda, go before it's too late, please." She hands me my coat.

I look off toward the stairs that lead to the attic, wishing I could barricade my room. "I will never forgive you if you are lying, Mama."

"Matilda," she cries. "I'm your mother."

"I know. That hurts the most," I tell her as I walk out the door.

CHAPTER 16

2018

I didn't realize I had been pacing the shop while reading, but I found myself needing a break while wishing I could warn Matilda not to trust her mother, my great-grandmother.

"How's the reading going?" Archie asks from behind the counter.

"This is intense," I sigh.

"Here, how about a cup of tea?" he suggests, dropping crystal-looking sugar cubes into a white porcelain cup, then pouring hot water from an antique kettle through a metal infuser. I watch the tea dribble over the sugar cubes and the sweet aroma warms me from the inside. He must notice my inquisitive stare. "These are Kluntje—sugar lumps like a sort of rock candy."

"It smells delicious." I rest the packet of papers on the counter. "I've only ever used a teabag."

"A teabag?" Archie questions with a cute chuckle. "My family, and yours, believed there was only one way to make tea and there are no shortcuts involved."

In Boston, I feel like all we do is search for the next best shortcut in life. I'm coming to realize how much we might be missing out on.

I press my hands onto the countertop, taking a closer look at what he's doing. "Well, if I haven't had proper tea before, I likely wouldn't know the difference, right?"

"Until now," he says, placing the cup onto a saucer.

I reach for the cup, but he holds a finger up.

"Hold on, I haven't added the final touch." He turns around and opens the short stainless-steel refrigerator and pulls out a glass bottle of milk or cream and retrieves a metal spoon from the stack of drawers next to the refrigerator. He spills the cream-like substance onto the metal spoon before dribbling it over the steaming tea. "You can't stir it. It must sit as is for the full effect of the three layers of tastes."

I had no clue there was an art form to making a cup of tea. I can understand why he might laugh at the thought of a teabag.

He slides the cup and saucer across the counter, then begins the process again to pour himself a serving. I wait for him before taking a sip, but he peers up at me while pouring the cream over his tea.

"Go on. East Frisian Tea is quite popular here and has been since the 1800s. This shop has always offered it to keep a tight hold on our roots and authenticity. The original owner's mother thought of it as a cure to all of life's problems."

I've never felt so honored to be given a cup of tea before. "Should I hold my pinkie up? Is that proper etiquette?" I'm partly joking, but a little serious. I feel very out of my element here when it comes to manners.

Archie drops his head with laughter while placing his cup down on a saucer. "No, you don't have to hold the teacup like that. However, I've been debating whether it would be polite to offer you a straw."

We're both quiet for a moment because I'm not sure if he's serious or making a joke, but he clears up my question when he bursts into laughter.

"I'm just teasing you."

"How about I just apologize now for any manners that might be lacking common formalities here?" I suggest.

"Don't be silly. There's no need to apologize for your way of life. I'm sure Boston has many unique traditions that I would be confused about."

I think for a minute, trying to come up with a unique tradition we have in New England, but nothing comes to mind. "We lack boundaries and rarely watch the words coming out of our mouths. We're kind of loud and can be rowdy. So, I'm not sure how uncomfortable that would make a visitor."

"Oh, yes, I've heard Boston is a lot like Ireland," he says with a wink, before blowing a bit of the steam off the rim of his cup.

"Yes, we have a lot of Irish culture in Boston."

"Well, it sounds charming." His smile is endearing and makes me smirk in return.

"That's exactly how I would describe it too," I say, stifling a laugh.

I follow his lead and blow on the steam before taking a sip of the tea. It's bold, and full of flavor. It's like nothing I've tasted before and it offers a similar feeling as if someone were draping a blanket around my shoulders.

"This is delicious. Thank you so much."

"My pleasure." His eyes glimmer beneath the hanging lights and he holds his gaze on me as he takes another sip. He feels so familiar, yet how can he be?

I'm walking along the street, staring down at the handful of marks in the cup of my palm. If my parents knew about Hans hiding in the crawl space, I can't understand why they have let this go on for so long. They have known Hans since he was small. I would like to think they have a soft spot in their hearts for him, especially after watching what happened to his family. He has never been rude or disrespectful to us. On the contrary, he always showed us gratitude and kinship, just as his parents had. There's no explanation for a changing view of someone who we all know to be an innocent man.

I need to get him out of the attic before tonight. It isn't safe for him to be sitting directly above where we will share a meal with the Nazis from downstairs. Any creak or slight movement would cause an uninvited inspection. That's what these men do. They are essentially the exterminators—except they aren't hunting mice. No one is hunting for rodents right now—it's the Jewish people we are supposed to trap and remove.

I'm not sure where to hide Hans or how easy it will be to get him out of the building without being seen. There are no Jews left in the town now. If anyone recognized him, they would know he should not be here. Hiding the truth from officials is treason.

I feel like we're being chased toward a barricade, a brick wall, a ledge. Yet, it isn't me who is being chased: it's Hans alone.

The sun is breaking through the clouds for the first time in what feels like weeks. The Arctic blast of air has lessened, but the snow-covered streets are now dirt-covered slush. I pull my coat tighter over my chest as I focus on a truck creeping toward me. It isn't until the wheels splash me with cold sludge, passing me by in the opposite direction, that I recognize the men in the vehicle.

I thought the men in uniform would be at work at this hour of the morning.

Just as I'm about to enter the outskirts of downtown, I spot Papa's car. He isn't at work. He is driving toward our home.

He's following the soldiers.

A paralyzing sensation knocks me down to my knees, straight into an icy puddle. Mama told me to leave.

As if the sky is responding to my fears, the clouds swallow the sun, stealing its chance to offer any more warmth.

I twist and look over my shoulder, watching the taillights of Papa's car. He drove right past me. He must have seen me walking. I press myself up to my feet and run as fast as my legs will carry me.

Puddles are soaking my legs with every pounce, but I don't feel the temperature. Nothing can mask the unwavering fear filling every nerve in my body. I clench my eyes as I push myself to move faster, praying I don't trip. As I reach our building, I find the soldiers chatting with Papa outside of their parked vehicle, enjoying each other's company, laughing.

A minute doesn't pass before Papa spots me pulling into the parking area. He narrows his eyes in my direction with clear inquisition. "Matilda, why are you not at school?" he calls out.

"Why are you not at work?" I counter his question.

"I don't see how it's any of your business."

The soldiers have their eyes on me. It's as if they can smell a person's weakness.

"What's going on?" I ask.

"Matilda, you shouldn't be here," he says calmly.

"I live here," I respond.

Papa glances back to the soldiers, then nods his head, and they walk on toward the entrance of the building. "Matilda, go wait in my car, please." He points to where he parked, but refuses to look at me while making such an odd command.

"No. I'm going upstairs." I spin around to follow in the path of the soldiers, walking directly past Papa.

"Matilda," he scolds, grabbing me by the wrist. "I have warned you. Do not force me to make a scene."

"A scene?"

"I'm protecting you," he mutters through gritted teeth.

I'm breathing so hard I can't form a response to his words. "Papa," I cry.

"If they think he has snuck into our attic for a place to hide, they will not hold you responsible. If they find we have been helping him, the story will be much different, Matilda. Is that boy worth dying for? Have you asked yourself this question?"

I'm staring into my father's eyes, trying to find anything I might recognize. The man who used to carry me around on his shoulders while we ran through meadows picking flowers, the role model who would bring me gifts every time he brought something for Mama to thank her for taking such good care of him, he's gone. There is nothing left within the blue sea of his once-bright eyes. He has lost his compassion, faith, and hope. He has chosen the side of evil.

"How could you do this?" I whisper, tugging my hand against his tight grip.

"You will thank me for your life someday, Matilda. A father's job is to protect his child from harm, and that's what I'm doing."

"You are protecting me by hurting another person. What is that teaching me? I should hate everyone but myself, or that I'm the only one who matters? Maybe it's just that no one could be more impor-tant than me?" I press my free hand against his arm, trying my hardest to escape from his hold. "No, Papa. I'm not selfish, I'm a helper, a lover, a friend, and I am loyal, unlike you. I'll never be like you."

Papa opens the door of his car and shoves me inside, then slides into the driver's seat, closing us both in. I shuffle to the other side, trying to reach the door handle, but I find the door to be locked—he never locks the door.

"How will you live with yourself, knowing what you are doing? You are just as bad as they are, you know that? Let me out, Papa."

"Stop this childish behavior at once," he snaps, glaring at me.

I feel like the roof is caving in on me as the front door of the building opens. The Nazis have Hans. His eyes are open wide with disbelief. Maybe he's hoping this is another nightmare he will wake up from. Though his pale complexion, the loss of color in his lips, and the sheen attracting a glow of sunlight on his forehead tell me every little thought going through his head.

He isn't fighting to escape. I don't understand why he isn't pulling against the hold of these men. Instead, he's walking as if in agreement. Hans is a fighter, the sweetest of all fighters, but he doesn't just give in. He would never give in. He would run, if necessary, but he's not trying to free himself. He must know it's his only chance to get away.

I pound my fists on the window, screaming his name, but no one looks over at Papa's car. We might as well be hiding behind a wall.

"Where are they taking him? Where?" I shout.

"Matilda, I didn't ask such a ridiculous question. How is that any of my business?"

"You don't understand what you're doing. Let me out of this car. Let me go right now. I need to tell him. He needs to know. He needs to know, Papa." My voice is becoming hoarse the more I shout. Every one of my words is in vain, unheard, ignored, blocked out.

"What is it you must tell the boy, Matilda? Really? What could be so important right now?"

"Let me say goodbye, Papa," I demand.

"They will know you were protecting him, Matilda. This will all be for nothing. They will not spare his life or yours if you speak out at this moment. Do you understand me?"

"No. I understand nothing. I hate you for this. I will always hate you for what you have done."

"You're just angry, Matilda. This too shall pass," he laments as if this is nothing—as if I'm not watching Hans being shoved into the back of a wagon so they can transport him to some place in hell.

"They're going to kill him, aren't they?"

"He's a child. I doubt they will kill him."

He's eighteen. He's not a child. We celebrated his birthday in silence by candlelight only three weeks ago. I'm not sure what we were celebrating, but it felt normal for just a moment. I gave him a new notebook and pen, wrapped in a piece of linen, and made a bow out of ribbon. He opened the gift and smiled as if I had given him everything he'd ever wanted, but then handed the notebook back.

"I still have so much paper left, Tilly. A gift to me would be your words. For whenever we are not together, I want to know you are saving each thought to share with me the next time we see each other.

I could see life through your eyes, and it would help me through the dark hours in here. Could I ask for that gift instead?"

"I can't write like you. You have a talent that I cannot possibly match," I told him.

"When you close your eyes, Tilly, the words will find you. Just write what comes to mind, and it will be perfect."

I agreed with a slight nod, realizing he must have run out of topics to write about. A person can't possibly find inspiration when sitting in a dark hole all day. "Of course, I will write for you. I will keep track of everything I see when I'm not here with you, and I won't miss any details. I promise."

"That is the best birthday gift I could receive, Matilda. I love you so very much."

I curled into Hans's side and tilted my head back to kiss the spot beneath his ear that makes him smirk. He embraced me tightly, shielding me from life outside of the small space. Sometimes, I felt as though I couldn't possibly be close enough to him, even when we were together as one.

I spot Hans in the back of the truck's wagon. For a moment I question if he can see me through the window, but I see him mouth the words: "Write for me. I love you." He gestures with his hand to write, then places his fingers on his lips for the kiss I cannot have.

I pause for a long second, fearful that a soldier witnessed the exchange, but it seems they aren't paying attention for the moment. I cup my hand over my mouth, wishing it wasn't the last thing he saw of me, but I've never felt so much agony. There's no way to put on a front or hide the truth of what this moment is doing to me. I inhale a deep breath and hold it in my lungs as I mouth back, "I love you. So much."

The moment the soldiers pull away from the building, Papa releases me from the car. "I need to get back to work. Mind your mother, Matilda," he says, his words strangled within his throat.

Though my chest throbs as if I've been impaled by a sharp object, I hold my shoulders back and my chin up, refusing to appear weak, succumbing to his cruelty. I can't understand how Papa, of all the people in the world, has managed to break my heart so irreparably. It's obvious he couldn't care less that he stole a piece of my heart and threw it to a pack of hungry wolves.

I'll never forgive him, not ever. "I hate you," I tell him again.

"My God, Matilda, get a hold of your emotions. If you want to make decisions like you have, you will learn to live with the consequences after."

There's nothing left to say when I back away and race toward the front door. I'm breathless by the time I run up the stairs to the front door of our building. I can't breathe. There is not enough air to take in right now. With every ounce of strength I have, I rush into our flat. I ignore the tears running down Mama's face, the pain she is portraying while holding her arms around her waist as if someone beat her with a stick. No one has laid a hand on her. It's a reaction of shame because she knows what she did. She knows she betrayed me, and she knows I will never forgive her either.

My bedroom is in a shambles. They threw everything I own across the floor. The mongrels even tore away the pretty wallpaper near the crawl space.

I grab my school bag and toss a few items inside before leaving the mess behind.

Mama still has nothing to say as I run past her again. I slam the door on the way out of our home.

I locate my bicycle against the side of the building and I cut through the woods, hoping the dirt will keep me from sliding along the snow patches. If I can make my way through the trees fast enough, I can catch up to the truck. I can find out where they are taking Hans.

CHAPTER 18

GRACE

2018

I've exchanged a cup of tea for a handful of tissues I've needed over the last hour of reading the demise of Matilda's family. I'm drawing conclusions of my own, wondering about what I will read next, if it will break my heart as much as the last few pages have. Matilda sounds like a good person, which leaves me feeling more confused about how she could have given up Mom as a baby.

I place the pages down on my lap and press the tissues beneath my raw eyes. "This is a lot to take in," I tell Archie. He's straightening books on a shelf a few feet away from me.

"I assumed it would be, and while I know about your grandmother's history, I don't feel right providing the details when they are so accurately described on those pages."

I want to ask him a million questions, but he has made it clear that he doesn't want to be the bearer of news, and maybe it's for the best. If I were to take this all in at once, it might be harder to digest. Although my spiraling thoughts may be in a far darker place than necessary too.

"My grandfather and Hans were best friends," he says. "They went through a lot together, some of which I didn't know until after my father passed away. Their generation—what they went through, it was too hard for many of them to speak about. Of course, we know how important it is to talk about our traumas as a form of healing, but life back then is nearly impossible for us to understand. Our minds can only comprehend snippets, and nothing can come close to the atrocities so many in this town experienced."

I stand up from my seat, finding my legs have fallen asleep from the position I had been sitting in for too long. "Ms. Cora mentioned other areas of the shop, a living quarter?" I ask.

"Yes, of course. Give me a moment to put a sign up on the door. Many people visit for a history lesson and if I'm not downstairs, well —they will explore," Archie says with a grin.

"I can imagine." As he locks the front door, I say, "What questions do you get asked the most?"

He chuckles quietly and turns toward me as he drops the keys into his back pocket. "Where is the next closest café? That's the question I receive the most." His response is unexpected and makes me laugh too. It's a much-needed break from the tension tugging at every vein in my body.

"Well, maybe I can understand that since the digital maps don't seem to work very well around here," I say.

"That's true. This area doesn't have a full satellite perspective available online. If anything, it will hopefully teach folks how to use a map again."

"Thankfully, I know how to use one."

"I'd say you have an excellent sense of awareness. I'm not sure I'd have the—ah—I'm not sure I know the right word—nerve—to travel to the United States alone and expect to find precisely where I need to go within a few short days."

"You might be surprised to learn what a burning question will cause a person to do," I respond.

"I suppose I can't argue that fact. Here, follow me. I'll show you around."

I follow Archie through a back door, one that looks older than the main entrance. The wood is worn and discolored but still beautiful and distinct. It makes me wonder how many times my grandmother placed her hand on the worn spot above the bronze doorknob.

I press my fingers to the oak-colored wood, wishing I could sense a connection of some sort. But that only happens in fictional stories and movies.

Archie catches my brief pause as I stare at the one spot on the door. "Are you all right?"

"Sorry, yes," I say, continuing to follow him up a narrow stairwell.

"You don't need to apologize," he says. The stairs whine and moan with each step. "You might wonder why there appears to have been minimal upkeep over the years."

"Well, beyond the laws of some historical zones I know about, thanks to my years in architecture, I can imagine someone might think twice before taking a hammer to the aged wood."

"Both are a part of the reason." He pauses. "I didn't know you were an architect?"

"Yes, I've been with a firm since I graduated from college, so I've had to become intimate with zoning laws and historical landmarks. But I assume laws may be different here than they are in the United States."

"Well, after learning about your cultural etiquette and rowdy ways of life, I might assume the same," he says, quirking a smile to one side.

"I would have to agree with you there."

"I'm sure no one ever wants to alter history, especially here in Dachau—not after all this town has seen following the fallout of the Napoleonic Wars and then World War Two."

"How do you feel about that?" I ask as we reach the top of the stairs. The ceiling drops into a sharp angle and Archie has to duck before continuing down the short, dark hallway. I fit beneath the drop by just an inch. It's a tight squeeze up here.

"My grandfather lived in the Dachau camp for nearly four years," Archie says. "He always appreciated them not tearing down all the remains. As painful as it was to revisit, it stands as a form of evidence for what hatred can cause. The memorial is life-changing for many people, and for that, I support the meaning behind its lasting existence, and as a Jewish man, I couldn't be prouder to live in this town. Hitler tried to eliminate our heritage and race, but I'm proof that he failed. Of course, that's not to say all residents are Jewish here, but those who are not stand for and believe in the same as I do. Without the memories of the fallen, we will fall again. Therefore, we keep this town as it should be—a reminder, and a chapter in a history book."

In a moment, Archie has answered so many of my questions. He's made me see this entire experience in a completely different light. "That's noble and very insightful."

"I imagine what you must have been thinking when you found out about this location," he says. "The question of why this shop is here is the second most asked from visitors." Archie twists his head over his shoulder to give me a quick wink before opening another worn door. Light spills out into the hallway, making the area feel bright and spacious with a homely feel. It's a studio-like living space with a bed in the center, a bureau, writing desk, and two armchairs. "There's also a washroom and toilet down across the way."

"Are you the one living here at the moment?"

"Oh, no, I live about a mile away," he says.

The bedroom looks as though it hasn't been touched in a while. "Does someone live here now?"

"No one has been occupying this space for some time now, but I've made sure to keep it clean and dusted for whenever someone might need to use it."

"But it looks like these are all someone's belongings," I suggest, moving past Archie to touch the quilt on the bed. It's a faded gray blue with a floral pattern, and there's a closet off to the corner concealed by a hanging drape. There are women's dresses on hangers. A jewelry box is on the dresser, surrounded by old bottles of perfume.

"There hasn't been an estate sale yet, so your grandmother's belongings are still here for now."

"I see." I make my way toward the window and peer outside, following the kaleidoscope colors of the village that weave around the hill's steep descent. My gaze moves toward the contrasting landscape of green pines against the backdrop of snow-capped mountains that flirt with a thin layer of clouds on the horizon. "No wonder it's so bright in here."

"Believe it or not, on a perfectly cloudless day, you can see the tips of the Bavarian Alps. They're quite stunning."

I step away from the window and circle around once more, feeling as though I can't take it all in at once because there are so many details I want to study.

"I should reopen the shop. If you need another minute, you're welcome to stay up here, of course."

"Oh, I'm okay, thank you," I tell him.

We make our way back down the steps toward the door that leads to the shop.

"There is also some storage space. It's the only part of the interior that has gotten a minor update since the items inside need to be kept at room temperature and dry."

"What's kept in this space—is it like a closet?"

I spot a new customer waiting in front of the door as we walk down the aisle of the shop.

"Oh, a variety of items that belong to various people."

Archie continues to unlock the front door, welcoming in the waiting queue of people. He apologizes in both German and English. Everyone seems understanding and then taken aback as they enter the store.

Then, there's me, standing here like a lost soul who must make an impossible decision. I cannot run a business in Germany from the United States, but how could I give up something that belonged to the biological family Mom had spent her life searching for?

I return to the chair I had been sitting on and retrieve the bound papers. Just as I open to where I left off, my phone rings loudly from my purse. I reach for it as quickly as possible, mortified at making such a racket.

Before I lift my finger from the answer button, Carla is shouting. I hold the phone up to my ear but keep it an inch away to spare myself losing my hearing. "Grace Laurent, answer me!"

"I'm sorry. I've been busy," I tell her.

"I've texted you like four hundred times. You were going to check in with me. Did you forget? You're in a foreign country alone and I'm responsible for you."

"You are not responsible for me," I whisper in response. "I'm a grown woman, just like you. You're acting crazy."

"If I'm not responsible for you, then who is?" she questions.

"Me, obviously."

"Why are you whispering?"

"I'm in the bookshop and there is a customer."

"And did you just say you are being responsible for yourself? Because if I'm not mistaken, you made a split-second decision to travel to a country where you don't speak the language or know a single person. Excuse me for assuming it has become my responsibility to watch over your crazy butt."

I switch the phone to my other ear so I can turn toward the corner, hoping to avoid anyone overhearing my conversation. "Carla, I promise you I'm being cautious. I've met with the attorney this morning, and now I'm talking to the gentleman who has been tending to the bookshop. I wasn't ignoring your texts. It's been consuming."

"A gentleman?" she questions as if it's the only word she heard out of my entire explanation.

I sigh. "Yes, Carla. A man runs the store."

"Is he good-looking?"

I place my free hand on my cheek, feeling the dramatic temperature difference from my cold palm to my warm face. "Possibly. I need to go. I will call you when I leave here later, I promise. Just relax, okay? Nothing is going to happen to me."

"You can't just leave me hanging like this, Grace," she whines into the phone.

"I don't have a choice. Someone is staring at me. I'll tell you everything soon."

I think I might have hung up as she was asking me another question, but Archie is looking at me like I'm nuts, hiding in a corner with my phone pressed up to my ear.

"Is everything okay?" he asks.

I stand from the chair and make my way toward Archie at the counter. "My best friend, Carla, is worrying about me traveling alone. If I don't respond to her messages, she jumps into mom-mode," I say, laughing off the situation.

"I'm glad someone is looking out for you. Your friend sounds like a good person."

"She is," I reply, but I'm itching to get back to my grandmother's story. "Where did they take Hans? The Nazis?" I ask.

He tilts his head to the side and reaches for the papers I am clenching within my hand. "Read. Please."

CHAPTER 19
MATILDA
MARCH 1941

I'm not sure how much longer I can keep up my speed on the bicycle. The wet roads are working against my legs, and I'm soaked, which is weighing me down more. But I need to know where they are taking Hans.

My legs feel numb as they move of their own accord and my hands are whiter than the snow with how hard I've been gripping the handlebars, but I've been so focused on staying out of the soldier's line of sight that I have paid little attention to my physical well-being.

Maybe it's only been a mile, but it could have been three or four for all I know. Out here, there is nothing more than farmland and outstretched dead grass covered with patches of snow, sporadic clusters of trees enveloping a road that looks as though it might lead to the end of the world. The distance is all I can manage.

The vehicle I've been following comes to a stop on the side of the road, forcing me to drop my bicycle into a mess of frozen brush. I lie low, peeking between shrubbery to see what's happening, but I only catch a glimpse of one of the two soldiers sliding out of the driver's seat.

"Ach mist! We still have twenty kilometers to Dachau," the other soldier shouts out the window. "Come on, comrade. We're on a schedule."

"It'll just take me a minute," the one walking through the snow says.

My heart sinks. Dachau. It's too far from here. It will take me hours to follow. Word of mouth at school was that most of the men over the age of eighteen were being sent to work at a Dachau camp while the women remained in the community, but that was only until the Nazis deported them to Poland. We weren't sure about Hans's family because there was no way to find out without putting him in danger.

I'll need to take a train. I wish I could tell him I will come for him. He must know I won't just let them take him.

The soldier in the middle of the snowy field relieves himself with his back toward the truck and me. He returns to the vehicle a moment later, and no sooner than the door closes are the wheels rolling again.

After all the effort it took to follow, I know I can't go as far as they can, and my heart is shattering into a million pieces as I watch for as long as possible until the truck disappears into the cloudy horizon.

I suddenly feel the chill from the snow and the blustery wind as if it hits me in the face like a bag of ice. My heart thunders, making me feel breathless, before I pull my bicycle up and out of the branches. If my head was not secure to my body, I would swear it's spinning.

The ride back feels like hours long, but it isn't. There hasn't been enough time to plan out what comes next. I need to get to Dachau, but once I leave home, there is no coming back. I don't have the means to support myself for longer than a week or two, and it won't get easier. Nothing will get easier.

The hike up the stairs is tearing at my muscles with every step I take, and the front door of the flat feels as if a heavy piece of furniture is resting against the other side as I push through.

Mama is still in tears, sitting on Papa's chair. It's like she was the one taken away by the two Nazis she wants to call her friends.

"You look like a fool, crying," I tell her.

"Where have you been, Matilda? I went looking for you. I even went to the school, but they hadn't seen you either."

"Does it even matter?" I ask her, taking my coat off one sleeve at a time.

"Matilda, you must know this wasn't my decision. I want you to believe me."

I shake my head as I hang up the coat and slide my sopping-wet boots off my feet. "Whether it was your decision or Papa's, you sat there and watched. That doesn't make you a better person, Mama. In fact, I'm not sure how to look at you and convince myself we are related. I don't ever want to become like you."

Mama stands from the chair, holding her arms over her apron. The fact she's still wearing it leads me to believe she didn't go looking for me. She wouldn't leave home the way she's dressed.

"What was I supposed to do? Claim I'm a part of the German Resistance, or better yet, admit to treason? How many times do we need to tell you what they do to anyone resisting orders? It's like you don't hear a word of what we're saying, and we're fighting to keep our nearly adult daughter safe. I don't know what's going through your mind lately, but it pains me beyond words I can express that you're going to get yourself killed, Matilda."

"At least I would be asking for it," I reply.

It's true. Hans and his family didn't ask for this treatment. They were born into a race and heritage that has become a genetic marker, labeling them as the enemy.

"Matilda! How can you say such a thing?"

"I assume it's like you having the ability to still look at yourself in the mirror every morning. I no longer care."

Rage fires through Mama's eyes as if I pushed her too far. She has never proven to be a robust woman, not beneath Papa's leadership in our family. She marches toward me as if she would strike me. She won't; she doesn't have the courage. Although sometimes I wish she did, because then she wouldn't have the excuse of being so weak-minded that she goes along with every poor decision made in this country.

She steps up to me, her stocking-covered toes nearly touching mine. "I will not tolerate the way you are speaking to me. No more, Matilda. I am still your mama, and I deserve some respect. You may think you can walk all over me when Papa isn't home, but you're wrong."

Her words form softly but with grit. But I'm not afraid. My entire life she has proven to be a coward. A person doesn't change overnight.

I stare her coldly in the eyes, waiting for her next move. She can say or do whatever she would like because nothing will hurt more than watching Hans being shoved into the back of a truck this morning.

Mama lifts her hand timidly and swings her palm against my cheek. I refuse to flinch at the burn or fall helplessly at the shocked look in her eyes. She takes a step away and her gaze drops to my hands.

"Why are you holding your stomach in that way, Matilda?" Her eyes are wide, unblinking, and full of terror, as if she has answered the question before I open my mouth. "Are you still ill?"

I stare back, my eyes drying without enough tears to fill the drought. "I'm not ill," I respond.

"Well, what is it? What's wrong?"

"Nothing's wrong with me," I respond. "Aside from a broken heart, which you clearly don't care about."

"Take off that sweater, Matilda."

"I'm cold," I say, swallowing against the lump in my throat.

"Take it off," she says, gritting her teeth.

All I can do is continue to stare straight through her. I won't remove my sweater. I will not answer the questions that are spiraling through her head.

Tears are running down her already raw cheeks when she rips at the buttons on my wool sweater, yanking the fabric from my arms.

Her hand flies up to her mouth as if she's spotted a decomposing corpse. "Dear God, how could you let this happen?" she cries out.

I tear my sweater back from her hand and replace it over my shoulders, pinching it across my chest. "I said I was cold."

I'm grinding my teeth so hard, my jaw aches. The pain travels up to my temples and the urge to scream is consuming every fiber of my body. "These are God's plans. Not mine, Mama."

"Do not blame the Lord for your actions, young lady. If you were to abide by our faith, you wouldn't have let such a thing happen."

"Are you rewriting the Bible, Mama?"

"This is a sin, Matilda. There are no two ways about it."

"This," I say, pointing to my stomach, "is a blessing. The only sinful person in this room right now is you, and you know it."

Mama wrings her hands through her hair, causing a mess she will have to fix later to look perfect for when Papa returns home, as if he has done nothing wrong today too. "You are not even eighteen years old, and you are with child, who I assume belongs to a Jewish man, am I wrong?"

"Which part is the sin, Mama?"

She wipes the tears from her eyes and steps away to begin her routine of pacing when she is searching for an answer that doesn't exist. "How are you so calm about this? Do you realize what this means?"

"Either I die for committing a sin—I'm sorry, *we* die for committing a sin, or you, as my mother, could choose to stand by my side, as I plan to do for my child." It's like staring through a piece of glass rather than looking into a mirror. There is no reflection of myself in her. I don't know who my mother is anymore.

She presses her hands against the protruding veins on her temples. "Go to your room," she groans through a gasping sob. "I need time to think."

"The decision is not yours," I tell her, keeping calm. I don't want her to think I feel the fear she wants me to.

"Go, Matilda."

I leave because I have nothing more to say. It was only a matter of days before the truth came out, but I was biding my time. That reason no longer matters because Hans is no longer here.

I'm not sure if he wondered or assumed, but he didn't ask. My stomach is still fairly flat, but as thin as I have always been, any change to my body may be noticeable. I have been wearing thick sweaters for the last couple of weeks to hide the hints of what I hadn't shared with him yet. I was waiting until the right moment to tell him. Of course, daily, he asked me if everything was okay. He told me I looked flushed. He mentioned his concern for my emotions fluctuating drastically. His questions made me realize the reality of our situation before I concluded it on my own. But I told him it was all caused by nerves, and I was fine. There was nothing to worry about.

If I had known he was going to be taken away today, I would have told him sooner. He, as the father, deserves to know, and I took that away from him.

Somewhere in my head, I assumed we could come up with a plan as the months passed. That we would be somewhere together and safe before the baby is born. But these were dreams I was filling my head with.

I'm scared. I know what's happening in the world, and I am aware

Papa will disown me when he finds out. He will send me away and I will go gladly, but without means, I don't know how to get by. Once again, I'm at their mercy while I also figure out how to help Hans, who is a train ride away.

The covers are in a messy pile on my bed from the room raid and I straighten out some of the evidence to eliminate the reminder of this being the longest and worst day of my life. It takes all my effort to clean after riding my bicycle for so long earlier, but the moment I'm content, I climb into the crawl space with my blanket and curl up in the very place Hans had been hiding for months—also the very place where we had laid together and made a new life.

I wouldn't know if it's morning, noon, or night from within the crawl space. I don't know how Hans maintained his sanity for so long here. The walls feel as if they are closing in after a few hours, constricting me like I'm in a coffin. This is how I forced him to live for months just to keep him safe. Now, it seems as if it was all for nothing.

I've been staring at his handwritten quotes hanging on the wall, imagining the way he holds a pen. He is left-handed so I've always poked fun at the way he folds his fingers over a pencil, but Hans seemed determined to prove that I was the one holding my writing utensils incorrectly. I suppose we never put an end to that childhood argument.

I rest my head back down into his pillow, holding it up to my face. He showered while Mama and Papa were at a town meeting last night. His pillow smells like fresh soap.

With a deep inhale against the sharp pains in my chest, I blow the air from my pursed lips, slowly, needing relief from the building tension. As soon as my lungs feel empty, I catch the sound of an argument growing between Mama and Papa. It must be near nightfall if he's home.

I climb out of the crawl space, avoiding all the creaking floorboards, and crack my bedroom door to listen in.

"Why would you do such a terrible thing, Arnold? He wasn't causing anyone any trouble," Mama says, but she sounds as meager as a mouse. She's afraid of what Papa will say. I've seen it before. "The Bauers have been our friends for so long."

"They are going to hear you, Johanna," Dad seethes. "You cannot be speaking this way about a Jewish family, or they will see you as one of them."

One of them. Dad should ask himself if it's better to be seen as a Jewish sympathizer, because those are the only two options now.

"Then why did you invite them over for supper? Why would you invite them into our home? What's the purpose?" she continues.

"We are an alliance, Johanna. We should remain that way if we are to keep ourselves safe. I can't understand why you are making me out to be such a monster when I'm protecting our family every way I can. Do I need to remind you how many hours I have missed at work because of these games? How stupid could she be to hide a Jew in our attic with Nazis living directly below us? I have listened to you for months, pleading the boy's case, hoping this will all end, but it's getting worse by the day, and I have heard the stories, Johanna. They are executing German Christians for going against Hitler's policies. There is no room for error. I feel the need to be home when they are downstairs. I don't trust them."

"So, you handed over a young man who we have known since he was four. Now you are chums with these men and we are safe, yes?"

"No, Johanna. We are not safe. If for one minute they decide we were hiding him rather than found him upstairs, any of us could— I don't understand why you aren't seeing this clearly. You can't possibly be this blind to what's happening."

I debate entering the conversation, not to defend Mama or speak my piece, but to make Papa see that no matter what he does there won't be a good outcome. In the end, he will still lose his daughter.

"Matilda will no longer be attending school," Mama says.

"What? Are you mad? She has two months left before she finishes her education."

"If our world is as dangerous as you are making it out to be, then she is not leaving this house. You feel the need to protect us with extravagant measures, and I will do the same."

"Are you siding with her now? Is this what it's all about?" Papa asks.

I step out of my bedroom and carefully descend the steep stairs down to the main floor. "What about what I want? Do either of you care?" I ask, feeling as though my heart is caught in my throat.

Mama is looking at me as if I'm holding a weapon up to her head. She is worried about what I will say. Papa isn't fearful of my words, but he doesn't know the truth.

"This conversation doesn't concern you, Matilda," Mama says.

"Well, of course it does," I argue. "Both of you have done nothing but decide for me without so much as asking me how I feel. I'm not ignorant. I see what's happening in the world, and I listen to the radio every day. I'm aware of how dangerous this war is becoming, but mostly for the Jewish people. Their lives are being stripped away from them while you two are arguing over how much attention we should give the Nazis downstairs just so they don't speculate that one, maybe two, of us don't agree with the methodical ways Hitler is destroying our country."

"Lower your voice this instant," Papa shouts in a whisper.

"They've already taken Hans. Should we tell them we hate Jews too? Would that tie us closer to them? Would they respect us more?"

Papa charges for me, with his finger pointing toward my nose. "Stop while you're ahead. I won't say this again. I don't know what's gotten into you, Matilda, but I will not allow you to be the reason we all become prisoners of this war." Each word he speaks is full of rage, and spit is flying in every direction. He's losing his mind. It's obvious.

"Arnold, don't touch her," Mama says.

Papa's eyes bolt between Mama and me. "Pardon me? I have never laid a hand on our child."

"I'm not a child," I tell him.

Papa grabs fistfuls of his graying hair, and his face becomes red. He bares his teeth, struggling to keep whatever composure he thinks he is capable of right now. "You are our child, Matilda. I'm keeping you safe."

"I'm afraid you can't do that any longer," I tell him.

I should feel fear for my father. I've minded him my entire life and never stepped out of turn until this past year. But he has changed: Papa is not the man I once knew.

"Are you threatening me?" he asks.

Mama is staring at me as if I'm a time bomb and the fuse is short. I'm sure she would like to run away and avoid whatever comes next, but she can't. Neither can I.

"She is with child, Arnold," Mama whispers, her mouth moving as the rest of her body remains still. "A child of a Jewish man."

Again, my hands curl around my stomach, an instinctive reaction.

Papa points at me, glaring down at my stomach. "See there, you are protecting your child, but you don't understand what it's like to do so when he or she is on the verge of getting themselves killed."

I'm surprised at his composure, but I should have known it was shock speaking.

Papa's hands fold behind his neck as he paces between the armchairs.

"I found out earlier today," Mama says. She's protecting herself from his next question of how long she was aware.

Papa stops pacing and leans against the wall next to the front door. He slides down, inch by inch, until he's sitting on the floor, holding his head between his knees.

Maybe I should feel ashamed, but I don't.

I could have been more careful, but I wasn't.

Love took a hold of my fragile mind, and I decided nothing else should matter outside of the moments I would treasure forever.

There are no rules when one man has the capability of changing them daily. There are no sins when living amid a catastrophe. There is only survival.

"Does Hans know?" Papa groans beneath his breath.

"No, you stole that from me too," I reply. "You have ruined my life, not saved it."

Papa's head snaps up straight. "How can you say I have ruined your life? Look at what you've done, Matilda. I didn't make this decision. You did, and now we must figure out how to hide you, just like you were hiding Hans. Not only are you a seventeen-year-old girl, but if the soldiers downstairs notice you are with child, especially after they turned a blind eye to your behavior in my car earlier, what do you think will happen to you?"

"I will lie to protect Hans. That's what people do for those they love."

"They won't believe you," Papa says, shaking his head as if he refuses to listen to the words coming from my mouth. "Why, Matilda? Why?"

I'm not sure what kind of question he is asking or how he expects me to answer, but there is nothing to say.

"This is your fault, you know this, yes?" This time he is looking at Mama.

"Mama had nothing to do with my decisions," I say. It will be the only defense I offer on her behalf.

"I wanted that boy out of here the moment I told her I thought I heard a family of mice. You didn't truly think I was stupid enough to assume there were mice in the attic, did you?"

"There is a mouse in the attic," I reply. "He was treated better than Hans. I've had to watch that reality while you have held yourself back from turning in an innocent man."

"You're going to regret your words someday, Arnold," Mama says.

"Never. I will never regret what I'm saying. I shouldn't have listened to you filling my head with absurdities that this will all be over soon, Johanna. This isn't over. It's only the beginning. You need to get her upstairs while I figure this out. I need to cancel supper and come up with a plan on how I will somehow keep my family alive. I am so very ashamed of you, Matilda. Of all the things you could have done, you have branded yourself for eternity. I have spent my life trying to guide you, but for the first time since you were born, I'm not sure I can help you this time. That is something I'll have to live with."

"Arnold, stop," Mama interrupts.

"Get the girl upstairs now, Johanna," Papa says, suddenly standing up and shouting louder than he has spoken throughout this entire argument.

Mama attempts to wrap an arm around me, but I shrug away from her touch. She won't step in and be a hero after she stood by watching as they took Hans. I understand the ideal of minding the man of the home, but we aren't worth much as women if we don't stand up for what's right and react against what's wrong. I, for one, could not stand by and watch an innocent person being dragged away from a living confinement of a hole to be taken somewhere far worse. He isn't an animal, and neither is this baby that Hans and I will joyfully raise together.

Somehow. Someway.

CHAPTER 21
GRACE
2018

To learn of a past that has been hiding my entire life, and to do so within a matter of hours, is too much to bear. I don't know what to do to relieve the pressure, stress, and suffocation.

I can't wrap my head around the fact that this story—my foundation—has been sitting here all this time, for all the years Mom was looking. It's here. All of it. Every grim detail.

When I look out the window from the chair I've been sitting in, I notice the streetlamps come to life. Darkness has set in and I've spent the entire day digesting words, re-reading lines and explanations that deserve more explanations. I'm heartbroken, angry, relieved, and confused. I feel like I know so much, but so little still at the same time. I'm terrified to know what Matilda went through, and I'm not even sure if the pregnancy has anything to do with Mom. If I had to wish up a scenario, this child would be the first of many Matilda and Hans would have together, but then I fall back to my senses, knowing Mom arrived in the United States as an orphan.

"You look pale," Archie says, kneeling in front of me. "It's a lot to read all at once. I might suggest a break if possible."

I slip the papers back into their stack and place them on my lap. "Yes, I agree. I'm not sure I'll be able to sleep after what I read, and instinct tells me that I haven't gotten to the worst of this story just yet."

Archie reaches over and places his hand on my shoulder, a touch of warmth to relieve the bone-deep chills. "As I mentioned earlier, my grandfather and Hans became the best of friends at Dachau. They were quite lucky to have each other."

I stand from the chair, needing to stretch every limb. "I didn't realize that's where their friendship formed," I say.

"It's just about closing time. Would it be improper to ask you to join me for evening bread?"

"Evening bread?" I ask.

"My apologies—dinner?"

I'm the one who should be apologizing for my lack of German knowledge.

"Evening bread sounds wonderful," I say with an embarrassed grin. The moment Archie mentions food, my stomach responds with a silent growl, reminding me I haven't eaten anything since the croissant I had this morning. "As long as I'm not keeping you from anything. Company would be nice."

"Wonderful," he says, with a coy side smile. "Give me just a moment to close up."

"Take your time," I tell him, pulling my phone from my back pocket. I'm shocked Carla hasn't sent me a hundred text messages over the last few hours. To pre-empt her concern, I'll send a quick message to let her know I'm alive and well, about to have dinner with a charming man who seems too good to be true. Though I'll probably leave out the last part. She'll suspect I'm walking into one of her beloved crime novels.

She responds with a line of x's and o's, thanking me for letting her know I'm still in one piece today.

"That should just about do it," Archie says. "What type of food do you prefer?"

I glance out the window, spotting several restaurants in the nearby vicinity. "I'm not sure since I know little about the food here."

"Well, I know a place that has a bit of everything. That might be a good option."

"That sounds great." I take my bag and sweatshirt to follow him out of the shop. "You said you live nearby?"

"Sure, just about a mile away. There are several blocks of flats there, so it's a nice little area. My flatmate works the night shift at a factory down toward the camp, so while I share the expenses with him, we don't see each other very often."

"I live alone too—in Boston, I mean. I used to live with my best friend toward the end of college and for a while after, but we both came to a point where we needed our own places, but luckily, we were able to find apartment units next to each other, so it's a nice little setup."

"How wonderful. It certainly sounds like the best of both worlds," Archie says, staring at me as if my explanation is fascinating.

The roads are much quieter at night. Fewer people fill the sidewalks. The chatter is at a low rumble, and there's a serene aura between the orange glow of the streetlights. Archie walks at a slow pace as if he's taking in the world around him, not in a rush, nowhere to be, just living in the moment. It's not something I'm familiar with after spending most of my adult life in downtown Boston. Everyone is always in a rush, late for wherever they're going, and avoiding eye contact at all costs. Maybe I had this all wrong.

Archie's gaze falls to the ground between us, and he wraps his hand around the back of his neck before peering at me. "Pardon me for saying so, but a lovely woman like you seems as if someone would have swept you off your feet by now, no?"

I can't stop the heavy sigh from spilling out of my lungs. "Ugh," I grumble. "Honestly, I haven't come close to meeting a man I can fathom spending more than a few hours with, and since I've had the pleasure of watching each of my friends go down the happy trail of marriage and family life, I often appear to be the happiest one of them. It's not that I don't want to settle down or that I'm against it, but it seems like my idea of freedom is a major sacrifice for a lifetime of marital negotiation and raising children. I've always wanted to find myself first, feel a sense of accomplishment, and know I can make it on my own before actively searching for the rest of my life. It probably sounds crazy though."

A short huff of laughter is Archie's initial response. "It makes perfect sense. This is your life, and you should love it before adding to it."

"Is that why you're living with a flatmate instead of a wife?" I ask, nudging him with my elbow.

"Me? No. I've had horrible luck with women. I've had a couple of long committed relationships I thought might lead to a future, and both times, someone better came along for my girlfriends. It is what it is, though. It wasn't the right person or time, is all."

"You seem very understanding. I hope you left them with a piece of your mind at least."

"A piece of my mind?" he questions. "I'm not sure I understand what you mean."

"Ignore me," I reply. "I'm not sure I understand me sometimes either."

Just a couple of blocks away from the bookshop, we come to a restaurant with outdoor seating. Decorative string lights brighten the dining area, giving off a casual vibe.

"After you," Archie says, swinging his arm out in front of the open door to the restaurant.

"Thank you."

The interior is made up of a dark wood finish, from the floors to the walls and even the exposed beams above us. Small hanging wrought-iron candelabras with short white lit candles line the space between the beams, offering a slight glow of warmth to match the cozy ambiance outside. Though each table in the restaurant appears occupied, there is a sense of peacefulness as if everyone has had a long day and needs a moment to unwind.

"Will you be warm enough to eat outside?" Archie asks.

"Oh, yes, I'll be fine, thank you."

The easy conversations I've had with Archie throughout the day seem to have shifted to a different level of formality.

A woman escorts us to the outdoor seating area. She places two menus down on the black wrought-iron table with a pair of matching chairs in the corner where two walls meet to block out some of the foot traffic on the sidewalk.

"You know, I find it very noble of you to come all this way to tie up loose ends for a family you knew nothing about. The act defines your character," Archie says, holding the paper menu up.

"It's more for my mom than me, but I would have done anything for her when she was alive, and I'll continue to do so. She deserves that much."

"My parents passed away within a couple of years of each other. My father didn't age well and had many health issues. To have a heart attack at sixty was nothing I could have predicted. My mother was very depressed after he passed away and depended heavily on smoking and drinking to lift her spirits, but she got sick, called it the flu, never saw a doctor, and a few months later, she too passed away. Bad luck, I suppose."

I place my hand on my chest, trying to wrap my head around the thought of losing two parents within such a short time. I'm not close with Dad, but the thought of losing him after Mom makes my stomach hurt. "Well, I'm so sorry for what you've gone through."

"I thought longevity ran through my veins," he says with a soft laugh. "My grandfather, Danner, he's still alive and kicking. He's the only one left though."

"He's still alive?" I question. "He was the one who was friends with Hans in the camp?"

"Yes, he speaks highly of Hans, even still after all these years. I suppose when a bond forms between two people in a horrific situation not much can come between that after."

"Does your grandfather talk much about his time in the concentration camp?"

Archie places his menu back down. "Oh, yes. It's as if he was there yesterday. He hasn't forgotten a detail. In fact, when he's feeling up to it, he will mosey down to the memorial site and offer his stories to anyone who will listen. The times he does that are becoming less frequent, but he feels he has an obligation to teach so we don't forget or leave behind his stories."

"Rightfully so," I agree. "I need to visit the camp before I go." Possibly sooner than that because I feel like I'm standing in between two stories, Hans's and Matilda's, and the gap is painful to consider.

"I wish everyone could visit a memorial for a concentration camp. It's a life lesson that can change someone's entire view of the world. To appreciate small things was a luxury then, but now it's overlooked so often."

"I can only imagine."

As I glance at the menu, I notice it's written in German. I would look crazy if I took my phone out to scan the page but asking Archie to read the options out loud might be more ridiculous.

"Do you like pork?" he asks.

"I'm not very picky. I just speak very little German—not enough to read this list."

"If you like pork, I would highly recommend the Wiener Schnitzel. It's a crowd-pleaser among tourists."

"Sold," I tell him, placing the menu down.

"Oh, you don't need to pay for it now," he says, placing his hand on my menu. "Don't worry."

I'm mortified, which is likely how I'll feel for the rest of this trip. "I just meant, that sounds great."

"Oh, I see," he says, snickering. His smile curls into two symmetrical dimples to the sides of his lips. It shouldn't come as a surprise that I would meet a man worth talking to on the other side of the world.

Below the blanket of darkness from the sky, the flickering decorative lights around us become brighter, setting a more intimate mood.

A woman brings us glasses and looks back and forth between the two of us.

Archie orders in German. "Wir werden beide das Wiener Schnitzel haben, bitte."

"Ja bitte," the woman responds, filling our glasses with water.

"I ordered the same," he says, lifting my menu from beneath my hand. He reaches the menus over to the waitress and waits until she steps away before picking up where he left off. "So, how about in the morning before the shop opens, I take you to the memorial for a tour?"

I shouldn't feel surprised by this question. But tomorrow morning feels so soon, and I may never be ready to face the reality of what I have only read in history books.

"You are Jewish too," he says, "it's important to know your roots."

I'm Jewish. I never thought I would find out the religion of Mom's side of the family. We didn't practice much of anything but learned about everything. She felt it was the right thing to do without knowing for sure. Dad wasn't raised with much insight on being Protestant, so we were blind to a lot of the practices and beliefs others were a part of. "I didn't know I was partly Jewish," I say.

"Of course. My apologies. I'm skipping ahead in the story you are digesting. But yes, you are partly Jewish."

"Hans, he's—"

"Yes," Archie responds. "Your grandfather."

Every turn down this road feels like I'm being hit in the gut with a blast of wind. "He lived in Dachau. How long was he there?"

"Quite a while," Archie says, keeping his answer simple.

"Then yes, I would like to visit the memorial tomorrow."

Archie places his hand on mine. "Everything is going to be okay. I can't imagine how difficult this journey is for you, but I wish to help you through it in any way I can. I know that sounds absurd since we just met today, but your family means a lot to me, and I can't imagine passing up the opportunity to help you connect to your roots."

My cheeks feel like they are on fire. No one has cared so much about my family tree before, aside from Mom.

"I'm making you blush, Grace."

He's very forward, I see, but certainly not wrong with his accusation.

"You're very sweet to help me. It means a lot."

"It's my pleasure," he says. "As descendants of the Holocaust, we have a role to fill, and that's sticking together in any way we can. That's what our grandfathers did for each other while they were living at the camp."

My chest is tight, and I want to cry, but instead, I force a small smile. I've never felt so much at one time before, and I'm suddenly very grateful I don't have to go through this alone.

CHAPTER 22
GRACE
2018

Sleep doesn't come easily to me. It's rare I make it through a night without waking up a dozen times. But last night I slept like a rock. I didn't stir once, and I feel rested. Maybe it's a sign of happiness or a sense of fulfillment, not that I have all the answers yet, but they are here, waiting for me. There are birds singing outside of the window, and the sun is bright, leaking through the curtains.

I considered reading more last night after dinner, but after a pleasant evening and letting some of the draining thoughts drift away, I embraced the calmness and gave myself a break. I clearly needed sleep.

Archie walked me back to the hotel and as we approached the arched gated entryway, my nerves sparked, recalling how most dates seem to end back home. No matter how nice the guy is, there is never the intention of a night ending at a front door. I'm not sure when things changed, but I sometimes wonder if gentlemen are only written about in books or acted in the movies.

Last night was different, though. Archie and I were not on a date, although there were moments it seemed plausible, and there is a sincerity about him I can't look past. After we stopped in front of the hotel, he kissed me on the cheek; a gesture I've noticed is common here. Then, he told me to have a nice night, and he'd meet me out front in the morning at eight.

My entire walk upstairs, I questioned if I was losing my mind, wondering if the day happened. I feel like I've lived eighty years within the last forty-eight hours.

I haven't managed to drag myself out of bed just yet, but I have about an hour before it's time to meet Archie so I grab my phone from the nightstand and click Carla's contact. Just before she picks up, I realize I've forgotten about the time difference. It's only one in the morning at home.

"Hey," she answers, her voice garbled. She was asleep, and now I feel like a complete jerk.

"I'm so sorry. The second you picked up, I realized it's the middle of the night for you. I can call you back later, when it's not dark out," I say, scoffing with embarrassment.

"Don't be crazy. I told you to call me at any hour of the day and I meant it. Are you okay?"

I'm pacing the hotel room, keeping my eyes set on the alarm clock. "Yes, I'm fine, which is why I feel awful. I didn't need to wake you up."

"How was dinner with Romeo last night?"

"Romeo? I'm in Germany, not Italy," I say, correcting her.

"My apologies—how was dinner with Prince Charming? He's from Germany, so don't start with me. Plus, you woke me up."

"It was very nice. Enlightening, in fact. I can't believe how much I've found out in the time I've been here. I know who both of my grandparents are. Of course, I still need to find out what happened to them because nothing is making any sense to me."

"Prince Charming won't give you the lowdown?"

"It's complicated."

"Uh, I'd demand answers, Grace. You need to know what's going on, why you're there, and what you'll do with a bookshop that's four-thousand miles away from here."

I plop down on the edge of the bed, forcing a sigh. "I'm learning all these integral parts of my grandparents' history and from the words I've read so far, I can't imagine asking anyone to tell me this story. It's brutal and painful. To know it's all the truth and was real life for them, it's made me feel sick at moments. I'm taking in as much as I can handle at one time, but I'm not sure I can just move on from this. There's something inside of me craving every detail, afraid of missing something important. I've waited my entire life to find out about this history and I owe it to myself to take my time."

"Sweetie, this is gutting you. Is it worth it? I just need to ask you."

I don't have to take the time to think about her question. There isn't a doubt in my mind that I should be here right now. "Even if I didn't have to decide on what to do with the bookshop, I would have come purely for the answers I'm finally learning. I'm okay, I promise."

"Okay, well, I still wish you'd let me come out and join you, but I understand. I just want to be there for you."

"No one could ask for a better friend," I say. "Go back to sleep. I'll talk to you tomorrow."

During the seconds I take to end the call and place my phone back down on the nightstand, I consider the sound of my voice. I don't feel broken; I feel empty and lost, desperate for a sign pointing me in the next direction.

I wasn't expecting a sign to present itself so boldly upon first sight.

"Arbeit macht frei."

I'm not sure what the words mean, but the letters melded from iron and displayed so intricately within the monstrous arched gate don't make me think it says something good.

"Work will set you free," Archie translates, his voice monotone and low.

"I'm sure no one believed this upon arrival," I say.

"It was a form of propaganda to hide what was happening to any outsider. No one was set free—whether they survived or died here."

We walk through the wide-open gravel-covered space, lined with rows of one-level white buildings with clusters of small twelve-panel bar-covered windows.

"This location is what was known as the 'roll-call area,' which was able to hold more than forty-thousand prisoners. Each morning and evening, there was a headcount to keep proper track of the population here." Archie sounds like he knows every detail about the camp.

"That must have taken hours each time," I say.

Archie doesn't respond, leaving me to believe it must be true. Instead, he leads us to the right side of the camp toward one of the many towers encircling the space. The closer we get, the more details I notice—the barbed wire, and a moat entrapping everyone inside.

"Guards would watch from the top of the tower and would shoot anyone who approached the barbed wire. Many of the prisoners found this to be their form of escape."

"Suicide, you mean?" I ask.

"Exactly."

My stomach churns with a wave of nausea, trying to digest everything at once.

"I can show you one of the blocks where common prisoners would live. Is that all right with you?"

I don't mean to pause before responding but every word is hard to digest. "Yes, of course."

We enter one of the long flat buildings, facing a farm of wooden structures in the form of bunkbeds. Each bed looks to be smaller than a common twin-size mattress.

"When the camp became overpopulated, there would be up to six people per bed, which is hard to imagine," Archie continues.

It looks impossible. I'm not sure how so many people could breathe in this tight space. My chest aches while trying to imagine such an inhumane sight. "This is awful," I say in a low voice.

"It's a lot to take in at once," Archie says. "Let's take a breather out in the open for a few minutes."

A cold breeze entraps us as we head back outside. "It's much colder and damp here than it was up near the village," I say. Would the sun even shine in a place like this? It's deadly quiet, likely because it's early in the morning, but there isn't the sound of birds, cars, or even footsteps from others around us. The only sound I hear is the crunch of the gravel beneath my feet. I suppose the silence must be inevitable with most people who visit the camp. I can't imagine there are many words dignified enough when seeing this all for the first time.

"Here, you should take my sweater," Archie offers. He pulls the navy-blue sweater off his shoulders and wraps it around mine before I have enough breath to argue.

"Thank you," I say, or try to say, but my words come out in a whisper.

"The prisoners occupied these buildings you see here, but the one ahead to the right of us held a particular set of prisoners who required a certain level of security."

"What do you mean? Why would some need security and others not?" I ask.

"Those particular prisoners were considered enemies of the state due to their resistance, trying to persuade people to take a better look at the truth. They stood up and spoke their minds and fought for what was right in an attempt to overturn German policies. Though one of the most famous inmates, Georg Elser, a German worker, is known for his assassination attempt on Hitler. He was held here for five years before being executed, just one month before liberation."

I can't imagine how he coped, knowing that such a life-changing and brave attempt didn't work out as planned. If only more had been like him.

We continue walking between the buildings, an endless row of repetitive patterns. The hairs on my arms are standing up, and I can't help but feel like I'm walking over the ashes of death.

I am.

I'm afraid to know what Matilda went through. The answer wouldn't have ever been simple, but this isn't what Mom expected to find. Not this—not here.

Archie has been checking on me every few seconds, as if I might explode with grief, but I'm able to hold myself together.

"There is some footage in a museum over there," he says carefully. "I'm not sure if you have ever seen documentaries, but it's up to you whether you feel up to watching the clips."

I should force myself to watch them over and over until I shatter. If not, how else could I understand even an ounce of what happened here?

"I'm fine. I should see the footage," I tell him. He points in the direction we're heading, and I notice a quiver run through his shoulders. "You look cold. Take your sweater back, I'll be okay."

"I'm not cold," he says, straightening his shoulders as if he were a soldier marching. "It's hard not to feel everything while walking through here. It doesn't matter how many times a person walks these paths, the feelings stay the same. Besides, the museum will be warm."

We enter the building, which appears much larger on the inside than it did from the outside. The walls are covered with artwork and there are different directions to take depending on what there is to see. "What purpose did this building have?" I ask.

"We are in the Maintenance building. This is where many of the prisoners worked, but it was also where the new prisoners arrived. They would wait in line to be registered, then they were told to strip off their clothes and hand over their personal items—they would likely not see their belongings again. The SS—or the Schutzstaffel—Hitler's protection squadron, would have them shaved from head to toe and disinfected in the showers." The way he speaks makes me believe he has said this a hundred times before. Archie must be used to shutting his emotions off, because my chest feels like it's caving in. Even though I have read about this, seeing the proof in front of me hits me like a sledgehammer.

We make our way to the area where we can view the footage, and I fear how bad this might get, but I must be strong for so many reasons at this point. My grandfather was here. Archie's grandfather was here. He's lived in this area, having to face the truth of these brutalities his entire life and I'm only now just coming to terms with it. This—everything surrounding me—it happened.

The video footage is of the history of Dachau, but also a showcase of forced laborers working in dirt holes, and skeletal prisoners undergoing medical experiments. Worse, the prisoners are on the brink of death, too weak to hold up their heads, starving, covered with bugs and dirt. Then, as if it isn't enough to see the torture of the living, we see the bodies of the dead being thrown into a pile as if they are no more than trash. Various limbs are all I can make out, and I can't believe what my eyes are seeing. These scenes are even worse than I expected and the pain in my chest burns.

"I want to ask you if he died here," I croak out. "But I don't think I'm ready to know the answer."

"Hans?" Archie asks.

"Yes."

"There is something to be said about everyone who has lived here. Whether they were here for a day or years, each of them is a survivor. The Jewish people, among other groups of prisoners, came together as if each of their fellow inmates were one of their family members. There was no survival of the fittest among them. If one died, it wasn't because they weren't strong enough. And regardless of who made it out alive, a part of each one of them died here. So, to be alive or dead is a relative definition when you think about what each person lived through."

"He was a survivor who also died here?" I repeat.

"I didn't say exactly that. Grace, there's much more to the story than life and death. As I've said before, I will gladly answer any question you have, but only if it's because you cannot continue to read through those pages."

I know we haven't seen the worst of what we will see here. I know that I can't leave until I stand where they stood, close my eyes, and imagine just a minute of what it felt like to live in their shoes.

For months, I have sat here, stuck upstairs in my bedroom without the option of leaving. Mama and Papa have essentially become prison guards. I lost the energy to fight months ago. The larger my belly grows, the more tired I feel. I've considered sneaking out at night. I even attempted to do so, but Papa has locked us inside with a key he always wears on his body.

I haven't been to a doctor, and I don't know if I'm healthy, and worse, if the baby is healthy. I feel the kicks, hiccups, and stretches, but it's all I can go by. My stomach is running out of space, and I sit here, waiting for something to happen.

With only time to think, I spend my days thinking about Hans, writing out my experiences, which aren't much, in my bedroom. Though, I've documented the growth of our baby and it's something I'm sure he'll enjoy reading, at the very least. I try to avoid the thoughts that haunt me at night. It's as if the darkness brings along a wave of reality I want to avoid—one I'm constantly fighting against. I had to stop listening to the radio for fear of what I will hear Hitler say next, but it's hard to block out the conversations I hear between Mama and Papa downstairs. Words about the deporting of all Jews and mass killings within ghettos in surrounding countries.

I wish I could avoid the thoughts of what Hans might be experiencing, seeing, hearing, or worse, fearing for what lies ahead, but I can hardly go a minute without a sour pain tearing through the pit of my stomach, knowing the reality of the world we are living in. The questions I can't answer are crippling. To think—to know the possibility that he might not make it, or has already... It hurts so much. I've never felt pain like this and there is no end in sight.

Mama is clomping around downstairs in her Oxfords. She hasn't taken her shoes off since returning from the ration line early this morning before Papa had to leave for work.

Her footsteps grow louder, informing me she's on her way up here, likely with food. She has kept me fed, clean, and clothed. Papa has clarified that this is the way our lives need to be. Everything inside of me wants to fight against him, but I'm scared for this innocent unborn child who doesn't have a say in what decisions I make on behalf of him or her. I'm doing what I must do to keep our baby safe.

"I have your breakfast, Matilda," Mama says, breathless as she enters my room. The stairs she has always despised have become her worst enemy over the last several months, as she has had to go up and down them multiple times a day.

"Thank you," I say, preferring to keep our conversation short.

I ease down onto the bed, positioning my back against the wall to pull the bed tray over my lap.

"You look very pale, Matilda. Are you feeling okay?" Mama asks.

"I'm fine." That's a lie. I hardly slept last night because the early labor spasms have been on and off for days, and one step away from the bed drains me of my energy.

"Are you in any pain?" she asks, sliding the bowl of oatmeal with sliced fruit forward.

"I'm not in pain. I'm uncomfortable."

She lowers each of my socks to check for the swelling she guarantees I will experience, but my ankles feel fine.

"You know, I'm leaving once the baby is born, Mama. I can't stay here."

Mama pauses for a moment, as if my words come as a surprise. She can't possibly think I would want to stay here after what I've been through—what they've put me through. She swallows hard, loud enough to hear, and reaches out for me with open arms I don't intend to fill. "Please, Matilda, you know that isn't a wise decision. Besides, you won't be able to go too far for a couple of weeks. A new mother is in no condition to venture out. After that time, you'll see... help will be a desire you won't want to walk away from. Give it time, please." It's like she feels remorse, but it's too little, too late.

I take a bite of the oatmeal, wishing there was enough fruit to divide between each bland bite. "How do you suppose we will explain the sound of a crying infant to the wonderful soldiers who live downstairs, Mama?"

It's hard to have a civil conversation with either of my parents. I'm not sure if they assumed my anger would subside at some point, but it has only grown stronger.

"I've already come up with a couple of solutions," she says. "Your papa and I are going to line these walls and the floor with quilts to add more padding to absorb the sound. It won't keep away all the noise, but it will help."

I snicker through a strangled cough. "How lovely, and what else goes along with this plan?" I realize there are very few options, but the thought of worrying about a new baby crying just infuriates me more.

Mama intertwines her fingers, pinching the bones of her knuckles against each other. "Well, the story is: my sister has died during childbirth, and I'm going to care for the baby."

Her statement takes me by surprise, and I drop my spoon against the bowl. The clatter of the metal against glass stings my ears, but my mouth falls open in response to her plan. "You don't have a sister," I say.

"I do now," she replies.

"Surely, they will question you, since you have had no family visiting in the time they have lived here, and they have likely wondered where I have disappeared to. You don't truly think they are that stupid, do you?"

Mama stands from the edge of the bed and folds her arms over her chest like I just insulted her intelligence. "What other choice do we have, Matilda?"

I don't have an answer for her. Truthfully, they should have let me go as soon as they found out I was with child. To live upstairs above two Nazis is asking for trouble, especially after they gleefully took Hans.

"Then what's your plan for when they ask why they haven't seen me?" I question.

"I have already told them we sent you to a finishing school in Belgium. They won't be wondering much when and if they see you at any point. That is why it has been so important to keep you up here and quiet all this time."

I take another bite of the oatmeal, but when I swallow the lump, I struggle to push it down my throat. A sharp pain bolts up through the center of my body. I try to reposition myself on the bed, hoping the sensation will subside, but it takes a moment to find relief.

Mama takes the tray away from me, placing it on the ground near the door. "You are even paler now. I think you need to lay down for a moment. I don't like the way you look."

"I don't want to lay down, Mama. I'm fine."

"Matilda, you only have me as a caretaker—that's it. You are free to argue with me all you want, but I'm trying to make sure nothing is wrong. You are my daughter and though you think I hate you, it couldn't be farther from the truth. Please, allow me to make sure you are okay."

Mama wraps her hand around my wrist, gently tugging, but I swing my feet off the side of the bed and push myself up so I'm sitting on the edge. After a couple of resting breaths, I pull myself up to my feet by holding myself steady against the nightstand. The moment I'm upright, another sharp pain causes me to curl forward.

"Matilda, I need you to listen to me. You are going to have this baby soon, and you will need to remain as calm as possible, no matter what happens. I'm going to clear the crawl space—so we can deliver the baby. The walls will block out some of the sound. I need to go prepare a few things for you, but it's time to make you comfortable there," she says, pointing to the wall behind my bed.

With an unsettling feeling reeling through me, I lose the ability to argue. Instead, I try to picture what it would be like if Hans were here, helping me through this. He would be so wonderful and supportive. I imagine he would have talked to our baby through my stomach every day, telling him or her stories. He should be here. He should be able to witness the birth of his child, and he should know he is about to become a father. Yet, I will be lying in the spot where he was forced to hide. I will give birth to our child—an innocent, helpless predetermined prisoner by means of a bloodline. It is already a fact that he or she will not be given a fair chance in this world—not in the state we are living in.

I watch as Mama moves the bed away from the wall, noticing a large spot of blood where I was resting. Immediately, I look down, finding my nightgown bloody beneath my belly. It hurts to stand up straight, and just as my mother lifts the wall panel away from the wall, a gush of fluid splashes over my feet.

"Mama," I call to her as she's climbing into the crawl space to straighten up. There is panic in my voice, causing her to knock her head on the wall as she backs away from the opening.

"It's okay, Matilda. This is normal. We just need to get you comfortable." If this is normal, then she should have an easier time hiding the sheer fright from her eyes. Mama had to help Frau Bauer when she was giving birth to Danya, but I'm not sure how much she had to do before a doctor arrived.

I won't have a doctor because I'm a walking sin. The thought of dying during childbirth haunts me and knowing Mama won't be able to do a thing to save me is incomprehensible. They act as if the baby will look half Jewish and it's absurd. No one could tell the difference between a Jewish baby and a non-Jewish baby. And unless I confess to whom the father is, no one would know it is Hans. My life and the baby's life are in jeopardy because of Mama and Papa's fears. They would have been better off sending me away to a place where unwed women go to give birth, but they claimed it was too dangerous. I can't even pick my poison.

Mama helps me into the crawl space. All I feel is the heaviness of my weight against my bare knees on the wooden floors. My back feels like it might cave in, and another pain is rooting from my core, leaving me winded, as if I can't pull in enough air to breathe.

"I have propped up the pillows, Matilda. Carefully settle down onto those blankets there and I will be right back. Take some deep breaths."

The pain seems to come quicker the next time as I wait for Mama to return. She's making a racket with whatever she is bringing upstairs, but I saw the soldiers leave for work a couple of hours ago. They wouldn't know what was happening up here, but Mama and Papa ensure they don't have a reason to ask any questions at all. Papa is sure they know I was purposely hiding Hans—they can think what they want.

Hours of excruciating pain have made me question if something is wrong, but Mama continues to tell me everything is fine. I'm not sure what to believe.

"I think it's time to push, Matilda. Are you ready?" she asks, kneeling between my feet. Mama is sweating and her makeup has run down her cheeks. Her hair is scraggly and damp, and she continues sweeping the strands away from her forehead.

A feeling defines pain, and I know no matter how much this hurts, nothing can compare to what Hans is living through right now. I can be strong like I hope he is being.

Groans gurgle in my throat as I push my feet against Mama's hands.

"Matilda, you cannot make a sound. Please. They might be home." I'm looking at her with my eyes wide open, wondering how a mother of any kind could say that to another woman, let alone her own daughter. "I'm sorry."

Mama hands me a washcloth as another urge to push takes me by surprise. The pain is like nothing I have ever imagined, and I want to scream at the top of my lungs to relieve the pressure in my body, but I place the washcloth between my teeth and bite down as hard as I can, pushing at the same time.

Relief rushes through my body as I become two different people: one who is seeing life for the first time from within an attic, and another who is witnessing the meaning of life for the first time.

CHAPTER 24
MATILDA
NOVEMBER 1941

Believing that a new life could change an old one has only set me up for disappointment. I couldn't help but think if Papa looked into his granddaughter's eyes and saw a minor reflection of himself, his outlook would change. It's clear I was being delusional. He refuses to even look at this beautiful little girl.

I don't know why God has watched over me or us, but baby Runa —she is my beautiful secret. It's been two weeks of rocking her in my arms, feeding her at nearly every hour of the day to keep her crying to a minimum. As much as I despise the padding around the bedroom, I believe it is shielding most of the sounds coming from up here. Thankfully, Runa gives me a small warning before fussing. Her coos, squeaks, and cries sound like a little bird. For as long as we can hold off offering the soldiers downstairs an explanation, the better off we'll be.

There is a sense of comfort in the crawl space and I don't mind curling up in the pile of blankets and pillows to rest while Runa does.

"Matilda, I have lunch for you," Mama says from the other side of the wall. "Is Little Bird asleep?" Mama calls her Little Bird more often than by name. She said newly hatched birds are a beacon of hope, like spring after a long winter, and maybe that's what Runa is to us.

"No. She's quite alert and staring at me as if she's waiting for something," I utter. I don't know what an infant could want aside from warmth, comfort, and a full tummy, but Runa has Hans's eyes, full of expression and windows to a mind full of wonders.

I scoot over toward the opening in the wall and Mama takes Runa from my arms, cradling her as I make my way out into where the sun is shining through the curtains. "You don't need to hide in there anymore, Matilda. We have a plan if the men downstairs hear a baby crying. If you stay up here until some of the extra weight comes off, there won't be a need to question anything."

Mama seems more confident now than she did a couple of weeks ago. I'm not sure what changed, but it doesn't offer me relief. I'm terrified for the safety of Runa and I won't do anything to cause suspicion. The moment I held her in my arms, I knew I'd do anything for her, even if that means living in this hole in the attic forever. I can give her all the love she needs, and I will do so at all costs.

"I would prefer the Nazis knew nothing of our lives up here, Mama."

"I understand, Matilda, but they are quite nosy."

"I wish they would leave," I say, making myself comfortable on my bed.

"I know you haven't been outside, but they are everywhere, all over town. There's no way to escape their existence. I don't think they'll leave anytime soon."

I take the pile of cloth nappies and fold them over my lap as Mama gently dances around with Runa locked between her arms. "Mama, I need to find Hans. I can't sit here much longer, wondering if he is okay. I haven't changed my mind about searching for him once I'm back on my feet."

Mama stops twirling from side to side, and her eyes widen with a look of concern. "It will be impossible for you to locate Hans. The Jews are being separated from all others, and you won't get anywhere close to him. The Führer has made it abundantly clear that he wishes to remove them from Germany at whatever cost. How could you even figure there is an ounce of hope in finding him?"

"If Hitler is trying to rid Germany of them, why was Hans taken to a work camp in Dachau? He's worth something, his strength; his ability to work. There has to be a reason they kept him in the country."

"You don't know if he is still there. From what I have heard among chatter, people are being transported and shuffled around daily. I don't want you to do something under false hope, not with Runa in your care. Hans would want you to look after your daughter." Mama's looking at me with endearment, her brows knit together along with a slight pout forming across her lips. I'm sure she'd like me to understand the reason for her fears. She'd like me to believe that Runa and I are her only concern, and maybe it's true, but Runa and Hans are what matters to me, and I won't let anything get in the way of protecting my family. "He's a man now," she says. "He can fend for himself. You must trust that."

Trust—it's a word no one in this house can tempt me with again.

I stand up from the bed and walk over to the window, needing an ounce of sunlight from between the drapes. "How can I love someone and not consider what else I could do to help?"

Mama follows me to the window, standing beside me, still rocking Runa in her arms. "To help Hans is seen as a crime, Matilda. It could be a death sentence for both of you. You are living in a world made up of dreams right now and though I wish this was not our reality, it is, and we must accept the truth to keep ourselves safe."

I take Runa from her, curling her into my chest. "She will not grow up without a father. Her life is my responsibility. I'll do whatever I can to make sure she has everything she deserves."

"Patience is the only solution, Matilda."

Runa has been asleep for a couple of hours, which leads me to believe she won't be sleeping well tonight. I have used the time to write every detail down, from the number of times she blinked her eyes today to the times she has whimpered from hunger. My words don't hold a flame to Hans's, but I must be able to give him an unrestricted view of every minute he has missed. I didn't think I could write so many pages. My hand aches when I fall asleep at night, and I have ink marks on my wrist that won't come off with soap and water.

I glance at the small table clock on my nightstand, finding the nighttime hours to be crawling in. Mama and Papa are downstairs arguing in a string of hushed shouts as they always are at this time of day. It's hard to make out what they are saying. Their arguments sound as if they are coming from beneath a heavy blanket. I used to be curious about what they were talking about, but I find it better now, not knowing.

"I'm going to talk to her," Papa says.

His words become more defined as his voice grows louder, warning me he is coming upstairs.

"Arnold, do not go up there," Mama says, sounding like she is following him. "This is the very last thing she needs right now. Have you no compassion for your daughter?"

"How dare you ask me such a thing, Johanna! Everything I do is to keep you both safe."

I hear him clearly. When he says he is doing everything to keep the two of us safe, he is referring to Mama and me, but not Runa, who he refuses to acknowledge.

"There are three of us, Arnold. Whether or not you like it, sin or saint, Runa is our granddaughter."

"They asked me about the child, Johanna. They heard the sound of soft cries and seemed concerned. Of course, I did as we agreed and told them it was your sister's baby, but you didn't see the look in their eyes. These men don't assume people are honest. It's just the opposite."

"Then, what do we do? Kick our daughter and granddaughter to the sidewalk and tell them to figure this out on their own? Is that your solution?" Mama's voice is growing louder by the second and it's causing me more worry than anything Papa is saying. The soldiers may very well be home at this hour. They could be listening. Even if all they can hear is muffled words, they will assume what they want. Papa isn't wrong about that. We try to be quiet, invisible to them, but we are not.

"You know what the solution is, Johanna," Papa says.

"Don't you dare go up there and utter those words to our daughter. Arnold, I will never forgive you."

I can hear Papa slap his hands down against the sides of his legs. He does that when he's out of energy. "Fine, Johanna. You win."

I feel like I'm standing in an elevator with broken cords, hanging from the very last frayed connection. I just don't know what waits below, and I'm scared to discover whatever that might be.

Mama couldn't face me tonight. Her anger often gets the best of her after arguments with Papa, and she retreats to her bedroom early for the evening. She set a tray of food in my doorway and left before I could get up to carry it over to my bed. Most nights, she offers to sit with me, but I have said no until these last two weeks since Runa was born. As much as I detested her company, I needed some level of comfort and I tried to let the rest go—at least for the time being.

After feeding Runa, I place her in the bottom drawer of my bureau, padded with a light quilt. I can see her from where my head rests on the pillow, which comforts me as I fall asleep.

"Runa, maybe we can make it for three hours tonight? Could we try, Little Bird?"

As if she understands me, she huffs a little sigh.

"I love you," I tell her. "Your papa loves you too."

I used to have difficulty falling asleep at night, especially toward the days leading up to Runa's birth, but when I have the freedom to steal a couple hours of rest, I'm able to sleep well. Of course, not well enough that I would sleep through her quiet cries in the middle of the night. At just two weeks old, there is no way she could make it through the night without needing food or being changed out of her wet nappy. Yet now, as I wake and glance over toward the bureau for my beautiful little girl, there is sunlight streaking across my cheek. The thought that Mama came in to care for her so I could sleep crosses my mind, but she hasn't done that before.

Chills overtake my body even though I'm warm beneath the covers. The hairs on my arms are standing up, and beads of sweat are forming on the back of my neck. Something feels wrong, and I'm scared to open my eyes. My heart pounds like a hammer against metal; it's deafening. I sit up and force my lashes to part, staring directly at the bottom drawer of my bureau.

The drawer is empty.

My heart stalls in my chest as I look in every corner of the room, knowing a two-week-old baby cannot move on her own.

"Runa," I call out.

I scramble out of bed, checking the drawer with my hands as if I need further proof.

"Mama!" I shout, praying she has taken her downstairs because I was asleep.

There's no response.

I open the door to my bedroom and hurry down the stairs into the main living area of our flat, finding nothing more than silence. "Mama?"

It takes me what feels like infinite footsteps to look in Mama and Papa's room. There I find an empty bed; unmade, and the drapes still closed.

I make my way into the kitchen, the last place either of them should be.

Mama is in front of me, sitting on the floor beneath the window over the sink. "I couldn't stop him," she says, sputtering through a strangled cry. She's on the verge of hyperventilating, shaking as if she just witnessed a murder, and sweating like we're stranded on a desert beneath the unforgiving sun. I can't tell if it's an act to protect Papa or a truth I'm dreading.

"What do you mean? Mama? Stop who? Where is Runa? What's happening?"

My chest feels like it's caving in, and my veins feel like they may burst. I can't breathe, yet my heart is beating so fast.

"He took Runa. He took her away. I told him not to, I told him I would no longer love him. He said he loves us enough to endure that pain for the rest of his life. But I didn't think he would wake up in the middle of the night to take her."

I fall to my knees because I have no strength left in my body. I'm not sure I can form words. A searing pain travels up my lungs, leading to a heavy sob I can't control. "Where?" I scream at the top of my lungs.

"I don't know, Matilda. I swear to you."

Of all the places Papa could have taken Runa, I wouldn't know the first place to chase him down. I have been interrogating Mama for the last three hours in the kitchen's corner. Her eyes are red and swollen, and her face is blotchy, likely matching mine.

"I swear to you, Matilda, I don't know where he went," Mama continues to croak out the same line over and over as if it will fix something.

Mama has no energy to stand but I can't sit. I can't stop moving. I have been pacing for these long unrelenting hours, waiting for Papa to rear his head. He'd better have Runa with him when he returns. So help me God, I don't know what I will do to him if he doesn't.

"He has been worrying that the soldiers suspect something," Mama says.

"They suspect everything, Mama. Half of which is not true, yes?"

"I don't know, Matilda. I know nothing, and I'm not sure what to say to you."

"I find it very hard to believe Papa didn't share any part of his plan with you. Forgive me for not siding with this naïve behavior of yours."

Mama tilts her head to the side and her nostrils flare while reaching out to take my hand, but I pull away, refusing to give her that desirable warmth. "Matilda, he wanted nothing bad to happen to Runa. I know this. He wanted her to be safe and cared for, but he didn't think it was possible here, not in Germany. We are all in grave danger. We've known this. I know you think your papa is a terrible man, but the truth is, he loves you. He loves me and Runa, and his only priority is to keep us all safe." She presses her hand against her mouth, closes her eyes, and silently cries while shaking her head. I'm not sure if she believes the lies she is speaking or if she's coming to the realization of what has happened, but I don't feel sorrow for her.

"That's a lie, Mama. My daughter is two weeks old, and he took her while I was asleep. He took advantage of the fact that I was desperate for a few hours of rest and he stole her from me. Don't you understand that I'm no longer a child, but a woman? I'm a mother and I should be the one to make decisions for my child. How could you let him do this?"

"I don't know," Mama says, shaking, her lips chattering as if she has been treading water in a frozen lake.

I'm questioning whether Papa could hurt an infant. I should never have to think about such a thing. He has never laid a hand on me. Though his verbal commands have been damaging enough throughout the years, he has never physically hurt me. I can't imagine he could do something so unthinkable to Runa, his flesh and blood. But what I don't know is if Papa sides with the Nazis—if he has a hatred for Jews as much as they do. If so, I don't know what he might do to Runa, my half-Jewish daughter.

"I was asleep when he left, Matilda," Mama says.

I'm not sure I believe her.

My mind is reeling with thoughts of where he could have taken her. If he was seeking safety and shelter, possibly the hospital. The established German *Kindertransport* would have been a safe haven, a program sending children from Germany to Great Britain for care during the war, but that has ended. There is no logic, no suitable solution. Papa has caused turmoil and destruction; he is as bad as the Nazis downstairs. He has taken everything, leaving me with nothing. He is treating me like a Jewish person, one without rights, one left to rot in a prison without medical care, and he has stolen my child. I don't know who he is trying to protect, but it seems the only one he cares for is himself.

Pain throbs through my engorged chest, needing to feed Runa. The thought of expelling milk and disposing of it feels like stealing food from my child, and this is what Papa is forcing me to do. I will suffer. I will wait.

I place pressure where the pain pulses and Mama finally stands from the floor and reaches for a pot. "I will heat some water. It will help the pain."

"I'd rather feel the pain," I tell her.

Every few minutes, I race through the family room toward the windows that overlook the street, searching in every direction for a hint of Papa's vehicle. It's almost noon by the time he pulls up to the sidewalk and has the nerve to step outside.

I run out of the flat, realizing the door is no longer locked like it has been. My feet hardly touch every other step down the stairs, and by the time I make it out the front door, I feel as if there are two sacks of bricks throbbing against my ribcage with every move I make. I meet him halfway between the front door and the sidewalk and throw my fists into his chests. "Where did you take her?" I shout at the top of my lungs.

Papa cups his hand over my mouth and pulls me to the side of the building. "Are you trying to get yourself killed?"

"I don't care," I tell him. "Where is Runa? Where did you take her? Tell me at once. Tell me now."

Papa clamps his hands on his hips and inhales a lungful of air. With his eyes closed, he continues with his disgraceful statements. "She is safe, Matilda. Isn't that what you want for your daughter? I did what you could never do, rightfully so, but it is what will keep her alive." His chin quivers and I wonder if he's feeling a morsel of regret. Because if he isn't, he must not have the same kind of soul I do.

"No, I will keep her alive. Tell me where you took her!" My voice is echoing off the side of the building, and I don't care. "Nothing matters to me. Nothing except Runa and Hans. And without them, I don't want to live."

Papa looks as if I just ripped his heart out of his chest. His forehead wrinkles as his lips pinch so tightly together they become white. He tries to speak, but a broken croak is all that comes out. He clears his throat. He acts like a coward, unable to look me in the eyes. "She is—"

"Say it, Papa. Where is she? What have you done?"

"Matilda..."

"Are you such a monster that you can't even give me an answer about where you took your granddaughter, the newborn baby you stole from her mother?"

He expels a mouthful of air, huffing as if he is the victim. I won't break my stare from his eyes until he tells me. "She is safe."

"I won't give up, Papa. I won't let this go. I will not stop until I have her back. Nothing can undo what you have already done, but the very least you can do is tell me what you have done with my daughter."

A sob bellows through his throat, a sound that has no effect on me. I couldn't care less about his turmoil. "She's—she's going to America. Someone will take care of her there and give the child a proper life. I had to pay a lot of money, Matilda. A lot more than what we can afford, but I did so she would survive and live a good life. You may never believe me or forgive me, but I know what I did was right. I will know this when I take my last breath."

I shove my palms into Papa's chest, pushing him back with all the power I have. For as strong as I have been and try to always be, the tears are unstoppable. I can hardly pull in enough air as I shout through explosive cries that feel as if they are the blood draining from my internal wounds. "This was not your decision to make. You know this. You know this and you did it secretly and in the middle of the night, taking advantage of my exhaustion. How could you do this to a mother? Never mind your daughter, you sick bastard! Tell me where you took her. Tell me now."

"She's gone, Matilda. There was an opportunity to get her on a transport and she was taken early this morning."

For all the anger that has built up inside of me, there is still an ounce of hope left. "Where in America? You don't even have papers for her. How will they know her name or her birthday? How will they have any information so I can find her? What did you do?" I scream.

"I'm sorry, I had to say that I found her. It was the only way."

My heart is in pieces. I can't even feel it beating. In fact, I wish it would stop—I wish I could die right here. My chin quivers uncontrollably and I fall to the sidewalk, feeling as though there isn't a muscle in my body capable of holding up even an eyelash. "I hope someone makes you feel the eternal pain you have caused me—pain I will live with until I die," I whisper through my gritted teeth.

"Matilda, please. Let me explain why I had to do this," Papa pleads.

It's the first sign of weakness I've seen in him, and I don't know if it's from the words I've said, from the look of destruction slashed into my face, or the realization of what he's done, but I don't care. I don't want to hear him speak again for the rest of my life.

I pull myself to my knees, scraping them along the sidewalk as I try to stand. It takes everything I have to make my way back upstairs and into my bedroom that smells of my sweet baby. I pull down the handwritten quotes from Hans, the blanket I wrapped Runa in the most, and some clothes. The marks I have left over from the jewelry I sold will be enough to help me for a bit. I will make it last. I must get my family back. If it's the last thing I do, I must.

Neither of my parents deserves a goodbye. I can't even look at my mother and father when I pass by each of them in a separate room because I feel nothing for them. I feel nothing inside at all. My heart is dead.

Mama and Papa don't chase after me. They don't ask me where I'm going or when I'll be back. I'll never allow them to find me again. If Mama helped him, she knew his intentions and didn't warn me. I would never have gone to sleep. I would never have let Runa out of my arms. It is just as much her fault as it is his.

Though the train station is only a couple of miles from home, it feels like hours have passed by the time I arrive. My mind is empty, my stomach hollow, and my chest is in agonizing pain as breast milk leaks through my dress.

The train I need doesn't leave for an hour, but there is no difference between an hour and a hundred now. I most likely won't find Hans, and I don't know how to begin ever finding Runa. I just need to be near Hans at the very least. I don't plan to give up until I find out where he is now.

The train contains a mixture of passengers. Soldiers likely heading to wherever they work, civilians in fanciful attire that depicts an ignorance of being at war. The thought of people dying every day must not cross their minds. Then there are people like me who look guilty, lost, scared, and furious. We are the people being asked for identification first. We must prove we are not Jewish. Once I provide proof, I receive a commendable head nod as if I have done something right, as if I was born into the right body rather than the wrong one.

I'm sitting next to a woman in a day dress made of expensive fabric. Her hair must have taken an hour to pin into perfect curls that glisten with a finishing spray. The perfume she doused her neck with is pungent and burns my nose. She must not be able to smell herself. Her leather gloves are tailor-made for her nimble fingers and she is sitting as if there is a wooden board nailed to her back. I want to ask her why she is acting so perfectly, who she is trying to impress. Does anyone truly care at this point? We are being hated or hating. This isn't life.

The woman's peripheral gaze falls to my chest, soaked with breast milk. Her nose crinkles and her cold stare returns to the seats in front of us.

"It is milk for my baby, in case you were wondering," I say. The word baby burns against my tongue.

"I don't see a child anywhere around you," she says, her voice soft but smooth—unaffected.

"Someone took her from me this morning. That is why."

The woman offers another glance in my direction, this time at my face. She can likely see the red stains webbing across my eyes. "I'm sorry to hear that," she says, before clearing her throat and turning her head toward the window. She doesn't want to know. I can't say I blame her.

CHAPTER 26
GRACE
2018

There's a path here in Dachau that led the prisoners to a yard where they queued up for roll call. Archie said they forced the men and women to plant the trees that line both sides of the gravelly road. The intention, derived from the Nazis, was to create a facade for anyone outside of the camp who might look in. Today, the trees stand tall, all of which bear witness to the footprints left behind, those who are paying respects, and then, the loved ones who have gone two generations without knowing where they came from. I have found comfort under the blossoming branches where I sat and read more of the unraveling pages that are kinetically forming a story—the real story I wanted to know.

Archie didn't seem comfortable with the thought of leaving me here but agreed because I need to feel a connection now more than ever. I'm certain Runa is Mom's birth name, which means my roots are here.

The heaviness in my stomach doesn't leave me with a feeling of closeness to Hans or Matilda. All I feel is a sense of helplessness. Matilda didn't know what was happening on these grounds. I'm not sure anyone could have assumed the truth of what I've learned today. A part of me is grateful she felt hope, but to see the images of corpses and people on the brink of death within their skeletal figures is a sight I'll never be able to erase from my mind. I will carry the images with me forever, as I should do. No one should go through life without knowing the truth of what our world is capable of, and to understand that I'm part of this place—everything I've ever known seems insignificant in comparison.

I still don't know if Hans survived or if Matilda found him. I only know neither of them ever found us.

As if in a trance, I exit through the black iron gates that inform all entrants that work will set them free.

Work will set you free. It was a lie, even for those who survived. No one could ever be free from this.

The bus ride back toward the old village of Dachau is quicker than I expected. It hasn't been enough time to collect my unruly thoughts, but the bookshop is already in front of me. Matilda must have been here while Hans was in the camp. I wonder if she was waiting, and if so, how long, and how much of that time she held on to hope.

The bells above the door jingle as I step inside, finding Archie telling a story. His hand motions seem to be integral to whatever he is talking about, but the visitor is holding an old book in his hand. He's holding onto it as if it's a rare diamond. It's obvious Archie enjoys being here in the shop. I couldn't do anything that would pull him away from this place that he's grown up in. It's another layer of an impossible decision I must make.

"Ah, you're back," he says, noticing me as I walk inside.

The visitor looks over at me as well, but with a confused look on his face.

"Herr, this is Matilda Ellman's granddaughter, Grace. Grace, this is—"

The man clears his throat, seeming uncomfortable for a moment. "People call me Al," the man says.

"It's very nice to meet you, Al," I reply.

Al places the book down on the table beside him, taking his time, careful not to mishandle the antique. "You are Matilda's granddaughter?" the man asks, as if that truth is impossible.

"It's fairly new information to me, but yes, sir," I reply.

Al makes his way over to me, his eyes wide and glossy. The closer he comes, the more I notice his age. It is easier to tell now that he's standing beneath the ceiling lights, casting a faint spotlight around him. I imagine he's in his eighties by the deep grooves across his forehead. His beard and mustache mask all other hints of age, but his eyes

—I can tell they have seen a lot. "Your grandmother, she found something that mended pieces of my broken heart. Of course, this was many moons ago, but people like her—they aren't common."

I take a step closer, feeling drawn to this man. "If you don't mind me asking, what did she find for you?"

The man's lips quiver as he dips his hand into his pants pocket, then retrieves a bronze watch, one with a detailed design engraved on the cover.

"I was just a boy, teetering on the edge of being able to forget everything I saw and having the ability to recollect everything. Some parts of living in Dachau I don't remember, others I do. They took me from my parents, separated us like many children were from their families. I can vividly recall the look on my mother's face when they pulled me from her arms. It matched the pain I saw in my father when the Nazis took him from us a couple of weeks earlier. At that age, I was sure we would become reunited again, but that wasn't the case. Anyhow, my father left this watch with my mother and she intended to give it to me when I was being taken, but when she searched for it in her pocket, it was missing. Not only was my father taken, and I was about to be taken, but the one thing she had left from my father was lost, too. My mother had been holding onto it as if it was her only hope. She even slept with it clutched in her hand each night. It hurt the most to know she lost everything that day and it's the last I remember of her."

Hearing this man's story is overwhelming. The need to release all the pain in my chest is fierce, but something within me refuses to break. There is an urge to be strong, a feeling I lost years ago when Mom passed away.

I inhale through my nose, slowly, silently counting to five to recompose myself before I fall to pieces in front of this man.

"But you have the watch. Is that it?" I ask.

The man smiles, baring his teeth that are stained by what looks like years of coffee and tea. "It is, with thanks to Matilda. This is my father's watch. Inside, there is a note to me on the back of a small photograph of the three of us from our last family trip to the Bavarian Alps."

He holds it out to me, and I brush my hands on my sides to make sure I don't leave a trace of dust on this beautiful watch.

It's heavier than I expected. The chain attached is cold and clammy. It must weigh his pocket down, but I suppose the reminder of it must be comforting. "This is beautiful," I tell him.

"Go on, open it."

I press the small knob on the side, allowing the two pieces to part. The photograph inside is just as he described—a black-and-white image of two cheerful people holding their young son, surrounded by a blanket of snow. I notice the watch has stopped moving.

He must see me glancing at the frozen mechanisms because he says, "I disabled the watch when Matilda gave it to me. I don't need a reminder of the minutes that pass, just the moment I had a piece of my family back."

"How did she find this?" I ask. I can't imagine how she came to find such an important heirloom and then trace who it belonged to.

"I haven't shown her yet," Archie tells the man.

Al smiles again and places his hands around mine, the one holding his pocket watch. "May I?" he asks Archie.

"By all means," Archie responds.

"Follow me, dear." Al removes his hand from mine, allowing me to continue holding the watch as I follow him across the shop, toward the back wall. I soon find out one of the tall bookcases is a Murphy door. I suppose I shouldn't feel surprised about anything new I discover in this shop.

Al takes a step in through the dark opening and pulls on a string attached to a hanging bulb. The space is like a decent-sized walk-in closet. He waves me over to where he's standing, and as I take a few steps closer, I find three walls lined with shelves, all with baskets of trinkets. "These are the missing belongings from the former prisoners of Dachau. I was one of the first people to be reconnected with a lost treasure found in the debris left behind in the camp. Thankfully, my parents had written my name on the back of the photograph. Matilda is the one who found the watch. I still wonder about the odds of someone finding this special treasure, but I consider myself lucky for it. Of course, I wasn't the only one she reconnected to lost items. There were so many, and these are what remain. All of them are a mystery, but all of them belong to someone."

The closet smells like a combination of brass, copper, and a hint of mildew. I suppose it's the scent of lost memories.

"Who knows, maybe you will find where some of these pieces belong," he says, tipping his head. I hold out his watch, and he carefully lifts it from my hand and returns it to his pocket. "It was a pleasure to meet you, Grace. If I didn't know what year it was, I would think you are Matilda by the stark resemblance. Those are some strong genes."

In silence, I step away from the closet, allowing him to walk out.

"Archie, my good fellow, I will see you next week. Take care, son."

"Have a nice day," Archie says.

We watch as Al leaves the shop, waiting for the door to close before either of us says a word.

"I'm sorry, I wasn't expecting his visit today," Archie says. "He moved here about ten years ago after living in the United States for most of his adult life. He feels closer to his family here, so he has made it his home." His explanation clarifies Al's English, with no hint of a German accent.

"I didn't know Matilda collected lost items," I say.

"You'll get to that part of the story soon," Archie says, looking away from me as if there's something he wants to say but is refraining. "Anyway, how was the rest of your visit? Are you okay?"

"No, but I don't think many can say they are okay after leaving there."

"Very true," he replies.

"The more clarity I seem to get, the more confused I feel. This bookshop—it feels like a lost memory intended for me."

Archie grins and lowers his head for a pause. "Precisely."

I slip off the sweater I've been wearing all day, the one that belongs to Archie. As I pass it over, our hands brush together, causing an unexpected spark from static.

"A miniature lightning bolt. Since you are a part of Matilda and Hans, this is no surprise," he jokes.

Archie takes the sweater from my hand, and I intend to release it, but I move with it as he pulls closer. My heart is beating out of my chest, and I have no clue what is going on right now or what I'm doing, but the connection I was looking for earlier is here, and Archie is part of it.

I'm staring at him with wonder and so many questions and though I think he knows all of the answers, it seems as if he has questions for me as well.

I put all thoughts on pause when my phone buzzes in my back pocket. I snap out of my haze and reach for the phone, finding Paul's name on display. "Sorry, just a moment—my boss is calling," I tell Archie.

"Take your time," he says.

"This is Grace speaking," I answer.

"Hi, Grace," Paul says, his calm words are full of attitude. "When are you planning to return to the office? We have a massive project that we've taken on and it's all hands on deck right now."

I turn around and lower my voice, embarrassed to be talked to this way in front of Archie even though he likely can't hear Paul on the other end of the line. "I'm not sure right now. I'm handling something with my family. It's only been a few days, Paul. I haven't taken a vacation in over a year. I didn't think this would be an issue."

"You left without notice. You created an issue, Grace."

Paul left without notice last year after he had to put his dog down and didn't return to work for over a week. It was unexpected, too. "Yes, like I said, something with my family came up."

"Look, Grace, I don't want to play hardball, but I need you back in the office by Monday."

I fling my hand out to the side as if he could see my gesture. "That's in less than forty-eight hours," I tell him.

"Okay. Great. See you then," he says, ending the call.

I power my phone off, livid, but decide to let it go for the moment. I don't need to bring my insignificant problems to this place that deserves every moment of my attention.

"Is everything all right?" Archie asks.

"No, but—it doesn't matter right now. Nothing matters except this moment, this shop, and the stories left behind for me."

CHAPTER 27
MATILDA
NOVEMBER 1941

Somewhere in my head, I imagined there would be a sign pointing toward where the Jewish people are being kept, but I couldn't have been more wrong. Life is moving about as if nothing out of the ordinary is happening. Perhaps there is nothing happening here. It has been nearly eight months since I heard a hint of where the Nazis were taking Hans. With a world containing a million doors spinning around me, waiting for me to decide which way to turn, I wish some kind of higher power would point me in the correct direction.

While circling the train station for directions, I spot a tall peak off in the distance. I've heard the historical stories about the Dachau Palace, the gothic appearance that remains, and how the Napoleonic Wars were responsible for destroying two-thirds of the building, but I have never been. As insignificantly small as I feel compared to the hill beneath the palace, it may be my only hope of a broader view of the town.

The pain of understanding nothing is worse than feeling helpless.

The window of the train station's ticket booth is open, and I take the opportunity to ask the only question I will probably find an answer to here.

"Pardon me, but could you point me in the best direction to travel up to Dachau Palace?"

The man doesn't lift his head to acknowledge me. He continues jotting down notes on a pad of paper, mouthing thoughts to himself.

"There is a bus," he says, pointing off to the right. "There is a stop in Dachau Old Town. You will find your way from there."

The urge to ask him where all the Jewish people are falls to the tip of my tongue before I stop myself. We shouldn't ask, and no one should tell. It has been the motto for years now.

"Thank you," I say to the man.

Without a response or even a momentary glimpse from him, I head in the direction he pointed. Just as soon as I round a corner, I spot a sign for the bus.

If the palace didn't look to be several miles away and so steep, I might walk to keep my mind busy, but I'm running low on energy and I'm miserably sore and wet from my chest down to my waist.

About an hour passes before I'm standing on a full bus waiting for my stop. Only a few others on the bus depart at the same time I do.

There's a historic look and feel to the small area. If I wasn't so distraught, I might find comfort in its beauty, but there is nothing beautiful about the place that is a purgatory for hundreds of Jewish people.

With an ache in my feet and a worse one in my chest, I follow the uneven roads, hoping the path doesn't end before I reach the peak and palace. Every breath left in my body feels as if it has gone missing when I spot the top of the buttercup yellow and white facade of the palace. By the time I reach the courtyard sprawled out before the enormous structure, I fall to the ground, desperate for a rest. But if I sit or stand still for too long, emotions will return and leave me falling to pieces again.

I glance out at the horizon; the view overlooks the town of Dachau and a hint of the Bavarian Alps hiding within the low-bearing clouds. Everything is a blur, not because I'm having trouble seeing, but because nothing stands out as abnormal. Rows of shops and homes, buildings, and factories seem to make up the town as if this is any other town, as if I have not traveled for the past several hours. I'm no closer to Hans than I was this morning. I might run in circles until the day I die, but giving up is not a possibility.

The longer I stare out into the distance, the sun fades deeper into the clouds, carrying along a shadow of darkness that will soon become the night's sky. I don't have a place to stay, nor do I know a single person in the area. I could fault myself for rushing every decision I have made today, but I would rather sleep in the dirt here than in the destroyed home I left behind.

With sluggish steps, I travel back down the steeper part of the hill to where the brightly multicolored shops line the street. Each store looks like it is the foundation for a flat or maybe a place for a traveler to spend a night.

I take my time to peer into the windows of each one. Many of the shops are empty, but some are lit up with visitors. I pass a woman sweeping the front step of her store, offering her a slight smile in return to the weary, haggard grimace she might have unintentionally given me. I step off the sidewalk onto the street so I don't walk through her cloud of dust, but she stops the broom mid-air. "Young lady, you seem lost. Is everything all right?" It might have been my false smile along with my damp dress that gave her this impression.

"I've never been to the area, and I was hoping to find a place to spend the night." Maybe she can point me in the right direction.

The woman tilts her head to the side with a look of curiosity. "You don't have any baggage with you?"

I have my satchel, but it isn't quite large enough to hold the contents for a proper overnight stay. "I must look like a mess," I reply. "There is an explanation, but not one you would likely want to sit and listen to at this hour, or any hour really."

The woman presses one hand over the other onto her broom and relaxes her shoulders. "Dear, I am about to turn seventy. Aside from running this old ratty shop, eating and sleeping, I have enough time to do all things I should have done twenty years ago." She nods her head toward the door. "Come on in, you look like you could use a cup of tea."

I'm in no position to turn down any form of hospitality, so I follow the woman inside. Her hair is silver with shimmering streaks of white and I can't help but wonder how long it must be given the number of times it's twisted into a neat bun at the base of her neck. She continues walking through the shop full of odds and ends, some trinkets, souvenirs for travelers, and a variety of old books. Her gray-blue dress swishes with every step, and the floors remind me of the ones at home with how noisy they are. The memory of hopping over floorboards to avoid the creaks stings my heart, wishing those silly boards were all I still had to worry about.

Behind the main counter where people must check out, there is a small bar-top with a large teapot, a stack of cups, and saucers. "My mother, may she rest in peace, always taught me the importance of having tea on hand because I will never know when someone might need a cup. In all the years I've run this shop, I have come to find that more people come here for talk and conversation than they do to purchase any of the items I sell. Of course, I refuse to turn the shop into just another café, but tea and coffee do seem to keep me in business. Maybe my mother knew something I didn't," she snickers. "Don't all mothers?"

I should be able to chuckle at her joke, but I will never know for sure how much Mama knew, and I don't think I truly want to find out. "I would like to think so, but I'm afraid I can prove that statement wrong."

The woman stares at me for a long moment, almost as if she's trying to read my eyes. "I'm Galina Fritz," she says, placing the broomstick against the wall in exchange for the teapot.

"I'm Matilda," I offer. "I prefer to forget my surname, if you don't mind."

A rush of pain reels through my chest and I wonder if a woman's body can erupt when it's full of breast milk. With subtlety, I press my forearm up against my chest, wishing for the pressure to offer relief.

Galina twists back to me with a cup of tea and a saucer. I release my arm, feeling a breeze of cool air rush against the damp areas of my dress. In hopes of avoiding the topic, I take a sip, appreciating the warmth after living through so many varieties of coldness today.

"Where are you traveling from?" Galina asks.

I move the cup from my lips, just far enough away to answer. "Augsburg," I reply.

"Oh, what a lovely little area. Or, it used to be, I suppose," she says with a tired sigh.

"There has been nothing lovely about that town in a while, I'm afraid."

"Is that why you're here? Are you an artist looking for some scenery? Most of our visitors come here for the view."

I rest the cup back down onto the saucer; the clink is a reminder of a time I would enjoy sitting with Mama at our table sharing a pot of tea while talking about my day at school. It's been so long, I don't remember the feeling of having someone to talk to like that.

"No, I'm here to find someone," I say, keeping my gaze on the swirling dark water.

"Maybe I could help. Does the person live in Dachau? I know many of the residents in the area."

My response might lead me to trouble, but I'm not sure I care now. "No, the man I'm looking for is also from Augsburg, but the soldiers brought him to Dachau about eight months ago."

"I see," she says.

With a quick glimpse down at my dress, I feel embarrassed to think she might have me figured out so quickly.

"He's Jewish, but more importantly, my best friend, and the father of our child."

Galina places her hand on her chest. I suppose she didn't assume as much. "Good heavens, where is the child?"

"I can't say," I utter against the teacup.

"Matilda, I understand the common courtesy of living without assumptions on one person's beliefs, but I don't think differently of you for trying to find your friend." She takes my free hand and closes it between her soft fingers, offering me a momentary feeling of comfort.

"My papa didn't feel the same. He took my daughter, Runa, and turned her in as an orphan last night, ensuring they—whoever that is —would transport her to the United States to receive proper care. Whether he is telling the truth, I might never know... I don't know if there is even a chance of finding Hans, my friend, and worse, my daughter. I'm completely lost at the moment." The urge to let the tears form and fall is strong, but I swallow hard and clench my eyes.

Galina takes the teacup and saucer from my hand and places them down on the small table. "I'm not sure there are words suitable to respond," she says.

"Words aren't necessary," I agree. "Nothing can undo what he has done."

"You mentioned looking for a place to stay tonight, yes?"

I take in a shuddering deep breath. "Yes."

"I'm about to close the shop for the day. I live just upstairs. You can stay here with me. I have clean clothes you can borrow and something to prepare for supper."

I press my lips together, touched by her offer. "I would be most appreciative, but I don't want to get in your way, Galina. The tea has already been more than I could have asked for, and listening to my story—it's more than anyone has done for me in a long time."

"As a mother to a son who doesn't treat me very well, I think I would be the lucky one to have company tonight. This world is a lonely place, Matilda, and there aren't many ways around it right now."

CHAPTER 28
MATILDA
NOVEMBER 1941

Before I open my eyes, I pray I have been living in a nightmare and that I'm finally waking up. I tell myself that I will take the horrors that I dreamt about and ensure they never become reality. I wonder if there is a way to pray harder than I ever have before.

My eyelids are hard to force open; a raw heaviness makes me stay where I am and never want to face the light of day. My eyes burned from weeping while I fell asleep. I tried to keep myself together all day yesterday, but no mother could not shed a tear after being separated from her child. Part of me is missing, dismembered, amputated, and left behind. It's impossible to just go on.

I stare toward the window, focusing on the dust sparkling in the ray of light. The dust and debris of this world already outnumbers the population, but to understand that an insignificant particle of matter has more freedom than so many humans—it's incomprehensible.

Galina made up a bed for me on the other side of her living quarters. She had a spare mattress beneath the frame of her bed and extra sheets with blankets. It's more than enough after the past eight months.

"Matilda, would you like some breakfast?" Galina calls out from the galley area outside of the main bedroom.

I don't want to be a thorn in her side. She's already been so kind to me. "I'm sure I can find something in the village. I wouldn't want you to have to cook for two," I reply, sitting up against the wall. For a bit, I forgot about the relentless pain in my breasts, but the moment I'm upright, the ache returns with a vengeance.

"I told you I was not going to put up with your nonsense," Galina says, appearing with a plate of eggs and fruit. She places the food down beside the mattress. "I have tea for you, too, but I'd like to ask you a question before I pour you a cup."

"Of course, and thank you. I'm not sure how to repay you for your generosity," I say.

Galina pulls the chair in front of her vanity mirror to my side and takes a seat. "This is none of my business, but I can't imagine how much physical pain you are in from the buildup of milk. This is difficult to ask and for you to answer, but I'm curious if you are waiting for the pain to stop or hoping to find Runa before then? Either way, there are ways to reduce the inflammation."

I pull the blanket against my stomach, feeling an emptiness in the loose flesh that hasn't tightened since giving birth. My gaze falls to my waist, watching the habitual sweeping motion of my hands caressing the barren area. I'm not sure I ever stopped feeling for Runa even after she was born. My subconscious is not ready to come to terms with the truth. I try to take in a full breath, but my lungs won't allow for such movement. The air just sputters out like a deflating balloon, and I can hardly lift my head or open my eyes enough to see past my wet lashes.

"I want to lie to myself and say I'll find her. I was sure my father took her to Munich to turn her in as a lost child, but he could have taken her anywhere and I don't have a clue where to look, especially if she really is on her way to the United States. He left her without a name or any papers. All I could do is tell someone that my baby with a few strands of brown hair and eyes that are dark blue is missing. I don't know whether to grieve or act like a madwoman calling every fire brigade and uniform force. My father said it cost him a lot of money, which makes me believe it was a private exchange."

"I will help you compile a list of phone numbers. You will always question yourself if you don't."

"I suppose I will both grieve and make those calls," I say.

"In the meantime, you can express the milk for relief. It will return, but if you aren't ready to give up hope, it's the best way to maintain your supply. However, if the pain is too much, I have some herbs I can put in your tea that will help. The choice is yours, dear."

I was afraid to waste the milk. I wasn't thinking my body would realize Runa was missing. As if I'm not already suffering enough, I must decide on whether there's a chance I might find her or if it's more likely that I will never see her again.

"Runa must be hungry," I utter, staring down at the eggs and fruit.

"Matilda, if you don't care for your body, there is no chance of finding her. I apologize for being so blunt, but it's the truth."

It's all I needed to hear to consume the food on the plate, which I do in a matter of minutes. "Do you mind if I excuse myself to the toilet?"

"By all means. I'll begin working on the list of numbers from the telephone directory."

On the way down the short corridor to the washroom and toilet, my mind turns to Hans. I had hoped to find him, to help him, and to tell him he is a papa. But now I'm left to hope I find him, only to break his heart more than it already is.

I spent the entire morning listening to different women at a switchboard saying: "Number, please."

Every location I contacted said that they had not encountered an orphan baby in the last few days. The more numbers I connected to, the less hope I felt. I knew in my heart it wouldn't be so simple, but I had to try, like Galina said.

"I'm so sorry, dear," Galina says, scooping my hair behind my shoulder. "I know this won't help you much, but at my age, life has a wondrous way of patching holes. You might not have found a trace of Runa today, but it doesn't mean you won't ever find her. Hope is something no one can steal from you."

"Yes, of course," I say, swallowing the air lodged in my throat. "Would you mind telling me how to prepare my tea with the herbs you mentioned this morning? The pain is too much to continue enduring."

Galina places her hand on my cheek. "I'll fix a cup for you."

Behind the front counter of the shop, I glance around, my eyes taking in the sights while my mind spins in thousands of different directions. It would take someone a year to see every item in this small storefront. Nothing has a matching pair and I wonder where Galina collected everything from.

The bell on the door chimes, and a brisk wind travels through the opening as someone walks inside. I can't see around the small table holding displays of maps, but it isn't long before the common sight of a Nazi in his olive-green wool uniform has stolen my breath. They are everywhere and it should never surprise me to turn a corner and find a soldier, but my reaction never changes. The question running through my mind always feels trapped behind my gritted teeth, waiting to pour out, but I remain still, waiting for them to pass by me as if I'm as insignificant as the last person they walked past.

"Who are you?" he asks. The man has somewhat of a sad look within the depths of his translucent blue eyes which are thickly overshadowed by his blonde eyebrows. His mouth seems to be permanently drawn into a grimace, forming a cavernous dimple between his bottom lip and chin. Misery is all I see.

I suppose I won't be so lucky to escape a conversation with this one. While I'm aware of how quickly I should respond, the answer doesn't come out as easily as it should.

"Erich, what are you doing here at this hour?" Galina calls out from the back of the shop.

He allows his glare to linger on me for an extra second before turning toward Galina's voice. "I'm looking for something," he says.

Galina makes her way over to my side and places the cup of tea down in front of me. "Go on, dear. It's hot, be careful."

"Who is this?" he asks again, this time to Galina.

"This, as you are referring to her, is Matilda. She is going to be helping me in the shop," Galina replies. It's clear she has no fear of a man in uniform. I wish I could feel the same. "Matilda, this is my son, Erich, the one I was telling you about last night."

I almost spit out my sip of tea. Galina only spoke briefly about her son, explaining that he didn't treat her very well. She told me that he visits, typically because he needs something from her, which happens often. She didn't mention he was a Nazi.

"I didn't know you were looking for additional help in the shop, Mother," he says, resetting his glare on me. "I would have found a suitable person for you."

"Erich, did you come here because you needed anything in particular, or did you come here to be a nuisance?"

"Do you have any peppermint leaves?" he asks. "My commander

has come down with an illness and asked me to find something to help him get through the day."

Galina shakes her head. "No, I'm out of peppermint leaves. Find another remedy for your commander. Perhaps he can take the day off from torturing innocent people?"

"Mother," Erich snaps.

Innocent people.

"I won't be of service to anyone there, as I have said before," replies Galina.

To keep myself from looking anything less than shocked, I take another sip of my tea, recognizing the peppermint flavor Galina must have added.

Erich straightens his shoulders and lifts his chin. "Very well. I shouldn't have assumed you could help me either way," he says.

Galina stares at him with clear pain folding into the creases of her eyes. "No, you shouldn't have."

Erich glances at me one last time before twisting on his heels and leaving as quickly as he arrived, without so much as a goodbye to his mother.

The moment the door closes behind him, Galina's shoulders relax, and she inhales a long breath. "I apologize for his behavior," she says.

"No need," I reply, keeping my focus on my tea.

"After Erich's father passed away, he felt an obligation to become a stronger man, one with a certain level of importance. His father would never have wanted him to become a soldier—not the kind he is today. I'm ashamed of him, Matilda. You must know this. I don't agree with his choices, nor his daily duties. A mother could never hate her son, but I dislike who he is."

"He's a Nazi," I state, still taken aback by the revelation.

"Yes, a guard at the work camp—the one they forbid us to talk about. We all know there is a place where they are holding people prisoners to work like servants in our country, but it's a secret; one the Nazis and the Führer intend to hide. For every citizen still living in this area, there seem to be just as many Nazis."

"He might know if Hans is there," I say without thinking through my words.

Galina presses the palms of her hands down on the counter, leaning forward as if she is out of breath. "He may, but from what I have heard, they don't know most prisoners' names, only their numbers. I'm not sure I trust my son to find out sensitive information that could affect Hans's life," she explains.

I shouldn't be able to understand how a mother could distrust her son, except that I am a daughter who will never be able to look at her parents again.

"He may be my only hope," I say.

Galina doesn't respond. She stares through the book-covered shelves across the way as if she is looking through a window at a horrible sight.

CHAPTER 29
GRACE
2018

"This is where Matilda was—in this shop with Galina?" I ask Archie while he's typing something into the computer at the front counter.

Archie's lips curl into a smile, but he doesn't peer away from the screen. I stand from the chair I have become one with over the last couple of days and make my way across to the counter, staring at him with desperation, needing this answer.

"You are very impatient, aren't you?" He thinks he's being cute with his question. I can tell by the light pink hue warming his face.

"I read all the pages. That means you have to tell me the rest of the story."

"You haven't read all the pages," Archie replies.

"I don't understand." I thumbed through each of the papers, one by one, making sure there was nothing I missed, but there was nothing more to read after Galina's son came into her shop.

"I thought it might overwhelm you if I handed over a large stack of papers, so I have more now." Archie takes a step to the side, standing directly across from me with only the counter between us. "I'm being mindful of the amount of information you're handling at once. I'm not sure how to help and I can't imagine going a lifetime wondering about your family and suddenly having it all pour down on you at once."

I drop my head, trying to compose my frustration. He's trying to do the right thing, but I've traveled halfway across the world in anticipation of answers, and it's been like watching sand fall through an hourglass in slow motion. "I have waited a lifetime and spent hundreds of hours researching, knowing I would never find answers. They sent my mother to the United States without a name or any other information. It's impossible to find a person with no trace of where they came from. Yet, here I am, finally uncovering the answers she spent her entire life looking for, and she's gone. She should be able to read these words left behind, not me. I should be here to comfort her as she finally learns who her parents were, but instead, I'm here in her place, alone."

"You're not alone, Grace," Archie says.

I pull my phone out of my pocket, remembering I had powered it down after receiving Paul's phone call. "I'm not even sure I will have a job to go back home to. If I'm being honest, I'm not sure I want a job to return to. I feel like I'm at this place—a fork in the road, and I have no clue who I am, who I'm supposed to be, or where I should be going. Everything I have based my life's decisions on was temporary foundations that gave out when my mother passed away. Our pasts should mold our futures, and I'm not sure how that's possible for me now."

Archie's gaze seems lost in the distance as he stares beyond me, touching his fingertips to his lips. "You don't enjoy what you do for a living?" he asks.

No one has asked me this question before, and an answer doesn't form as quickly as I would have thought.

I tug at the sleeves of my shirt, pulling them down over my knuckles. "I wouldn't say I don't enjoy what I do, but I'm not sure I ended up working for the right company. Architecture has always been my passion. Until this week, there wasn't a day I considered the thought of going in a different direction. I'm fascinated by the history of old structures and bringing those ancient designs to modern-day styles."

"Is that what you do? Back at home, I mean."

I shake my head, wondering how our conversation veered so far off track. "Yes, I design blueprints for an architecture firm, but I had dreams of running a business of my own. I assumed if I did my time working for someone else, I would eventually have the chance to spread my wings and start a practice of my own. Yet," I lift my phone and squeeze it the way I wish I could wring Paul's neck, "I'm living under scrutiny and following rules I don't agree with."

Archie leans over the counter and takes my clenched hand that's still clutching my phone. "Your grandmother would tell you it's never too late to find what you're looking for."

I let out a huff. "She might have told me that, but in reality, it became too late for her and my mom to find each other, didn't it?"

"I suppose that might depend on your theory of evolution," he says.

"The evolution ends with me, Archie."

He releases my hand and I return my phone to my pocket, forcing myself to take in a couple of deep breaths.

"Just a moment," he says, walking toward the back closet where the lost mementos are stored.

He returns with an old envelope that looks as if someone has handled it a million times over the years and pulls out another stack of papers.

"Here is the rest of the story. It's all here." He hands me the papers and I take them with a careful grip.

I stare down at the words, blurring my vision as I contemplate what more I could uncover, or how much more I can handle. I already know how the story ends: It's with me, here, alone with no family left to reunite with.

"Come with me, I'm going to take you somewhere," Archie says.

I look around the empty store, wondering how many visitors shop here daily. It's been so quiet since I arrived. "What about the shop?"

"No need to worry," he replies. "Come."

I follow Archie out the front door into the midday sun. He hangs a sign on the front window and locks the door with a skeleton key.

"Is that key for fun?" I ask.

"We've never had to change the locks and, fortunately, no one has lost the key."

"It's hard to comprehend that a woman I never met thinks it's a good idea that I inherit this key."

Archie snickers in response. "I'm sure if it's something that's important to you, you won't lose it."

The keys jingle as he drops them into his sweater pocket and points up the hill. "It's just this way."

"What is?"

"You'll see."

The hill is steeper than I thought, but the palace on the top is smaller than I expected and closer than I imagined. "I thought this was much larger."

"The original owners constructed it as a medieval castle, back in the year 1100, before it was demolished three hundred years later. It wasn't until the mid-1500s that the new rulers of Bavaria rebuilt the structure as a renaissance-style palace, intending to use it as their residence. However, after years of passing down the property to newer generations and the end of the Napoleonic Wars, three-quarters of the palace saw another bout of destruction. This part of the structure in front of us is the only part remaining, and they didn't restore it to its former baroque style until 1977. Of course, the exterior has been used for many backdrops over the years, and the beautiful gardens have been a setting for artists from all over the world to keep the view alive through photographs and paintings."

Archie sounds like a tour guide, but I appreciate the history, especially the rise and fall of the renaissance and baroque architectural styles. "Are we able to go inside?"

"Certainly," he says, "but I want to show you the view first. The gardens are beautiful this time of year."

The surroundings make me feel as though I've stepped into a fairy tale. The vibrant greenery and scents and colors of the maintained flowers have a surreal feeling. It's peaceful and the only hint of sound is the buzzing of bees.

I have tried to walk at a slower pace to match Archie's relaxed way of getting from one place to another, but I'm so used to being in a rush I have forgotten what it's like to take in the surrounding details. I can only imagine what else I've been missing out on by flying by the seat of my pants.

The path through the garden continues beneath an arched opening bordered by neatly trimmed shrubbery. As we step through, it's like a doorway to yet another world, one with a view spanning hundreds of miles of villages, industrial space, and winding roads that greet the Bavarian Alps, where the white snowcaps become one with the blur of clouds.

"This is where she sat," Archie says.

"What do you mean?"

A smile presses into his lips and he dips his hands in his pockets, rolling back onto his heels to take a breath. "Matilda—this is where she came to look for Hans, at the highest peak in the area. She sat here day after day."

"She couldn't find him though," I clarify, having already read that part of the story.

"It's a lot to take in all at once. No one would know where to look with so many fragments of the world displayed on the horizon. Matilda returned many times, hoping to spot a hint of where Hans might have been. She spoke highly of this landmark. It was her favorite place to be."

"And you? Are you only here to show me the sights?" I ask.

"Of course, but I have many memories from this very location, too. My parents would bring me up here for picnics and it inspired my grandfather to paint. He was never very good, but he always said that sitting up here made him feel like he was bigger than everything else in the world, and it gave him a sense of peace he was so often desperate to feel. Until recently, he would still come up here once a week to take in the sights."

"He's still here—your grandfather?" I ask.

"He is."

"I would love to meet him. Would that be possible?" He must have known both Matilda and Hans well.

"Possibly, but he's a bit fussy about his schedule and routine. I'll see what I can do." Archie seems fidgety as he shifts his weight from foot to foot, gazing in every direction as if there is too much to look at and he needs to take it all in as fast as possible.

"That would be amazing." I spot a bench a few feet away and I take a seat. "Honestly, I couldn't imagine staying in Dachau after what he lived through. It must have been painful to have reminders around him all the time."

Archie takes a seat beside me. His leg brushes against mine, even though there is plenty of space around us. A feeling of belonging, having him close, fills me with a warmth I've never felt before. "He doesn't want to leave because he feels as if that would mean abandoning his parents and two sisters who perished during the war. He also said if he left, he would give Hitler what he wanted, which was control over who should live here with freedom. My grandfather outlived Hitler, and to him, Dachau needs to be a place he has reclaimed as a Jewish man—something that shouldn't have been taken from him or the other prisoners. We don't forget what happened, but we stay to ensure history cannot repeat itself."

CHAPTER 30

MATILDA

My Dearest,

This letter may never find you, but I pray nightly that you are okay, wherever you are. I'm not sure where to send this or if there is a way for you to receive any. I just need to write to you. Of course, I have continued to write out all the details of day-to-day life, but I'm afraid my words might not make for the best story.

I miss you so dearly and I would do anything to know you are well. I've come out to Dachau hoping to find the location of wherever you are, but it seems everyone keeps their lips sealed tightly around here. No one knows where the Jewish men and women live, yet the Nazis flood the streets daily. I'm not sure what kind of world we are living in, but it's hard to see an end in sight or light at the end of this tunnel. I realize how much I have depended on you to help me see through the hard times and train my mind to focus only on what I wish my world to look like. It's as if I've forgotten what you've taught me because I can't seem to think of anything but you, fearing the worst.

There is so much I want to tell you, but I want you to know that I'm fine, and I will not give up looking for you until I somehow find you. That's what love is, and you taught me so. If you are still in Dachau, we are within a few miles of one another, no matter where you are in this town. We are looking at the same stars at night—they are our beacon of hope. If only they could deliver letters, too.

If by some miracle this letter finds its way to you, I will be grateful for that much. The person who will hand you the post can take one from you as well, but only if it is safe to do so. I only wish to know you are alive, but not at the expense of endangering your life.

I am here. I will never leave, not without you.

I love you so very much.

Tilly

I fold the paper neatly into thirds and slip it into the envelope. There is no postage or address because I must rely on an untrustworthy courier and pray that I'm not putting either of our lives at risk.

I have been here in Dachau for a few months now, but no matter how many hours I spend searching the town, I only have an inkling of where the work camp may be. I've noticed the Nazis are like packs of ants, one following another in a trail of breadcrumbs to their hole in the ground. Of course, someone like me couldn't make my way as far down the dirt-covered roads since they guard those heavily, but where there are guards, there must be something to hide.

I intertwine my fingers and place my hands down on top of the sealed envelope, considering how the following conversation will go. But I have to hope for the best.

I glance up at the clock on the wall. It's just before five, and it's almost time to close the shop. It's also Thursday, and one of the three days Erich drops in to visit Galina. His visits have become more frequent over the couple of weeks since she has been ill with a case of influenza. The time I have spent tending to her and caring for the shop has been a welcome distraction, but the quiet moments between our conversations when she is awake have given me a lot of time to think, too.

The door chime startles me as it always does and I lift my hands from the counter, noticing I've left a smudge of ink on the backside of the envelope. When I turn my hand, I find the usual source of stains that I rub away on my dark dress. I always wonder if Runa will be left-handed too, just like her papa.

"How is she today?" Erich asks.

"The cough doesn't sound as raw and she is breathing better," I reply, keeping my answers simple, like I always do with him. Less is better.

Erich places his hand on his chest as if my words offer him relief. "Good, good." He removes his cap and runs his fingers through his hair. "I'm going up to check on her."

I appreciate his effort and I'm sure it has made Galina feel better, considering the sour feelings she has toward him. "I'm just going to close up the shop, so shout down the stairs if she needs anything."

"Will do," he says. Erich's gaze falls to the envelope on the counter. "Is that mail for my mother?"

I take the envelope and hold it behind my back. "No, it belongs to me."

Erich stares at me, his eyes narrowing. He must think I will change my answer if he makes me nervous enough. "Why are you afraid of me?" he asks.

"I'm not." That's a lie. I didn't realize my feelings were so apparent.

"Good, because I wanted to say thank you for taking care of my mother. She has been lucky to have you by her side. If there is any way to repay you, I will gladly do so."

Erich isn't expecting a response. No one in their right mind would ask a Nazi for a favor, no matter how much gratitude there is to go around. He continues making his way toward the back of the shop.

"There is something," I say, my voice hardly audible.

He stops and twists on his heels. "Go on," he replies.

"I'm looking for someone."

My heart is racing. The questions running through my mind are endless, knowing this request could end badly. I have nothing left to lose and Erich might be my only hope, which is difficult to process, seeing as he is the enemy.

"Who are you looking for?" he asks.

"A worker," I reply, breaking eye contact.

"A Jew," he corrects me.

I lift my gaze, trying to hide the anger that must be so apparent within my eyes. "That is not what I said."

"But it is what you meant, yes?"

I wring my free hand around my other wrist as I grip the letter a little tighter. "Are you familiar with the names of—"

"Jews."

I'm breathing in slowly through my nose, trying my best to keep calm. "Of the people conducting the labor at your site."

"We have records for that, yes."

"Would you be willing to find one particular worker and give them a letter?" I feel faint the moment the words come out of my mouth. If Galina cannot trust her blood, I certainly should not do so either.

"I could get in a lot of trouble," he replies.

"Not if you're careful."

Erich is not a typical model of a Nazi. He is older than most with his rank, overweight, and often out of breath when he comes into the shop. Looking at many of the Nazis I see around the area, the unfit, lower-ranking men seem to be a common trend. I'm not sure I understand why they would send the lower-quality soldiers to guard a place they don't want to be found, but I'm sure there are reasons I don't want to know.

"You're asking me to go against the Führer. This is treason, Matilda."

Ah, I'm surprised he remembers my name. It is the first time he has addressed me with any form of respect.

"Do it for me, Erich." Galina's voice startles me as she walks out from the back door.

"You're up?" I ask. "You should be in bed, Galina."

"If I don't get back on my feet, I will forget how to walk. I'm all right, but you are an angel for the care you have been giving me. She is an angel, Erich, did you hear me?"

Guilt runs through my blood because Galina and I have discussed asking Erich to locate Hans several times. She worries he will get Hans in trouble.

"Mother," Erich says, "you should be resting. You don't want to tire yourself out, especially on those stairs."

"I'm fine, Erich, but thank you for your concern." Galina expels a weak cough, a far cry from how awful she sounded earlier in the week. "I have felt nothing but disappointment in you for the last couple of years, my son. I'm not sure I can explain the grave difficulty of knowing that the boy I raised has become a Nazi. It sickens me more than influenza, I assure you."

Erich drops his head, shaking it with disdain. "Mother, you know my options are limited. I must provide for myself."

"Your father and I raised you to be a good man. What would he think of the person you have become?" she continues, making her way beside me.

Erich throws his hand in the air with exasperation. "Look around, Mother. There are more of me than there are of you."

"I assure you that isn't true, and I fear for the day when you realize this, too."

His cheeks burn red and the lights above him create a reflection within the sheen on his forehead. A breathy growl rumbles deep within Erich's throat before he states, "I will find whoever it is you are looking for, but I cannot promise this person is still working at the site."

Erich won't look at either of us now. I'm not sure if he's lying or worried about what his actions might cause.

Without thinking, I lunge toward him and clutch the sleeve of his uniform. My pulse drums fiercely within my ears as I stare up at him, my eyes wide with the thought of my terrifying plea. "Tell me you won't hurt this person or have him hurt," I demand.

"What is it you think I do all day?" he asks, his focus still seemingly glued to the ground.

"Something I'm incapable of imagining," I say.

"This world isn't like the descriptions in children's bedtime stories, Matilda," he replies.

"Erich, do you swear on my life and all that is holy that you will keep this person safe at all costs?" Galina follows.

The response doesn't come quickly. Erich paces in sets of four long strides, back and forth almost a dozen times before he stops.

"I will try my best," he finally says. "If the others harm this person, it will be through no fault of mine. I promise that."

I glance over at Galina, gauging her expression, wondering whether she believes him. She takes the letter from my clenched fingers and walks it over to Erich.

"Matilda, write down his name—jot the letters backward from right to left."

I do as she says. With a torn corner from a piece of notepaper, I take my time to make sure I don't make an error. Then I pass the scrap of paper over the counter toward Erich. "Thank you."

"I will let you know if I find him," he says.

"I knew my son was still in there somewhere," Galina says, patting her hand against Erich's cheek. "I miss him greatly."

Erich seems to have trouble swallowing the apparent lump in his throat. "I'm sorry for being such a disappointment, Mother."

She grabs his chin firmly in her hand. "There is no time like the present to repent your sins, Erich. What if two of those Jewish people enduring intense labor in the subzero temperatures were your father or me? Think about how you would feel."

He places his cap back on his head and slips the envelope and scrap of paper into the inside pocket of his coat. With a nod, he leans forward and gives Galina a kiss on the cheek before turning around to leave the shop. "I love you, Mama."

After watching the door close, I peer over to Galina, watching as she holds her hands in prayer against her chest.

It has been almost three months since we last saw Erich—the longest of all the months I've lived. He has not returned to the shop, and it is my fault. I blame myself for the sadness in Galina's red-streaked eyes. I have apologized dozens of times a day, each day, but she tells me I have nothing to be sorry for and the decisions Erich makes are of his own accord.

The other side of my thoughts are drumming in my head, causing me to question whether he found Hans and if the news was too horrid to report back to me. There is also the chance he got caught in an exchange with Hans. The possibilities are endless, and they are relentlessly haunting me every minute of the day.

The radio is playing softly behind the front counter of the shop while I wait for the Führer's daily rant and update. I'm not sure if I have been hoping for the war to end or if I would rather know the worst is happening or has happened—and I don't know what the definition of the "worst" is at this point. I should have considered the fact that news could come from other sources as well—sources that aren't tainted by a view that can only see in one direction.

This morning, on my walk back from picking up a couple of pastries from the café down the street, I spotted a crumpled piece of paper by the curb at the end of the road. At the same moment, a gust of wind curled around the corner of the shops, bringing along a foul odor I have started noticing over the last few weeks. The smell only arrives with the wind, but it's so strong I feel the need to cover my nose with a handkerchief. Others walking along the sidewalks do the same. No one knows where the aroma is coming from, but I'm not sure anyone would ask either.

I leaned down to retrieve the ball of paper. I could only make out a few letters from the top line marked in a heavy type. It appeared to be an informative memo, but to whom, I couldn't tell. I hoped it would be reliable information—whatever was typed out beneath the top line. After looking in every direction, making sure no one was nearby, I took the paper and ran back to the shop.

My hunger for breakfast was no longer important as I placed the bag of food down on the counter to unravel the damp, wrinkled paper.

A bulletin from the Resistance would offer insight I didn't want to know but needed to.

I only had to read a few lines in order to see what the writer had punched into the keys of the typewriter harder than all the other words: "1,000,000 Jews have already been killed by Nazis," as reported by the *London Daily Times*.

For the past hour, I have been sitting in the corner between the wall and counter, shaking while trying to wrap my head around how many Jewish people exist in Europe and how many have been killed. The bulletin doesn't go into detail about when this happened; if it has been occurring over the last couple of years or if there has been a sudden influx of murders. I shouldn't have to wonder why this wasn't a major headline in *The Reich*—the only form of news we should believe, according to Hitler. Controversially, I'm sure the Nazis and the Führer are proud of their actions and would want to boast about their accomplishments.

The longer I stir, the clearer everything becomes. This must be why Erich hasn't returned. *What are the odds that Hans is okay?*

I crumple the paper back into a ball, toss it beneath the counter behind a box full of used price tags, then scoop up the bag of pastries to take upstairs to Galina. Before I'm able to make it to the back of the shop, the front door chimes, welcoming in the first visitor of the day, another soul walking around as if the world isn't ending. We should all be so ashamed. Are we living in denial or fear?

The moment I turn around, my heart shudders from within my

chest cavity at the sight. Erich is standing just inside the front door, staring in my direction. The rim of his cap overshadows the sullen look on his face. His shoulders are straight, and his fists curled by his sides.

"Where have you been?" I ask.

He walks toward me, a clear warning to move out of his way. I step to the side as he makes his way through the shop.

"A lot has happened since we last spoke. My commander sent me away on assignments that weren't intended to take as long as they did."

I shake my head, confused. "Assignments?"

"I cannot go into more detail."

I walk away from Erich and run toward the back door to yell upstairs for Galina. "Erich is here, Galina. He's here. Can you hear me?"

Rather than respond, her barreling footsteps answer my question.

I turn back for Erich, meeting him in the middle of the shop. He reaches into his pocket and retrieves an envelope—the one I likely gave him three months ago to deliver to Hans.

"He is still alive. He's been tending to the land within the labor unit," Erich says, his hand shaking as I reach for the letter.

The sensation of pins and needles fills my face. The air I have been holding prisoner in my lungs for so long is spilling out of me all at once, like an overfilled glass. "He's alive?" I ask, my voice broken and hoarse.

Erich drops his gaze to the ground beneath us. "Yes, but I can't guarantee what the future holds for him or the others. Everything is changing quickly and by the hour, it seems."

I want to block out his words and the look on his face.

Galina wraps her arm around me rather than reaching out to give her son an embrace.

"I'll let you two be alone," I say, sniffling away the confusion of emotions running through me.

I take the envelope and hold it against my chest, scared but thrilled to have something—anything—from him. I glance down at it as I make my way through the back door to rest on the first step of the stairwell.

There is no writing on the front. I can hardly steady my hands as I peel open the flap and pull out the dirt-ridden paper. I'm careful to unfold the letter, worried about tearing the tissue-like texture.

I close my eyes and pray this letter is from Hans.

The lungful of air I had just released moments ago is back, filling up every inch of my chest, causing my muscles to tighten. I open my eyes, finding the familiar handwriting. There isn't a doubt that this beautiful penmanship belongs to the man I have missed so much.

My Sweet Tilly,

Your letter has given me reason to continue, to fight for every breath of air, crumb of food, and hope of a future outside of these iron walls.

I will tell you I'm okay because there are only two options now, and I'm grateful to be alive. Life is unusual here and nothing how I expected it would be. I do as I'm told. I keep my thoughts to myself and work as hard as I can. They promise us work will set us free, and yet I don't know what that means, but if there is any hope of freedom, I will continue to use every ounce of energy within me to make it out alive.

The work keeps my mind busy, which is a good thing. Otherwise, I would spend every minute of the day worrying about you, wondering where you are and if you are all right too. I don't like that you are in Dachau. It's not safe, but I understand nothing I say will make you change your mind. You are a fierce little warrior, Tilly, and I don't know what I did to deserve someone like you to love someone like me.

I write when I find paper and a pencil, and I hope you are doing the same. Our stories must come together as one someday. It's my one wish for us.

Thank you for finding me, but I must ask you to be careful of passing along communications. I'm sure you know this man better than I do, but I'm terrified to have given him a letter to bring back to you. There are eyes in every corner of this land, watching and waiting for someone to step out of line. I am hanging on, Tilly. I will hang on until I'm left without a choice.

I love you more than I could ever express through words, which is hard for me to accept because I can only express myself on paper, but you are different. You are a feeling that lives within my soul, the source of courage and motivation to have hope.

Stay safe, my love.

H

An icy chill weathers through my bones as I digest each word. My heart feels as though it's lodged within my throat, and I gasp for air as tears tumble down my hot cheeks. *Oh, Hans, hope is all we need.* After all of this and the time that has passed, he has hope. I wonder if he would feel the same if he knew about Runa and the fact that I lost our daughter before he even knew he had one. If he survives, I don't know how I will live, knowing I will cause more loss.

I slip the letter back in the envelope and place it in the pocket of my dress. There isn't a sound coming from the front of the shop, so I push open the door a crack to see if Galina is still having a conversation with Erich, but all I see is her holding the front door to let him leave.

The partially open door I'm peeking out of creaks and Galina turns around in response. Her face is pale, and her eyelids are pink and appear heavy.

"Are you all right?" I ask.

"Of course," she says.

"It doesn't seem so," I reply.

Galina presses her lips together and tilts her head to the side. "I'm not sure Hans will be there much longer. Maybe he will stay, but it sounds like the site is beyond its capacity and overcrowding has become an issue. There is talk of deportation, but I only know this because Erich might transfer to another location as well. I was doing my best to read between the words he was leaving out of his explanation."

I take Galina's hands in mine and inhale the small bit of air I can take in. "We'll pray."

"Of course, dear," she says, pressing her lips into a flat unconvincing smile.

"There's something else, isn't there?"

"Matilda, some things are better left unsaid."

I squeeze her hands a little tighter. "Please, I need to know if there is more. I can't live in this world where I am pretending there is a happy ending in sight. The truth is all I'm asking for. We all deserve at least that, don't we?"

"The truth is unfathomable, and it is why so many locals don't ask the questions that may have answers they fear."

"I cannot be afraid. I must be strong for Hans. I don't deserve to live in a state of ignorance when all the Jewish people cannot be so lucky."

Galina opens her eyes wider, looking directly into mine as her eyebrows knit together. She takes a moment to gather her words. For each second that passes, I assume something worse than the moment prior. "The odor outside—"

"Does Erich know what it is?"

"They are burning bodies in a crematorium on site. It is part of the solution to overcrowding. The smoke we have seen billowing into the air occasionally—that is what remains of the perished."

CHAPTER 32
GRACE
2018

I turn to the next page, wishing that this story is endless, but at the same time, if it's endless, I won't know how Matilda and Hans's life turned out. A few pages fall loose from the clipped binding, so I pinch my knees together to catch the papers from falling to the gravel.

"Ah, yes," Archie says, reaching over to help me collate the pages back into the order they were in. "I believe these are the other letters Matilda received. I'm not sure why they aren't attached to the rest of the papers."

"The letters aren't translated into English either," I point out.

"Hmm," Archie replies, scratching the back of his neck. "They must not have gone through the scanner for some reason. Here, I'm happy to translate and read them to you if you'd like."

I stare down at foreign words, wishing I could understand German. I'm sure Archie has read it all before, but the story feels so intimate—not the type to be read out loud. "If you're sure you don't mind."

His lips curl into a smile to just one side. "How could I mind? You've come all this way. The least I can do is read you a few pages."

"You've done quite a bit for me since I've gotten here. I'm not sure I'd ever be able to repay you for being so welcoming and kind."

Archie glances up toward the sky as if looking for his next words. "Is my cordiality unusual compared to how someone might behave in

America? I don't feel I'm doing anything differently than anyone else in my shoes would do for you."

I stifle a laugh, keeping the first thoughts that come to mind inside because I've always considered my life in Boston to be moving forward in a line of offense rather than defense—like there are only two options to choose from. It's better to be right than wrong, and of course, if we all mind our own business, there will be less trouble to face. I suppose if I've learned anything life-changing this week, it's that this world cannot be seen as black and white.

"Don't get me wrong. There are plenty of wonderful Americans, but in the city where I live, unless you are close with a person, most people are too busy to stop and help a stranger. I suppose there are some exceptions, though."

"That's unfortunate, and your city sounds a bit terrifying to me," Archie says with a chuckle.

"Oh, no, Boston is wonderful. The city is so lively, colorful, and full of energy, but it can be an aggressive lifestyle if you aren't used to it, I suppose."

"Yes, I think I much prefer the village type of living," he says, straightening the pleats of his pants over his knees.

"I can understand why. This view from the palace is breathtaking." Though for my grandmother, the site must have stolen her breath in other ways. I can't imagine sitting up here, waiting for answers she must have assumed might never come.

Archie gently takes the group of papers from my hand and shuffles them over his knees to straighten the pile. "The first letter looks to be from February 1943..."

My Dearest Tilly,

I'm so sorry it has been so long since I've been able to hand a letter to this soldier—Erich, I believe is his name. He doesn't appear to be on guard regularly. I worry about his motives, as I mentioned briefly in my last letter, and I hope he is doing only as he says. Erich isn't like the others, that much I can tell. He's quite skittish and seemingly uncomfortable in his job, which I think every guard at this camp should be. With so much time to think, I find myself wondering how so many soldiers have found themselves in a situation of enforcing crimes of hatred. Surely, these people weren't all born as bad as they appear? I can't imagine what their parents must think of them either. It feels impossible to understand how our world has been tipped upside down and left on its back, unable to correct itself.

Time goes by very slowly here. Each minute feels like an hour. The nights are endless. Though the space in the barrack is pitch-black, there is no comfort. I share a wooden bunk with five other men. The only benefit for us is the body heat, especially during these cold months. The clothes we have been supplied, blue and white pajamas, are made of a cloth thick enough to keep a draft out, but too thin to keep me warm.

The food is as you would expect—meek, stale, tasteless. It's just enough to keep us going—most of us.

As for the labor, I'm still working mostly with the gravel pits. The work is exhausting, especially when we hit large boulders. We are responsible for moving them from one location to another, but I'm rather lucky to have an assignment. Others have not been so fortunate. The rate of deaths is high, and they have run out of space to bury bodies, so there has been a crematorium built and used right here across from the rows of barracks. It's unsettling. Sometimes I think I hear cries, even though they are supposedly burning people who have already perished. It's much like a nightmare I'm awake for—it's terrible and the remnants of smoke piping out of the building linger in the air for hours, making it so we can never forget the horrors we face.

Anyhow, you might find relief to know I've made a good pal here, Danner. The two of us have kept each other great company. In fact, he feels much like a brother of sorts, and it's nice to have another person to talk to. He's been displaced from his family as well, so we have that in common—both of us wondering if our families are alive and well. I've also told him all about you, and he can't wait to meet you when all this is all over.

I miss you so dearly, Tilly, and I will not give up hope of us being together again someday soon. The thought of your smile warms my heart, and when everyone is silent at night, I feel as though I can hear your beautiful laughter traveling through the gusts of wind. I do hope you find reasons to laugh. I want that for you more than anything.

The others are about to line up for supper, so I better wrap up my letter. I pray these words find you safely, and I hope you are doing as well as possible.

I'll do what I can to get another letter to you soon, but try not to worry if some time goes by.

I love you more than all the stars in the sky, Matilda.

Take care, my sweetheart.

—H

They could see the smoke in the sky and smell the burning flesh.

I stand from the bench as I make my way over to the short stone wall overlooking the view of the town and beyond.

"Matilda stood here, watching the smoke, wondering if it was his body making up part of the morbid sight, didn't she?" I ask Archie.

"Matilda wasn't one to close her eyes in the face of fear," he says. "She needed to witness whatever it was he was watching or feel what he was feeling. Matilda was a fighter, refusing to ever give up, and look how it turned out in the end..."

I turn to face Archie, wondering why he would say such a thing. "I'm supposed to look at how Matilda's life turned out? You mean me, all alone, with just a history of misery that has landed me in the very same spot my grandmother stood while wondering how much worse her life could become?"

"No, Grace, you're alive. You're here to carry on the memories of their strength and heroism."

CHAPTER 35
MATILDA
JUNE 1944

My Dearest Tilly,

It's been a while, sweetheart. It's January as I'm writing this, but I know it could take months before you receive the letter since I haven't seen Erich in quite some time, which means I haven't gotten any letters from you either. I'm afraid I won't see him much more, if even once more, since there has been a rumor that some of us are facing deportation. We aren't exactly sure why anyone will be moved, but I assume it's due to the lack of space we have, which is hard to fathom because there have been thousands upon thousands of deaths, whether from sickness, execution, or some sort of medical experiments we aren't supposed to know much about. Word travels quickly here, surprisingly. The Nazis talk louder than they should, and I wonder if they intend for us to hear. I wouldn't be shocked as they appear to enjoy the act of causing fear.

I do wish we knew whether life would get worse or better. It's hard to think in either way now. I have very little energy and I'm struggling to get through a day's worth of work, but if I can't, I will become a target too.

Oh Tilly, I wish I could ask you so many questions. I'm curious about what people in this town know of what goes on within these gates. I wonder if the entire world has turned against Jewish people. It's hard to believe Hitler has convinced so many to turn their backs on us. I also wish I could ask you if you have heard anything from my mama or papa. I worry so much about Danya. I'm sure you would have said so if you knew something, but on the chance that you are trying to spare my feelings, please don't hold anything back if you find the opportunity to write again. The more I know, the better off I will be. Of course, this is only possible to ask if I meet Erich again to give him this letter, and if he is willing to sacrifice his safety by taking it.

I hope you are well, Tilly. I sincerely do wish you the best and please know that if this is the last letter you receive from me, it isn't because I have stopped loving you, not even for a second. Pray for me, sweetheart, and stay safe.

Love always,

—H

This was the last letter I received from Hans, nearly five months ago, and it has become worn from the oils on my fingertips, and the stains from my tears have made the paper fragile. I'm afraid if I go much longer without hearing from him, this letter might fall to pieces in the very same way my heart is breaking. Still, I have this letter, and hearing his voice, even if just in my mind, Hans feels alive to me.

With care, I fold up the paper and place it neatly in the pocket of my coat, then lean back against my palms, taking in the view of Dachau from the highest cliff in front of the palace.

Like I do almost daily, I sit here wondering who has lost their life, what their story was—if they suffered. I wonder if Hans is making up the black cloud in the sky. Is it his ashes I'm inhaling?

I am living in the remains of so many, yet I'm alive and supposed to continue existing as if particles of corpses are not taking up space in my lungs. I'm part of them, and they are a part of me.

Why me? How come I get to live, and they don't?

I am weak.

They are strong.

I have nothing to live for.

They have everything to survive for.

How can this world be so wrong?

I wonder if the British and American war planes know what they are flying through as they pass over our snow-covered town like there is somewhere more important to be. Perhaps they are flying toward the New Year with hope of leaving this one behind. What an apathetic thought to have. I don't have the slightest clue how bad the war has grown in other areas, aside from the radio reports and various headlines scrolled across newspaper headers, but surely there is a reason we are being passed over.

For each plane I see, there is still an ounce of hope, but it's hard sitting here on the hill each morning, wishing for an answer to how many days remain of this war. I have been witnessing the planes for months now, with no end in sight.

When and if the war ends, I wonder if all Germans will be seen as one kind—killers of the innocent, a race responsible for destroying another. I recall a lecture in class years ago, just after they removed the Jewish children from school. We were told the Jews were monsters and their intention was to end the German race. They taught us to be fearful of those who are being murdered daily.

Now, in one small town in Germany, I can hardly remember what a blue sky looks like. Ashes from bodies are so potent, they have formed a thick smog in the sky, one that doesn't go away. The clouds and smoke lock us in with the cold, and when the wind blows, it's hard to know if we are seeing snow or human remains. The similarity is uncanny.

I hate wondering if Hans has heat within his shelter because I'm certain he doesn't. I only hope that the overcrowding offers warmth. This winter feels as though it may never end, and maybe it won't. This could be my last winter, as well as the last for all the people living in Dachau, prisoners or not.

Fear is becoming a feeling of numbness, like sitting in the cold for so long that the pain from the chill disappears.

The clock tower acts as an alarm each morning, telling me I've spent long enough staring out at the horizon, praying for mercy on Hans and every poor soul beneath the black clouds of smoke. Since I can't sleep well, I've made it a point to watch the sun try to break through the wall of ash— clouds each morning, but I only see a faint glow from what feels like another world on the other side of a mirror.

I tighten my scarf and pull the collar of my coat up higher as I make the slippery walk down the hill toward the shop.

A wave of grief passes through me when I find the store still dark. Galina used to be downstairs an hour before opening, dusting, straightening items and books, and preparing for the day, but it's been months since she's been able to do that. The bout of influenza seems to have had a lasting effect on her and I wish I knew how to help rebuild her strength, but I'm doing what I can—cooking, cleaning, and running the storefront. When she's up and about, she likes to take charge as normal and I'm happy to step back and give her the space she seems to want.

Part of me wonders if she might be heartbroken over Erich's coming and going. Ever since returning from the three-month assignment he was sent out on almost two years ago, his visits are sporadic. We will see him one day, maybe the next, and then it could be weeks before we see him again. For me, I only wish for no words when he arrives. We agreed that no news means Hans is alive. Therefore, with each day I don't see Erich, it feels like a smidgen of hope, but for each day Galina goes without seeing her son, it seems to take another day off her life.

After hiking up the stairwell behind the storefront, I start a flame beneath the burner under the teapot and set a small saucepan on the other burner to fix up some porridge for us. When I return to the bedroom, I notice Galina is awake but staring over at the window. "Are you all right?" I ask, kneeling by her side.

"Of course," she says without wasting a breath.

"Something is bothering you," I say with confidence.

Galina turns to look at me. White strands of hair loosen from her braid and fall to the sides of her pale face. "My heart hurts, Matilda. I try my best to be strong, especially for you after how much you went through, but I feel like I'm fighting a battle inside of my head and the good parts of me are losing."

I understand what she's trying to say, what she means, and how she feels, but the very last thing I have ever wanted from her was sympathy. She has enough to worry about without taking on the woes of my life, too.

"I saw more war planes this morning," I say.

While I realize they were not German planes, we are both hoping for the same outcome—peace and survival.

"They only fly over us, never to us. Besides, by bombing there is no way to choose who lives or dies. We would be a threat to Germany —our lives would become meaningless in pursuing relief. For now, we should consider ourselves lucky and pray Germany surrenders before those warplanes make us a target too."

Galina has a way of teaching me more than I could have ever learned in any class.

"What can I do to help you today?" I ask.

A faint smile tugs at the lines around her lips. "Sweetheart, what haven't you done already?"

"Fixed up some breakfast for you," I reply, tucking her hair behind her ear.

"Never in my wildest dreams did I ever think someone would care for me the way you do," she says as I tend to the burner on the small stove in the galley.

"Everyone deserves to be cared for."

"Words only a mother could understand," Galina replies.

So much of my time here in Dachau is spent in mourning for Runa. Though I pray she is alive and well, she is still missing from my life. I ask myself, what could a mother be without a child? But there isn't an answer. I have called every viable location within Germany, asking about their records from November, 1941. There are no matches between those midnight hours to dawn of a man dropping off a two-week-old baby girl. Galina says I am a mother because I have yet to give up hope of finding her. It's a hard truth to agree upon when I don't think Mama or Papa deserve the endearing titles they embrace just because they put me on this earth. What they did is nothing a real parent could do to their daughter—one they claim to have loved. They have taken my parental title and given it to someone else, and I will ensure the same for them.

Just after placing a bed tray over Galina's lap with a cup of tea and a bowl of porridge, I hear a succession of taps against glass coming from the floor beneath us.

"Do you hear that?" I ask Galina.

Her forehead wrinkles as she struggles to listen for another sound. We still have a half-hour before any visitor would expect the shop to open.

Again, I hear tapping. This time Galina hears it as well.

"What on earth could that be coming from?" she asks.

"I'm not sure. I'll go down to the storefront and look," I say.

"Matilda," Galina stops me before walking out of the bedroom, "in the top drawer of my bureau, there is an old pocketknife. It's probably rusty, but hold onto it just in case."

Galina has never armed herself or suggested I do so when inside these walls. I could have a false sense of safety here, I suppose, but I'm not sure what I would do with a knife if I had to use one. We hear noises all the time—usually a racket out on the streets late at night, but never this early in the morning.

I take the old knife; the silver handle is etched with deep lines but each groove has a filling of dirt solidified within the metal.

"Erich's father took the knife from a comrade who didn't make it out of the First World War. He kept it as a memory of his fallen brother, but I haven't felt the need to touch it. I have always seen a weapon as a symbol of a war between someone who may live or die, but we are in a new time now, I suppose."

I wrap my fingers around the knife and slip it in my pocket. "I'm sure it's just a common beggar, no need to worry," I tell her.

Despite my words, the blood in my veins grows hot and beads of sweat form on the back of my neck. I'm all wound up over a silly noise after watching the world crumble in front of me this morning, like I do most mornings.

I'm quiet when I make my way toward the front of the shop, peeking out the side windows for a hint of where the noise might come from. Again, the tapping grows louder, but the motion sounds weak rather than authoritative.

When I reach the door, I spot Erich, but something isn't right. I unlock the bolts as quickly as I can, opening the heavy door with the help of a strong gust of wind. He is hunched over, his hand against the door frame and blood dripping down the side of his face. It's as much as I can see with his cap hiding the damage.

"What in the world happened?" I ask, whispering my words as I pull him into the shop.

Erich slides down against the wooden beam just within the front entrance and I relock the doors.

With one look at him, it's clear he was in a fight.

"I tried—" he says.

I strain while staring at him, kneeling to his eye level. "You tried what?"

"He was starving. I gave him some bread left over from my supper, but another guard spotted me from a tower. I didn't think I was in sight."

"He?" I question. My heart is in my throat, knowing I should help Erich with his wounds, but I cannot seem to move until he answers my question.

"Your friend—I have been trying to help. I never meant to be a bad person. I don't know how I ended up here, like this. It's no excuse, but it's the truth. I was stupid. We are all stupid puppets without meaning in our life, bred to hate. But my mother, she has only taught me how to love and I don't know where I went wrong."

"Is he all right, Hans?"

"Yes, yes, I took the blame. I made Hans hide when I realized another guard spotted me."

I want to feel relief, but it's impossible. There is no such thing as relief, or so it seems. "Then the guard beat you?" I ask.

"Yes. He called me a traitor, told me not to return or I will be seen as a Jew too."

"I'm going to get you some compresses and bandages. Sit still until I return," I say.

Galina has trouble standing for more than a few minutes at a time, but she is coming through the back door as if ready to fight off whoever is keeping me.

"Erich?" she calls out after spotting him.

"I'm okay, Mother."

"The hell you are," she bites back. "Who did this to you?"

"It's not important," he says.

I return with the compresses, rubbing alcohol, and bandages.

"Erich, it's not like you to fight," Galina says. I think she has tried to forget who he has become and what his job entails.

"I was trying to help; I've been trying to give the Jews scraps of food because I don't want to be a bad person anymore, and I don't want to live like this or see what I'm seeing. I can't do it—I just can't. The sights, they are worse every day. They are suffering more than any human should have to suffer and I can't do a thing to stop any of it from happening. I am a living sin, Mother," he says, his eyes bulging from their sockets as if he has just come face to face with his future ghost.

Galina's hand shivers as she places it over her mouth. "What do I say, Erich? To right a wrong doesn't undo what you have done, but to change is growth, and with growth, you can do more good than harm."

"No, Mother. I could never do enough good to outweigh the bad I have been a part of."

CHAPTER 37
GRACE

2018

"You didn't have to continue reading, but I appreciate having someone to sit through the story with."

Archie holds his gaze to the papers he's gripping. "I suppose I couldn't stop myself. It doesn't matter how many times I read these pages, each time it feels brand new again even though I feel like I own photocopies of some of their memories."

It's unfathomable to comprehend, and even worse to know it happened not far from this spot where we are sitting. If the world could once be so cruel, there isn't much stopping it from happening again, and that's the scariest part of all this.

"Are there more letters?"

He flips over each of the three pieces of paper he has, acknowledging that he has read each page already. "That's it, I'm afraid. I always look for another, even though I know there are no more. It's a hard reality to accept, even all these years later."

"You really loved my grandmother, didn't you?"

"Even if I hadn't met her, I would love her just from reading her story. She was one of a kind, a unique soul with the gift to love unconditionally. I only wish more people were like her. The world would be a much better place."

I wonder how much I'm like her by way of DNA. I'm not sure if kindness and generosity is something learned or engrained in our blood. If I could be a quarter of the person she was, I would be doing right by this world. Yet, I feel as though I've accomplished very little in comparison so far. All I've done is fought for a career that forces me to feel like a square trying to fit into a round hole. "I couldn't agree more."

"We should return to the shop. The town might have had a sudden desire for tea and books while we've been gone," Archie says with a sigh as he stands from the bench.

My knees silently whine as I rise to my feet, making me feel as though I've been sitting here like a statue for hours. "Thank you for bringing me up here. I'll never forget today." The words come on their own. I feel like Archie deserves to hear the impact he has had on my life in such a short time. He isn't just telling me a story of where I came from, he is helping me experience it—something I didn't think was possible.

We walk along the exterior gardens toward the path that leads back down toward the village. The wind blows briskly as we travel down the steep sidewalk and we dodge the low-hanging trees along the way, but when we reach the bottom of the block, Archie takes my arm, stopping me from continuing across the road. His grip is hot, embracing, and shouts silent words I wish to hear. I glance up, finding a look of concern narrowing his eyes as he peers down the road to the right. "Bicycles can sometimes be more aggressive than cars. Let's allow him to pass first."

Before he finishes his statement, the cyclist flies by us, forcing my hair to wrap around my face like a scarf.

Archie laughs quietly. "Told you," he says, swooping his finger around the waves that have flown into my face. The gesture takes my breath away and leaves me without a response. "You all right?"

I must look as flustered as I feel. My mind is racing in so many different directions, and I feel as if the world is spinning around me like a ride at an amusement park. It takes me a minute to reset my bearings and focus on where we are walking.

"We have lots of cyclists in Boston too. I just wasn't expecting to see someone riding so quickly down these cobblestones."

"There are plenty of us around here who enjoy a fast-paced life and some adventure, despite what you might see."

"I never assumed otherwise. Life is just very different here, but in a beautiful way."

Archie takes my hand to cross the street as if I might end up getting run over by another cyclist. He clasps his other hand around the one he's holding and squeezes gently before releasing me as we step onto the next block. "Oh, I think we just appreciate the uncommon moments, maybe more so than others. It likely comes with the territory of living on top of a burial ground."

As months pass, I feel as though I have aged a decade, and each day makes me feel more detached from the world outside of these walls. The meaning of life—a definition I thought I understood—should be erased from the dictionaries now.

When the shop is empty and there are no visitors, I stare through the shelves of books across the way, wondering what Runa might be doing at this exact moment. I imagine what she might look like now —how much she has changed, whether she still has blonde hair like me or dark hair like Hans. Her eyes were blue, but Mama said they might change. Maybe they are hazel like Hans's. Is she happy? Does she know I love her? Does she know I exist?

My heart aches when my questions fall one after another in an endless list that I would die to find answers to.

The sound of shouts echoing in the streets pulls me from thoughts of Runa and I make my way to the window. Maybe Erich has finally come home. We haven't heard from him in so long, it's hard to know where he is or if he is all right. There's no telling after the last time we saw him.

At first, I'm not sure what I'm looking at, but after a moment, I spot the American flag wave in the wind from a passing vehicle. My eyes grow larger than saucers with the understanding of what's happening.

"Galina!" I shout as loudly as I can, hoping she hears me from upstairs. She's been spending more time in bed, but I know this information will be more than enough encouragement to come downstairs. "Galina, come down at once. Can you hear me?"

A rustling sound from upstairs follows my second shout, so I keep my eyes frozen on the scene of vehicles parading down the streets.

After a long couple of minutes, Galina scurries to my side. "What is it?"

I move to place her in front of me, gripping my hands on her shoulders. "Do you see that?"

"Americans," she mutters. She holds her hand to her heart. "Please Lord, keep us all safe."

"Of course they will. They're here to help us, aren't they?" I reply.

"Come away from the window, dear," Galina says, twisting around, forcing me to take a step back. She scoops my hand into hers and squeezes with a weak grip.

"This is hope," I offer as an explanation. "It's the first sign of hope. Can't you see?"

"Matilda, come this way," Galina says, tugging me behind her.

"But why?"

"You know why," she says. "We are their enemy and until they decipher who they are here to free, we will only be their enemy."

"No, they must know. We're good people."

"How could they know who is good versus who is bad?" Galina follows.

"Isn't it obvious?" I ask. I don't want to be fearful of those who are here to free the prisoners of this war.

"Nothing is obvious—nothing at all. Where is the shop key?"

I reach into my dress pocket and retrieve the small brass ring the key hangs from, handing it over to her. She ambles to the door and locks it from the inside.

"Upstairs. Let's go," she says.

Before making our way through the back door and up the stairs, Galina takes a moment to hide a few of her beloved tea ingredients in a box, then clutches it against her chest before leaving the shop dark. She closes us into the bedroom, taking a spot beside the window to watch what is happening from above the street.

"We have no reason to hide," I say.

"They don't know who has a reason and who does not though, and until they have everything figured out, we must lay low and stay quiet. Trust me, dear."

. . .

It feels as if hours have passed and we are still staring wide-eyed out the window, convoy after convoy traveling down the streets. American soldiers have been banging on doors all around us, including ours, but we have stayed put. I don't know if that is incriminating us, making us look guilty, but I'm not sure what the best solution is either.

"They just broke into the café," I say to Galina, watching a soldier kick the door open across the street. "They will do the same here if we don't allow them inside. We're not hiding anything, Galina. We have nothing to keep from them."

For the first time since I've known Galina, there is a look of loss swimming through her eyes. If I must guess, I think it's because she doesn't know what's right or wrong.

"I'm going to allow them to search for whatever they are searching for," I say. "We haven't seen them taking civilians away. They are seeking enemies, that's not us."

Galina takes slow steps toward her bed and gently takes a seat on the edge. "Do as you must," she replies. "I won't argue. I'm not sure what we should be doing."

My heart says we should allow them inside. The quicker they find their answers on this side of town, the quicker they will find the labor camp, if they haven't already. I will do this for Hans, even if it's only for a smidgen of hope.

I unlock each door on the way down the stairs and walk straight for the front entrance. The only light spilling into the shop is from the windows, directing me to move straight ahead and do as I think is best.

My heart races as I unbolt the locks and twist the knob to open the door.

Two soldiers, dressed in camel-brown and gray-green uniforms, ones that are much bulkier than what our German soldiers wear, stand guard across the street as the others with them break into the storefront window. The two facing this direction give each other a quick glance before moving toward me at a quick pace. Unlike what we are used to around here with our soldiers, there is a sense of hesitation written into the look of their eyes.

I hold my hands up, hoping they will understand my gesture as a sign of innocence. "What is happening?" I ask.

"Wir—müssen jedes Gebäude—uh—auf der—Straße..." One of the soldiers struggles to speak German, but I know enough English to understand whatever he wants to say.

"I understand English," I say, offering to help.

"Oh, thank you," he replies with a sigh of relief. "Yes, we need to secure each building on the street, and in town. We need to inspect this building."

I step to the side, allowing them to walk in.

"We have done nothing wrong," I say. "It's just me and the shop owner. She's elderly and upstairs in the room we share."

The men look at each other again and nod. "We won't take much of your time."

"Of course," I comply.

I lead them up the stairs and show them into the bedroom, where Galina is still sitting, facing the window.

"Ma'am, we need to secure the shop and make sure no one comes in or out at the moment."

"Very well," she says without turning to face them.

"We're going to search around before we leave, but you need to remain indoors until further notice," one of the two men tells me.

"I understand."

Two days have passed since the American soldiers secured us within the shop. They have only left us to listen to the radio for updates about what is happening outside of these walls.

I'm watching out the window when Galina shouts from the other side of the room. "They're about to make an announcement," she says.

She hasn't moved from the radio since yesterday.

I sit down beside her and clasp my fingers together tightly, waiting for what I hope to be a positive update.

I'm staring at Galina's profile when a man introduces himself as Admiral Karl Doenitz. I can't seem to blink as each word is garbled with static, but the words we need to hear are as clear as day.

"German men and women, soldiers of the German Wehrmacht, our Führer, Adolf Hitler, has fallen."

. . .

It has been days, each filled with less hope than the one before. The streets have become quieter with citizens and louder with the rising number of American soldiers. Most residents wear a look of shock on hearing the truth so many were hoping never to know. We stand along the sidewalks, waiting for news, but the movement never stops. Our town has been taken over by bands of military forces, and it's clear we are not in control of what happens. The whispers on every corner are filled with speculation, but it seems more people have questions than answers. I assumed everyone silently knew what was happening in the very center of the town we live in, but apparently that isn't the case.

The reports of skeletal bodies stacked in train carts outside of the prison camp have changed everyone's sense of curiosity to a high level of uncertainty, fear, and disgust. Yet all we can do is sit and wait for further information on what's to come next.

I have been sitting on the front step of the shop most of the day. Erich told Hans where I was staying, I know this much. If the Americans liberated the labor camp, I would like to think that Hans could have found me by now, but I don't know what condition he is in, nor do I know if he made it out of there alive. After they dismissed Erich from the camp, all I have left is hope.

Hope. I'm not sure what form that may come in or look like now. It's hard to know if I would recognize a sign of such if there were to be one. I pray for hope. It's all I ever pray for, really.

Amid the gray world I'm surrounded by, a small yellow bird swoops down from the sky after spotting a crumb of some sort in the middle of the road. I watch the only source of color peck at the food it has found. When there is nothing left, the bird walks in a small circle, possibly in search of more, but then it seems to look at me as if I'm the animal in its world. The poor thing looks to be just a baby, one maybe seeing this terrible world for the very first time. Even so, I'd choose to be a bird over a human without a second thought.

The bird hops over toward me, looking at me as if I'm the source of the crumbs. "I have nothing, little bird, to give you," I say, gasping at the end of my statement.

Little bird. "Newly hatched birds are a beacon of hope like spring after a long winter, and maybe that's what Runa is to us." I'd almost forgotten Mama's words.

"Is that why you're here? To bring me hope?" I'm not sure I can believe in such a theory after Papa took Runa.

The little yellow bird must have gotten bored as it flaps its cottony wings to take off down the street. The departure is a sign to return inside the shop and stop looking for something that isn't outside.

Inside, I lift my cup of lukewarm tea from the countertop and sip it slowly, watching the time pass on the clock. I'm not sure what I'm waiting for now. The minute hand and the hour hand are always inching closer to whatever comes next, but what if there is nothing next?

"Dear, there is no use in conjuring stories in that mind of yours. We will know what is happening soon enough," Galina says, walking up behind me. I had no idea she was downstairs. She's so quiet unless she's struggling through a fit of coughs, something that has been happening more frequently it seems. I think the tainted air is aggravating her lungs, understandably.

"It feels impossible to be patient," I explain.

"Of course it does," she replies, placing her hand on my shoulder. "Of course. I understand just the same."

As if the universe is responding to my sad question, the bell above the shop door chimes, but not with gusto, as it usually does when someone is eager to come inside. The bell stalls for a brief second as the door pushes against the metal and then releases its hold.

I peek around the corner, finding a disheveled man limping toward me in a pair of blue and white striped pajamas. Every other button is missing, and the fabric hangs from his body like a heavy blanket weighing him down. The man tries to smile as he approaches, and I notice his teeth are rotting and the skin of his cheeks is buried within the depths of his skull. He's bald and without eyebrows, but there is a look of relief, or maybe it's a hint of happiness, glowing from his tired gray eyes. "Can I help you, Herr?"

"Yes, yes, I hope you can," the man says. "I'm looking for Matilda Ellman. Do you know where I might find her?"

To hear my name on a stranger's tongue sends a flurry of unease through my body. "Yes, I am she. I'm Matilda Ellman," I clarify.

The man walks in closer, making me feel nervous. "I have something for you," he says.

I don't know what this man could have for me on his ravaged

body. I'm terrified of whatever it is he's here to give me, or worse, to say. "Do we know each other?" I ask.

"I know you very well, Fräulein, but I'm afraid you don't know me much at all."

I feel faint, trying to understand the riddling words he's speaking, and grip onto the stack of used suitcases we have for sale. "I don't understand."

"Hans and I were the closest of friends," he begins.

I understand the past tense of his sentence, and I feel the hot tears burning from behind my eyes. Part of me wants to tell him to talk faster and the other part wants to tell him to forget I exist—to leave me with the last bit of faith I have that Hans is still alive. Hope is better than the truth, I see that now.

"'Were,' you said?"

"The Nazis sent Hans away from Dachau a couple of weeks ago. When they found out the American soldiers were searching for the camp, the guards tried to hide as much evidence as possible. They separated us. Hans went in one direction just before the Americans arrived, and I was fortunate enough to be brought to the hospital for medical care."

"Where did they take him?" I beg for an answer he may not have.

"I don't know, but they were forced to walk wherever it was they were going, and we had already been starving to the brink of death."

I cover my mouth and squeeze my eyes shut, assuming the worst because it seems impossible to think any differently. "Please, no," I cry. I'm not sure who I'm pleading with. God doesn't seem to listen, and it hurts more than anything because He is all we have left.

"I truly don't know his status, Fräulein, but when we went in different directions, he had more hope for me making it out alive than for himself. He asked that if I survived, if I could make sure you receive something he wants you to have."

I can't stand any longer and I care little about what this man thinks of me as I allow my knees to give in and fall to the floor, using the stack of suitcases as a wall to lean up against.

The man bends to his knees too and scoots next to me, struggling with each move. He pulls a roll of papers out of his coat pocket and hands them to me. His knuckles have dirt caked within each line and his fingernails are raw, shortened to the redness of his untouched flesh.

My hand trembles as I take the papers and unravel the stack.

"Hans said you would have matching papers to his and together, they would make up—"

"Our story," I say, completing his statement.

The man huffs a small laugh. "He was right, you two are just alike."

"Thank you for bringing this to me," I offer.

"I'm Danner Alesky," he says. "It is my honor."

"I owe you more gratitude than I'm able to offer. Allow me to make you some tea and prepare a meal for you. We have a toilet, and a shower, though it doesn't work well. You are welcome to stay as long as you need," I offer. Galina would say the same, I'm sure of it.

"I couldn't possibly impose, Fräulein."

"Matilda, please."

"Matilda."

"I insist," I tell him, holding the papers against my chest, touching something Hans has touched. His words are all I could ask for if I can't have him.

CHAPTER 39
GRACE
2018

A siren blows by the window, screaming at me to wake up. Except, I don't recall falling asleep. I blink a few times, finding myself in an unfamiliar bed with hazy surroundings. I'm trying to recall what happened, but I was so caught up in reading the pages that it's like I'm having trouble deciphering my life from Matilda's.

I sit up in the bed, feeling the coarse springs from within the mattress. Oh my gosh, I'm in the room above the bookshop. I'm in Galina and Matilda's former bedroom.

The only thing I did for most of yesterday was move from one location to another while trying to ingest these words. Determination to finish reading is all I can focus on.

I find the stack of papers draped over the side of the pillow, opened to the spot I must have left off. There are only a few pages left.

I can assume why. Much like Matilda, I would prefer to remain in denial, but there would be much more to write about, had Hans survived.

A knock on the bedroom door startles me into pulling the quilt up to my chest even though I'm dressed in the same clothes I fell asleep in last night.

"Grace, it's me, Archie. May I come in?"

Archie. I've been so rude compared to his hospitality.

"Of course," I say, my voice scratchy from sleeping so hard.

He opens the door, bright-eyed, a morning glow across his high cheekbones and a slight smile. He's holding two cups of tea and taking slow steps toward me. "How's it going? Are you still all right?"

I take the stack of bound papers and fan them down on top of my lap. "I'm not sure I want to finish reading—I don't know if I can bear the truth, yet I want to know every little detail about my grandmother from this moment in the story until her story ended."

"That's quite understandable," he says, handing me a cup of tea.

I close my eyes and press my lips to the lid of the cup, inhaling some of the steam before tasting the smooth floral flavor from the tea leaves. "Archie, I could never repay you for what you have done for me this week."

"It's only tea," he says, trying to hide a smirk behind his deep dimples.

"True," I reply. "I'm so glad I flew here for tea. It's unforgettable, truly."

"I would have to agree," he continues, staring at me like he's waiting for me to snicker. For the sake of being honest, I try to hold myself together so I can explain what I'm trying to say.

"Seriously though, I'm so grateful for the trouble you went through to allow me to digest this information in my time. To know the story and be sitting with it while I learn about each detail at an excruciatingly slow place must be hard on you too."

"If I were to just tell you a story, it would have less meaning, and when you repeat the story for the next person, more details will fade. The way you are learning of your roots is by a deep-seated connection through original words. I couldn't fathom stealing the opportunity from you. It would be unfair to Matilda and you."

I pull the quilt off my lap and place the papers down on the pillow. "I can't believe I slept in her bed."

"Her?" Archie questions.

I stare past Archie's shoulder toward the dusty bureau against the wall. I didn't notice it before, but there's a small gold-plated picture frame resting behind a vase of dried flowers.

"What is it?" Archie asks.

"The photo," I say, making my way over to pick it up. I brush off the dust with the hem of my sleeve. "Is this Matilda?" She has long golden hair draped over her shoulders and bright eyes accented by sweeping dark lashes. Her wide smile shows a sense of excitement, or maybe it's just happiness. She's in a long dress, holding a bouquet of wildflowers in a field that doesn't look to end until it meets the sky.

"It is," Archie says. "See how much alike you two are?"

I run my fingers through my hair, recalling how much Mom loved to brush her long waves that fell over her shoulders the same way. I can't help but smile despite the pain and millions of questions still spinning around in my head. "She didn't have freckles like me."

"No, she didn't have freckles, but sky-blue eyes, long sandy curls and tear-shaped eyes—you have so much of her within you."

"Who are the others in the photo?"

Archie carefully takes the frame from my hands and places it back down on the dresser. "How about I read you the last of the pages?"

"I don't want to find out that Hans—my grandfather—didn't make it. I want to create the end of the story on my own and tell myself they found each other and lived a long happy life."

"What is the definition of a long happy life, Grace?" Archie asks.

I take a minute to repeat his words silently in my head, trying to understand what he means. I'm staring at him with so much confusion, the sensation is straining against my eyes.

Archie places his hand down on my shoulder. "We all have wishes, but as I'm sure you are aware, many don't come true without a sacrifice. It's how life balances out, yes?"

"We're running low on tea leaves and cream. Do you know when we'll be able to obtain more?" Danner asks from behind the counter, tracking our inventory. Galina has always kept a close eye on the supplies since we've been selling more tea than the assortment of small gifts. It makes sense. Unnecessary objects are not in demand and there's no saying when they will be again. I'm thankful we have access to at least something to sell. Galina has been under the weather for the last few weeks, so Danner and I have been doing what we can to handle the shop so she can rest. She swears the budding flowers are what's causing her trouble and congestion, but she refuses to contact a doctor or nurse.

"I'm going to meet the distributor early tomorrow morning to see what they can give us. I won't know how much until then."

"I see," Danner says, releasing a heavy sigh. "I wish there was more I could do."

"You are doing more than I could ask for after what you have been through," I say, meeting him over at the counter with the feather duster.

"This is nothing in comparison to the work I was forced to do in the camp. This is a holiday." Danner always has a way of holding the light over a dark situation. Even when it comes to Hans, his positive spirit, full of hope, keeps me going.

The front door chimes, which seems to be happening more frequently now. The American soldiers are fond of our coffee and tea and make up most of the reason we are in such demand for more inventory.

The man who has walked in isn't an American soldier. At least, not by the looks of his appearance. If I had to guess by his overgrown haircut, parted deeply to the left, along with his tan and white pressed attire, he was a German soldier who is now desperately trying to cover up his past to blend in with the locals. It's hard to know who is innocent since not all of the Nazis are being detained. It's hard to tell who has been imprisoned versus who hasn't and for what crimes. It's unsettling to see some still walking around the town. We all wish they'd leave.

"Can I help you?" I ask, folding my hands in front of my waist. No matter who enters the shop, I do my best to be polite and courteous.

"Yes, I'm looking to speak with Frau Fritz—Galina Fritz."

"May I ask who is calling for her?" I reply, tilting my head to the side with wonder as I study this man.

"I'm afraid she won't know me, but I have a message to give her."

I can't help but look over at Danner and his ghostly complexion. I'm not sure what he's thinking, but it must be simpler than the dozens of possibilities going through my head. "I will be happy to give her the message. She's ill at the moment and isn't seeing visitors."

The man pulls a letter out of his back pocket and pinches it tightly between his fingers. "I would like to insist on speaking with her myself. I will be quick."

"What does the message pertain to?" I continue. I'm not sure if I'm protecting Galina or feeding my curiosity. This man seems unsteady and nervous, which isn't giving me a good feeling.

"Her son, Erich Fritz," the man says, keeping his explanation shorter than the rest.

I feel Danner staring at the side of my face as I hold my focus on the man. "I cannot allow you upstairs and she is unable to make it down here. I will see to it that she receives the message."

The man drops his hand by his side, the letter still held tightly within his grip. "Very well," he says, reaching the paper over to me with a shaky hand.

I hold the letter against my chest, waiting for the man to leave as quickly as he arrived.

"He was one of them, I know it," Danner says.

He places the crate of sweeteners he was straightening up and tends to my side.

"I have a bad feeling about this message," I say.

"Are you going to read it first?" he asks, staring at the folded paper.

"I can't do that to Galina, but if it's bad news, it will only make her situation worse."

Danner rushes to the front door and turns the lock. "Come on, we'll be with her regardless of what's written inside."

I head toward the back door, feeling as though I'm walking a mile within just a few short feet. Each step seems higher than a small hill, and the heat rises by several degrees the closer I get to the bedroom. Danner is just a foot behind me, silent enough that I can hear my heart beating through my chest. Maybe it's his pulse I'm listening to.

With a slight shove, the door creaks open, revealing the same scene I've witnessed since spring began. A handkerchief hangs from the cuff of her nightgown's sleeve, and her hair hangs in a mess of gray waves, frayed from resting against a pillow for so long. She's pale and the whites of her eyes are pink. She's staring straight ahead at the papered wall hung with a few gold-plated picture frames of her family in their younger years.

"Galina," I say, taking gentle steps toward her.

She pulls in a shallow breath and opens her mouth to speak, but the words don't form right away. It takes her a moment. "When a woman has lived as long as I have, life begins to repeat itself. Younger people often confuse the elderly for having a deeper, more profound knowledge of the world around them, or a deeper connection to God as we make our way closer to the end of life."

"What is all this nonsense about being old and coming closer to the end of life?" Danner asks. "We've had many discussions about this, Galina, you and I—you know better than to speak this way. You promised me when I promised you that we were looking at a fresh start despite the lives we have lived."

Galina has shared these vows with Danner in the hope of helping him heal from what he's been through, but I doubt she was thinking much of herself when making such a pact. "I know what I said, Danner, but I don't think you understand what I'm trying to say now."

"My apologies," Danner says, clasping his hands behind his back.

"What I was trying to say is... after being approached several times throughout my life with handwritten condolences or messages, I've picked up on the details surrounding those moments. A person will have a slow, heavy step when bringing a person unsettling news. They will often hide a note behind their back until they have found their courage."

I realize the note is behind my back and I knew how heavy my feet felt as I climbed the steps.

"The lumps we swallow just before speaking, and the prominent frown lines—I've seen it before. I have seen it too many times in my lifetime."

There's nothing I can say and it's more than clear by Danner's silence—a man who has trouble keeping quiet even when he's asleep.

I hand Galina the note, watching as my hand shakes the same way the man's hand did downstairs. "I'm not sure what's inside. I only know it is regarding—"

"Erich is dead," she says, matter-of-factly. Her head wobbles as if she can't keep it straight while unfolding the paper.

"How do you know?" I ask.

"Haven't you been listening?" Danner mutters, elbowing me gently in the side.

He's right. She knows. Of course, she knows. He's her son, and when a connection is severed in such a way, it's a pain we feel through every nerve of our body, indefinitely.

Galina inhales sharply through her nose and closes her eyes, holding the letter over her heart. "My dear boy... I knew, and yet there was nothing I could say to stop you." A shuttered gasp hitches in Galina's throat. "You see, he couldn't live with what he has done, or what he has witnessed. I received a phone call from him last week and I could hear it in his voice. He could no longer find his way out, and for the first time in his life, I couldn't help him with that."

I cross my hands over my throat, feeling like I'm being choked.

Danner clears his throat and rushes to the other side of Galina's bed, kneeling by her head and taking her hand. "Look at me," he demands. "He couldn't live with himself. No one deserves to lose their child, but if he made the choice he has, it's because love overcame the hatred he was forced to understand. He's free of that now."

My chest aches, listening to Danner's explanation.

"A mother should never have to be without her child," I whisper. "I'm so very sorry."

I clamp my hand over my mouth, internally shouting at myself to pull myself together.

"She and I—we share a special bond," Galina says.

"Matilda and you?" Danner questions.

"We always have."

"I'm not sure I understand what you mean," Danner says, a frenzy running rampant through his voice. "Galina..."

I continue watching the scene as if it's a picture reel about to run out of film. He's holding the back of her hand against his mouth. Then I see that her eyes are closed ever so softly, her white lashes dusting over her cheeks.

"Galina," I call out, running to her side. I take her other hand between mine, finding a chill I don't want to feel. "Galina, open your eyes."

"My other son died at just two weeks old," she mutters. "My reason for being is no longer here on earth."

"There are plenty of reasons for you to be here," I argue. "I love you, I need you. Can't you see? You have been like a mother to me. You can't leave, Galina. You can't."

"Darling, I must, but I know in my heart you will be loved and never alone. You still have a purpose, and if things become difficult, have a cup of tea or give one to someone who needs it more."

I fall to my knees, selfishly begging God to let her stay. I need her more. Can't He see? Heavy sobs bellow from deep within my chest and I feel as though I'm releasing every ounce of pain I have held onto for the last four years of my life. "I will take care of this shop forever. I will make sure it is always a place of comfort for those who are lost, just as you did for me," I cry out.

"I love you, sweet girl. Take care of her, my boy, please," Galina says before trying to take in the last breath that would not find her lungs in time.

Danner pulls himself up to his feet and makes his way around to the other side of the bed, helping me up. "Death is a part of life, Matilda. Trust me, I understand more than anyone should."

He folds his arm around me as he pulls the quilt by Galina's feet up to her neck. The blood is quickly draining from her already pale skin. She's so still there isn't a question of whether there is a pulse still beating, but I check anyway.

She's gone.

Danner was kind enough to call the coroner and do what I should have done. We're sitting behind the counter, our backs up against the wall, hiding from the sight that left over an hour ago. No one wants to see a body carted away in front of them, and Danner has seen it again and again.

"Just before she passed, when she and I were alone for a moment, Galina said you two were very much alike and that you shared a special bond. I'm not sure I understand the context she was referring to," Danner says.

"I didn't know she had already lost one child. She never said a word," I reply without thinking through my thoughts.

"And you have lost a child as well?" He twists around to face me, a wildly confused expression tugging at the creases of his eyes.

"I lost Hans's child, and he may never know. She was taken from me just a couple of weeks after she was born and sent away without any record of who she belonged to."

Danner shakes his head as if he needs to straighten out the statements falling freely from my lips. I have only ever spoken about Runa to Galina until now. "Hans was a father—is a father," he stumbles over his words, correcting himself. "He's not gone. He's not, Matilda, do you understand?"

I nod for his sake, for his morale. I don't know what to think anymore, but I'm living here in this town while thousands of people fell to their deaths. What right do I have to happiness when there is not enough of that to go around?

"I never had the chance to tell him, and I couldn't write it in one of our exchanged notes. It would have stolen whatever strength he had left."

"You did the right thing, painful as it must have been for you. I'm sure she's out there somewhere, you know."

I squeeze my fingers together, feeling the bones pinch in pain. "I'm sure she is alive, but I'm not sure I'll ever be lucky enough to find her."

"We mustn't lose hope. Not ever, and I'm sure that is what Galina told you. Now, I will tell you too."

I twist my head to look over at Danner, grateful for the unexpected friend Hans selflessly lent me when he is likely the one who needs a friend more than anyone right now.

That is, if he's still alive.

"Matilda," Danner calls out from the bookshelf he is dusting.

"Yes, what is it?" I reply, straightening out the front of the counter.

"Have you heard the joke about the ceiling?"

"The ceiling?" I question.

Danner chuckles and shakes his head. "Never mind, it's over your head."

I stare at him for a minute, watching his fit of laughter as I come to understand the joke. "Oh, very funny, ha ha. You are full of the very worst jokes, you know that?"

"Clearly, you haven't heard many jokes before," he replies, his voice pitched in a higher octave.

"You have a good point, I suppose." I know he's trying his best to distract me from all that has happened, but despite his efforts, it's hard to lift myself up each day and carry on toward what seems like a dark, narrow path with nothing but a black hole at the end.

"I told Hans that my jokes, no matter how stupid they were, would be what kept us alive. In fact, I believed this statement too, even until the end when we were sent in two directions," Danner says, placing the duster in his back pocket.

"Did he laugh?" I ask. Hans had the best laugh. It was pure and never questionable. If he found something funny, I would laugh because of how happy he was. The sound was contagious. His face would light up, each freckle would squish together, and his eyes would squint. It was like his face was brighter than the sun... until the storm clouds took permanent residency in our lives.

"Not always, yet some of my jokes were so bad that he couldn't help but laugh. Maybe it was for the sake of my sanity."

"He was a good man," I say.

"Is," he says, continuing to correct me.

I wish I had as much hope as Danner has, but it's hard after what I've seen and heard. The daily reports on the radio are filled with nothing but numbers of additional Jewish deaths in almost every nearby region. They are being unearthed daily in unthinkable places and finding piles of human remains that have turned to ash is a more common sight than dirt, or so it sounds. Of course, Danner has seen it for himself, but understanding how slim the chances are at finding a survivor now, it's difficult to hold onto. I also believe false hope will only prolong pain. I know so from spending so many years trying to find a connection to Runa.

"You're right," I agree. I shouldn't be the one to take someone's hope.

"Oh, Matilda, I meant to ask you a question. I know a fella who owns a collection of books by Jewish authors that were kept safe during the mass burnings of books. This shop is so eclectic and unique that I thought it might be nice to house some of them here. We have plenty of shelf space."

I drum my fingers on the countertop for a moment, thinking about the books that were saved, realizing I could never bear to sell one, but understanding that people should be able to sit and hold them too. "I think that would be lovely, but I'm not sure I'd have the heart to put a price tag on them."

"So, we'll put some more chairs over by the window and people can come in and read at their leisure while they enjoy their tea or coffee."

"I suppose that would be nice," I agree.

Danner has gone above and beyond to repay me and Galina for helping him after liberation. With the heartache of Galina passing away, it has been a blessing to have the company and help. I have taken care of the shop more and more over the years, but life is changing now. If there is one thing I can do to keep the love alive—the love which has grown from within these walls—it's offering every visitor what Galina gave me and now Danner. It's just a shop, but it's full of so much wonder and greatness. Galina would want this store to live on and do as it has always done.

"Did I say something that upset you?" Danner asks, tilting his head as he glances over in my direction.

"Not at all. I think I just need a breath of fresh air, that's all."

I walk around the counter, making my way through the maze of stacked suitcases and crates of trinkets, and push on the door while twisting the warm knob.

The breeze from outside is like a lasso pulling me out further than just one step, as if to show off the blue sky above. The clouds' tears are falling less and there is a brightness forcing its way back into our dark world.

I take a seat on the front step, straightening my dress over my knees. I lean back into the palms of my hands and allow the sun to warm my face. A tiny chirp among the quiet street grabs my attention and I look around, finding a little bird. There aren't many birds around here. It has been so infrequent that I recall the last time I saw one. The yellow bird was pecking at a stale breadcrumb in the middle of the empty road, right before the American troops arrived. As much as I hate to think of Mama and Papa, it's hard to forget Mama telling me that a little bird was a beacon of hope. I wonder if they made it somewhere safe and managed to stay out of trouble. Maybe, if they are doing well, they finally understand the consequences of their actions.

"What is there to be hopeful about?" I ask the bird.

The feathery little friend doesn't turn toward my voice, focusing on its hunt for worms in the crevices of the cobblestone.

Well, at least there is fresh air out here now. Though sometimes I feel like I still smell death, it seems fainter each day.

I stand and brush my dress off before reaching for the door.

"Pardon me, Fräulein," comes a voice. "I'm looking for a shop. Do you think you could point me in the right direction?"

I spin around, surprised to hear someone when the road was empty a moment ago.

A man has just turned the corner and is walking up the sidewalk toward me. He's wearing a cap that casts a shadow over his face. He's tall and thin, frail almost. I can't tell if he's old or young until he's standing in front of me.

"What shop are you—" If it weren't for the freckles, I might have continued my question. I place my hands on my chest because I think my heart has forgotten how to beat.

"Tilly," he says. "My sweet Tilly, is it you?"

My throat tightens and my cheeks fill with heat. My head aches, my chest throbs, and my stomach churns into knots. "Hans?" His name only forms on my breath.

"I'm so sorry it took me so long to get back to you."

How can he apologize? How can he say anything at all? He's here and alive, and I'm crying harder than I have ever cried in my entire life as I throw my arms around his neck. His long arms tangle around me, squeezing me with what I assume is every ounce of strength he must have in his body. He's taller than he was the last time we saw each other, and much thinner. He buries his face in my neck, breathing in my skin as if it is fresh air.

"I'm terrified I'm going to wake up at any moment," I whimper.

"No, sweetheart, no, no, I'm here now."

"Hans, I didn't think—"

"There were moments where I didn't think I would make it, but somehow, I was lucky enough to make it through. Most of us didn't. But, Tilly, why are you here in this God-awful place?"

"I couldn't leave you. If there was hope that you were here, I needed to stay," I say.

"You stayed for me?"

"I would stay anywhere for you and do anything for you, no matter what that means."

"You're an angel," he says, sweeping a fallen strand of hair away from my ear.

"Then, you're a saint and a warrior."

Hans pulls in a shuddered breath and drops his gaze for a short instant. When he looks back up, I notice something lacking within his eyes, like a piece of him is missing. I can only imagine how much of him is gone. "Tell me, Tilly, did my pal Danner find you?"

My chin quivers as I pull away from his hold. I press a weak smile onto my lips and take his hand. "He did. Come..." I open the door to the shop and Hans wraps his hand around the edge of the wooden slab, opening it a bit more so I will walk through first.

"What is it?" he asks.

Danner emerges from behind a display of postcards and spots Hans walking through the door. Danner's eyes grow large and round, his mouth falls open, and he runs to Hans, knocking him into the door. "You're alive," he screeches. "Dear God, you made it—you made it through the death march. Hans, you're alive. How?" Danner slaps the sides of Hans's face as if he needs physical proof he is standing in this shop.

A death march. Danner didn't refer to their different paths with those words before. Maybe it's best he hadn't.

"We were heading toward the Austrian border, but we were dropping like flies. Bodies became buried by snow and there was no end in sight until an American battalion spotted us and saved those of us who were still alive."

Danner closes his eyes and takes a couple of unsteady steps back, knocking into another display. He tries to right himself, but he shakes his head over and over. "I found Matilda for you," he says, still looking as if he's trying to shake some sense into his head.

"I see," Hans says, sniffling as his gaze drifts up toward the ceiling. Tears fill his eyes as he struggles to keep them from falling, but nothing else feels appropriate except crying out every morsel of emotion we are feeling.

"He brought me your words. I read them every night, it's kept you alive in my heart," I say. "I've taken care of Danner, and he's been helping with the shop."

"Thank you, Tilly. I don't know how to explain how lucky I am to have a family at this moment, but that's what we are. A family, right?" Hans asks.

The mention of the word forces Danner upright. He snaps out of his dizzying moment and clears his throat. "I'm going to get you something to eat and drink. I'll be right back." He has his hand pressed to his chest as he dashes toward the back of the shop.

"Did I say something wrong?" Hans asks.

"No, of course not. There's just so much for us to catch up on. I'm sure he wants us to have some space."

"Of course."

"Hans, have you heard any news about your parents and Danya? Do you know of their whereabouts? I have tried to look, but I couldn't find much at all, including your status."

Hans drops his head and folds his hands together. "I've been trying to collect information, but I've been unsuccessful so far. I fear the worst."

I'm staring into his eyes, knowing that after all this time has passed, I still haven't thought of a proper way to tell him about Runa. To add that to the unknown about his family makes me feel like a horrible person. How does one say such a thing, especially to a man who has gone to the brink of hell and come back by some miracle?

I take Hans's hands in mine, studying them for a moment, recognizing the freckles on his knuckles. It feels like a hundred years ago, when I used to stare at them because they make up the shape of a star. Although it seems just like yesterday that I would tell him he owned a galaxy right on the top of his hand, and if that wasn't a sign that he should be a writer, what was?

When the thought ends and I return to his question, knowing the answer he deserves, I exhale the words, "I was with child when the Nazis took you away. I had planned to tell you the very same day you were taken. It was my surprise for you, but I didn't know I was about to run out of time." My heart lurches into an unsteady rhythm, speeding then stalling.

Hans's shoulders fall, and his eyebrows knit together as he glances down at my stomach and back up to my face. "We have a child?"

I squeeze his hands a little tighter. "A girl. I named her Runa—her name means 'secret love'. She's our secret love."

"Where is she, Matilda? Where is our daughter? I want to see her?" Hans is breathless and I can't seem to get the words out of my mouth fast enough, but it's clear the damage is done. I'm going to end up hurting him.

I close my eyes, focusing on the fluttering of my lashes over my cheeks. "My papa took her away, turned her in as an orphan, and said she would have a better life in America. I have spent years searching for any trace of her, but my papa didn't leave her with a name, or even a birthday. It's been an awful thing to live with and you don't deserve this. I'm sorry, Hans. I am so sorry. That's why I left them. I haven't seen or spoken to Mama and Papa since that horrible day. I could never face them again. That's when I came here to find you—then to wait for you. I would have waited forever."

Hans pulls me in against his chest, cradling his hand around the back of my head. "Shh, shh. I'm here now. We will find her together. If it's the last thing I do, I will make our family whole again, Matilda. I promise you."

Without enough air filling my lungs, I gasp. "I live on the idea of hope, Hans, and I promise you I will never give up, but I don't know how it is possible to find her without a name or papers. No matter how many phone calls I've made or letters I've written, no one has any information on relocating a baby girl to America on the day Papa left her."

"He was trying to protect her," Hans says. I'm not sure if he's asking or trying to wrap his head around it.

"You know I would have kept her safe."

"Of course, I know you would have," he says. "Look at me, Tilly." Hans grips his hands around my arms and stares down into my eyes. "God wouldn't have allowed me to survive if it wasn't for a good reason. Together, we'll find our daughter."

"And your family, too," I add.

CHAPTER 42
GRACE

2018

Tears spill from my eyes. My grandparents found each other again.

"He made it?" I whimper into my hands. "Hans made it out of the camp alive?" I'm questioning it because it's hard to believe. The odds seemed impossible, and yet, there he was, back with Matilda with just as much love as they had when they saw each other last.

"He did. He and my grandfather, Danner, endured more than I could explain. It's nearly unbelievable, unfathomable; surreal."

I glance down at the pages in Archie's hands, noticing the brief paragraph on the page he's holding. With a gentle grip, I take the stack of papers and turn them around to see what the last sentences say, but they are the words Archie just read. "There's no more? That was the last page of their story? There must be more. It was only the beginning for them, right?"

Archie casts his gaze toward the bed behind me as if there's something he isn't saying. "Of course there's more," he replies. "You're here, aren't you?"

I hold the papers against my heart, trying to understand what he means by that. "Well, yes, but what does that have to do with my grandparents?"

"Will you come somewhere with me?" Archie asks, taking the papers from my hand.

I stare up into his eyes, trying to decipher every one of his thoughts. The man who was a stranger to me just days ago feels like someone I've known most of my life. "Of course," I answer without a second thought. "Thank you for the chance to learn about them in this way."

I wrap my arms around Archie's neck, squeezing him tightly as if he was an old friend I haven't seen in years. But maybe that isn't what I'm feeling. This is different. It's as though my heart has reached through my body to touch his. There's a connection, something deeper than I've known before. We're alike, but so different. He's lived with these stories forever, and I'm just inheriting them, but we come from a place where life isn't a gift—it's a miracle.

Archie reciprocates and wraps his arms around me, nuzzling his head into my shoulder. "Watching you go through the motions of learning about this story—the history—has been difficult. It's hard to explain to someone else how they should view life. Sometimes I feel like an outsider in my life, never truly understanding where I came from. I know nothing of pain and suffering, yet those are the fibers of what I'm made from. My grandmother was fortunate enough to stay safe, since she lived in a small village in Switzerland. They were unaffected by some luck, but the fear was something she understood well."

"I'm feeling a lot all at once," I say, unsure how to respond. "Where is it you'd like to take me?" I pull away from the embrace and sweep my finger beneath each eye to wipe away the tears.

"You'll see," Archie says.

"More secrets?"

"I wouldn't call it a secret," he says. "We can stop by your hotel if you'd like to freshen up first."

I immediately remember I fell asleep fully clothed in this room above the bookshop. "Oh, yes, please. Thank you," I say, staring up at him. My heart pounds as our gazes connect, and I can't seem to look away while wishing I could read the thoughts brewing like storms within his beautiful eyes.

We've taken a bus around the outskirts of Munich, passing through thickly lined forests that blend for miles into endless green pastures. With today being so clear and sunny, the horizon seems so far away. I'm not sure I've seen so much untouched land before. Then, as if someone placed a mountain range in the middle of the vast landscape, the foothills of the mountains draw my attention to its beauty. It's how I've always imagined this part of the world to look, with old wooden houses, all with red roofs, alongside farms filled with cattle.

The bus drops us in a small village. "Most visitors take this bus to continue on to the ski resorts up the mountain, but it works out nicely that there's a stop here too," Archie says as we step off the bus.

"Why is that?" I ask, wishing he would tell me why we're here.

"It's only a block away," Archie replies, giving me a glance as if he's deciphering my level of curiosity.

The backs of our hands brush together as we walk side by side and I'm not sure if it's purposeful or a mistake, but my heart skips a beat as we continue walking. Again, our hands meet in between our strides and this time Archie steals mine and encloses it between both of his.

"I'm so glad I've gotten to know you, Grace. I had wondered about Runa—your mother—for so long. I wish I could have met her, of course, but I'm grateful you exist and are here to fill in the pieces here too. After a lifetime of questions spinning around my world, these answers—you—it just feels like a dream—one I should pinch myself to wake up from. Or rather, one I'd prefer never to wake from."

I glance over at him, finding his kind eyes glimmering beneath the bright sun. "I've wondered about what life I could have had somewhere else had things been different. I didn't imagine having a friend to go through this with though."

Archie snickers. "What about your friend Carla? She sounds like quite a girl. In fact, is everything all right with her? I haven't heard your phone ding in almost a day."

I snort at this remark, having figured out Carla so quickly. "I asked her to give me a little time, and I promised to check in when possible. Also, I told her I was in excellent hands and not to worry."

"I appreciate the faith you have in me," Archie says. "She must wonder who I am."

"I explained, and she's hoping you will invite me to move into your castle and become the princess of a country she's never heard of before, too," I say with laughter.

"Gosh, I better figure out how to work my way into a royal family somehow," he replies with a coy wink.

"Yes, you better get busy with that," I continue. "But, no, I didn't mean I've gone through life without a friend—I just—I've never known myself, what makes me who I am, and it's been a lonely feeling, one that is very hard to explain to anyone. I think that's why I've been so independent and focused on a career. I'm a stranger to myself, or I have been, so it's hard to let others into a world I often feel blind in."

Archie lifts my hand and places a soft kiss on my knuckles. "I can only imagine how difficult that has been." The slight gesture sends chills up my arm and for the first time in my life I feel lost in the right place rather than found in an unknown destination.

We turn the corner, finding a beautiful set of buildings colored with a rosy red and white edifice. The structure looks new, with gardens in every corner and lining the brick pathways toward various entrances. "Where are we?"

Archie releases his hand from mine and presses his finger to his lips against a growing grin. "Just another minute, okay?"

For the life of me, I can't figure out where we are. There aren't many people outside and those who are have found a bench and are reading.

We walk through a wide set of open glass doors into a foyer with a hotel-like front desk and a lobby with lounging chairs and lots of greenery. It's beautiful inside.

"Herr Alesky, how are you today, young man?" a woman asks from the front desk.

"Well, thank you," he says. I find it interesting to see some locals speak German right away while others begin a conversation in English. I appreciate those that start in English.

"Right out back as usual," she says.

Archie dips his head in gratitude. "Danke," he replies.

I can't help but keep my gaze glued to his face, trying to figure out why we're here. The unknown is unsettling once again. My heart is pounding, and I'm not even sure why.

Archie leads us into a long room with a glass ceiling and filled with fresh flowers. His steps are slower than I'd prefer as we continue walking, but I try to calm myself by taking in deep breaths. When we are halfway through the open corridor, I spot two elderly gentlemen sitting side-by-side in front of the window overlooking a wide field of greenery. They're engrossed in a discussion, using several hand gestures to get their point across. They're enjoying each other's company, which is obvious by the laughter between the strings of German I can't decipher a word of. Archie seems to find whatever they're saying humorous according to the smile growing across his cheeks. He must know them. In fact, one of the men appears familiar to me, as well.

Archie stops short in his step and places his hand around my back, giving me a quick wink before returning to his view of the men. He clears his throat, making it known he's standing to the side of them. "Grandfather, Hans, I'm honored to introduce you to Grace. Vater, Hans, das ist Grace."

My lips part as I struggle to find air to breathe. My heart is pulsating so loudly, I can hear it beating like a drum in my head.

Two gentlemen sit in chairs. Both are in dress pants and button-down shirts, their hair combed. The one on the left has dark-framed glasses, but the one on the right, he has a face full of freckles. My freckles.

My face burns and my body trembles as Hans presses his hands against the chair's arms and brings himself to his feet. He's looking at me as if he's witnessing the world's most fascinating wonder.

"Meine Enkelin," Hans says. "Mein schönes Mädchen."

"He said: My granddaughter, my beautiful girl," Archie translates.

"Yes. I mean, Da," I respond with a hitch in my throat.

"Ich habe ein Leben lang gewartet," my grandfather says.

"I've waited a lifetime," Archie repeats.

"Me too," I say.

Hans reaches for me with unsteady hands, places his palms on my cheeks. His lips quiver and tears fall from his eyes. Sobs shudder through his chest as he pulls me in against him, holding me so tightly, filling me with a type of warmth I didn't know existed. I feel the love we've unknowingly shared. I feel it so much it hurts. He's shaking and I worry he might become weak, but neither of us move. Two strangers, but destined to meet through impossible barriers spanning two generations.

"This—is," he says, having trouble with English. He pulls away for a moment and takes my hand. "Danner, this is—my girl. Kannst du Matilda nicht in ihrem Gesicht sehen?"

"He said: Can't you see Matilda in her face?" Archie continues.

"I sure can. I see you, Hans, as well," Danner says, his English clearer than Hans's.

"You were the gentleman in the shop this week with the pocket watch, weren't you?" I ask Danner.

"Oy," he relents. "Yes, some refer to me as Al, short for Alesky—our last name. And the watch—the one your grandmother found for me—it was me. In any case, my grandson here threatened me to keep my mouth shut. If I didn't go along with his plan, I'd have to listen to them kvetching about ruining Hans's 'big plan.' The two of them have been in cahoots for months. Archie helped him with the DNA test process, and he was off running the moment those results came back. I think I raised a good man. What do you think, Grace?"

Danner's question makes my cheeks burn, knowing what I honestly feel about Archie and how amazing he has been. "I completely agree. Archie is wonderful. More than wonderful, really," I say, smiling shyly in Archie's direction. It appears I've made him blush a bit, too.

Hans walks across the small area and pulls a chair over for me, pats it, and nods with a smile.

I take a seat, sitting across from him, ready to stare into his eyes and wait for the rest of my questions to be answered. Then I pull the stack of papers out of my bag and place them down on my lap. "I read Matilda's story, but it all ended so abruptly. Is there more?"

"Sie will das Ende der Geschichte. The rest of the story," Archie tells Hans, pulling a chair up for himself.

"Ah, da." Hans looks up at Archie for a long minute before twisting around in his seat and pulling something out of his sweater's sleeve that is draped over the back of his chair.

"Archie, read?" Hans asks, handing him the papers.

Archie hesitates before leaning over to take the papers.

"I want to know all about your life with Matilda," I say, hoping Archie will translate if necessary.

"Sie will mehr über Matilda wissen," Archie says.

The three of them take turns looking at one another and I'm not sure why, but when that moment ends, three sets of eyes are on me, smiling with kindness. "What is it?" I ask.

"Oh, no—nothing. I'll be happy to translate these pages for you," Archie says, stumbling on his words.

CHAPTER 43
MATILDA
AUGUST 1947

It has been two years since Hans found his way back to me, and a year since we learned the heartbreaking news that his parents and sister did not survive. The three of them were taken to Auschwitz, the death camp. From what we know, they lost their lives by means of a gas chamber.

Hans was numb when we read their names on a never-ending list. He stared at a wall for days in silence. I was worried he was imagining what they might have gone through, and I believe I was right because after the first few days, he was inconsolable. It was hard to watch while knowing there was nothing I could do to help.

After some time had passed, all we could do was agree that we would never waste a day we have left on this earth. We promised to do that on their behalf as well as our own. We have a daughter to find, wounds to heal, and a shop that was left to me by Galina. Our path is clear yet foggy, but navigating through the unknown is nothing new to us.

We married each other just after he found me—something small, something just between us and a few close friends, a commitment never written on paper because it was scripted into the stars.

And our forever will live on well after we are gone because we are a story of everlasting love, patience, strength, and bravery.

I give you my all, every part of me, my heart, and soul.

Together as one, we shall conquer the world.

Our words, vows, and promises are something I will never forget.

No one needs to tell us we belong together when we know. I took his last name, and this is our life now.

Sometimes I think about the number of days I sat in the shop, helpless, wanting to help in some way, knowing there was nothing I could do. I knew more than I should have known because of Erich, which was a blessing and a curse. I was terrified, but that feeling was not something I could accept, not while people were suffering and dying in the most unimaginable ways.

Life isn't fair—it's such a simple statement to make, but I will never know why it was him over me, or Runa rather than another child, or why there is even good versus evil in this world.

I thought the feeling of helplessness would fade after some time, but it's like a poisoned weed sitting at the bottom of my stomach, growing out of control, taking over everything inside of me. Maybe I should have done more, tried harder, been louder. I don't know if it would have made a difference, but could it have? No one knows. No one will ever know.

"What's going on in that head of yours, Tilly?" Hans asks as we walk hand in hand between the barracks of the Dachau concentration camp. Some of the buildings are temporary holding areas for imprisoned members of Hitler's commandants who are waiting on hearings. Other block units remain empty and untouched since the camp was liberated. There is nothing much to see aside from barren cement blocks, gravel, barbed wire, and watch towers, but at a closer look, it's hard to ignore the bloodstains on certain walls, the random single shoes buried beneath a pile of rubble, buttons that had fallen from pajama coats, and on occasion a small personal memento someone must have lost along the way. It feels like a ghost town, something I assume it will always be. The silence is deafening and the crackle of rocks beneath our shoes echoes between the buildings. The smell is the worst of everything. It never fades.

People think we're absurd for coming here a few mornings a week, but Hans finds peace in knowing he was able to conquer the horrors that lived within these gates. It was hard for him at first and I begged him to stop. He would break down. He would stare at a wall, one that looked so insignificant, but no one could possibly know what impact the stone had on him or anyone who lived here for those years.

"Execution—there was one there," he told me during one of the first few visits.

"Tilly?" Hans calls again, waving his hand in front of my face.

"Sorry," I say. "I was thinking we haven't looked in that building over there yet." It's just another random barrack cell, a location where too many people slept on wooden shelves, cramped so tightly there was hardly enough air to breathe.

Hans leads the way into the barrack block and stops just inside the entrance. "Wow! There's a lot in here."

I open my small tote and begin searching for items that prisoners were separated from or forced to leave behind. I have overfilled the closet in the shop with treasures we have located around the camp. They may look insignificant, but to me, they are someone's precious belongings. They were only allowed to keep a few personal items, which means they are important in some way, a way I may never know or understand.

While I fill my days writing letters to family services departments in the United States in search of Runa, I also try to find who the owners of these belongings are. I know it may be impossible to reconnect someone with a lost item, but since I refuse to give up on Runa, these missing treasures deserve a chance too. Some have initials engraved. Others have photographs. I believe someday I will have a way to find their missing counterpart, even if it's a family member of the prisoner.

"When we get to America, do you think we'll have an easier time finding her?" I ask Hans. It's one of those questions I don't expect him to have an answer to, but one I still ask almost daily.

"Of course," he says. "We will find our daughter. It isn't an option, Matilda. We will."

A year ago, Hans was determined to travel back to Augsburg, our former home, in search of Mama and Papa. I refused to join him inside as I have no desire to ever see either of them again, but he wanted to ask the questions I should have been able to force out of Papa the morning after he took Runa.

There was another family living in our home. They said the flat had been abandoned and the landlord said the residents picked up and left one day, then never returned. I'm okay with that.

There was a new family living in Hans's old flat too. It was a relief to hear that rather than those insidious monsters who lived below us for far too long. In the end, though, we still had no more answers.

I blame myself a lot, knowing that had I been more careful when

Hans and I were young, we could still be here, ready to start a family, rather than preparing to spend a lifetime searching for the little girl who made us one. The thought of having more children is not something I can come to terms with. We both agree on this. Runa is our child, forever and always, and with or without her, she is our only one.

"Matilda, why do you have such a sullen look in your eyes? I can feel your pain," Hans asks, taking my hand and pulling me out of the barrack block.

"Oh, it's nothing," I tell him.

"I don't believe you," he says.

I place my hand on his cheek and stare into his eyes. "I see her when I look at you. I bet you she has freckles like yours." I trace my fingertip from the tip of his nose to the lobe of his ear, touching each defined spot. "Maybe that's how we'll find her."

"Many people have freckles, Matilda," Hans says, chuckling quietly.

"Not like yours. With the galaxy on your face and your hands, you are one of a kind, and maybe she is just like you."

He places his hands on my shoulders and leans down to kiss me. "My sweet Tilly, I think we've seen enough today. Danner is expecting another large order of books and we need to help him take inventory. Come on, let's go home."

Home. In the town of destruction where so many are buried within the earth, and yet, we remain, holding a figurative flag of triumph.

"You there, what are you two doing on these grounds? This area is forbidden and condemned. Surely you saw the signs out front," a man calls out. He's dressed in similar colors to what the soldiers wore during the war, but his shirt is not pressed or tucked into his slacks. He looks as if he just woke up on a bench. I can't imagine what he must be doing here, just as he's wondering about us. Indeed, I might ask him the very same question since I know no one lives or works on this property. He's right. It is forbidden and condemned, which means no one should be here, including him.

"We're leaving," Hans says.

"Hold on now," the man replies, walking in closer toward us. He's dressed in street attire, dark pants and white T-shirt. He doesn't look to be anyone of importance. "I remember you."

I'm not sure who he is talking to, Hans or me, but I surely don't recognize this man. He looks like he has been drinking all night and into the morning. His hair is greasy, and he doesn't look to have shaved in months. He can hardly walk in a straight line.

"I think you must be mistaken," Hans says, taking my hand and pulling me behind him.

"No, no, you are that Jew—I never forget a face, even with all the ones I watched die. You were the Jew my friend Erich helped," the man huffs, snickering. The soft laughter turns into a rolling hysteria rooting from the bottom of his gut. He seems quite crazy.

"I'm not sure what you are speaking about," Hans continues.

"Do you know what the others did to Erich after they found out he helped you?"

Hans shakes his head. "We need to be going now. Have a good day." Hans tugs my elbow, moving me behind him as he intends to step forward. He's acting as if he needs to protect me. I shouldn't need to be protected, not after all he has gone through.

"Erich shot himself in the head, right in front of me," the man continues. "I watched my friend murder himself for no good reason. You are the no-good-reason."

I assume this man was a Nazi, but why he isn't in prison or somewhere far away from this town is beyond me. They didn't stay. They were imprisoned and put on trial. Only some were released without proof of murder. None of them should have been released as they were all accomplices in some way. Hans wasn't murdered, but he will forever live with the damage done by these monsters.

"Good day, Herr," Hans says, continuing to push right so we can create more distance from the man.

It's clear he doesn't intend to let us by yet as he follows our every move. He pulls a cigarette out of his pocket and places it between his dry, chapped lips and lights the end. I debate if the few seconds it takes him to spark a flame is long enough to run, but Hans seems to know better than that and we stay still, cold with fear.

"It's always been one life for another, right, Jew?"

"The war is over now. Let's be on our way, shall we? You move on and I'll move on, yes?"

The man scoffs and shakes his head. "You are in the wrong place at the wrong time, again, Jew."

I can hear Hans swallow a lump in his throat, and I realize I can't figure out how to swallow against the dryness in mine.

The man reaches around behind his back, retrieving a pistol. He doesn't take a moment to think about his actions, and neither do I.

He lifts the weapon, pointing it directly at Hans and I shove him out of the way and step into his place, taking the bullet that was intended for him.

An ice-cold numbness spikes through my body as I fall to the dirt-covered ground, forced to stare at the man who is still holding the pistol. He puts a bullet through his head next, ending his life because it's one life for another, not one life over another.

"Matilda," Hans shouts, falling to his knees, shaking me. I don't feel my body moving. I can only hear him, see him, smell his sweet scent. "Why did you do that? I'm not worthy of your life, Matilda. I'm not." I cannot speak to tell him otherwise, but he knows that's not true. "What about our family? I'm going to fix our family, Matilda. I will. Please, don't leave me. Please. I love you so much. I love you, Tilly. My sweet Tilly."

I wish I could tell him I love him too, but in my heart, I'm certain he knows. My purpose in life was to make sure he knew how much he is loved after surviving the cruelness of this world, and though she isn't with us now, I have faith he will find Runa in some way and have a piece of me like I had a piece of him. Life is about the connections we make living and the ones we leave behind after we're gone.

Hans's face is turning purple as every ounce of pain he carries around weighs him down even more. The veins on the sides of his temples inflame as they pulsate. Sweat forms between the strands of his dark comb-slicked hair that have fallen over his forehead. His eyes bulge as tears stream down his cheeks. All he can do is stare at me in sorrow. He's in misery, again. It's my fault.

Hans grits his teeth and screams wildly from the bottom of his gut, releasing the most horrific sound. "Help me! Please, someone help me! My wife, she's been shot. Help me, please! Someone help! I can't do this without her, I can't. Matilda, please, I need you. Our story isn't over. Can you hear me? It's not over yet."

CHAPTER 44
GRACE
2018

"Why did you stop reading?" I'm lunging for the papers in Archie's hands because I can't understand why he would stop reading. There's no way this is the end. It's obvious. Matilda, my grandmother, left me her shop, but how? It's Runa's Shop of Wonders. "Archie, I need to know what happened. Please."

Archie releases the papers from his hand without a struggle. I take them onto my lap and flip to the last page. For a minute, I forgot why he was reading it to me in front of his grandfather and my grandfather —it's in German, and even after almost a week, I still know barely a handful of words.

"Hilf mir! Bitte, jemand hilft mir! Meine Frau, sie wurde erschossen. Hilf mir bitte! Jemand hilft mir. Ich kann das nicht ohne sie tun. Ich kann nicht. Matilda, bitte. Ich brauche dich. Unsere Geschichte ist nicht zu Ende. Können Sie mich hören? Es ist noch nicht vorbei."

The amount of explanation marks in the text makes it clear he read the words to where the story ends.

"Archie, what happened? Why did the story end?" I ask again.

"Darling," Danner says.

"Was ist los mit dir?" Hans asks, sounding concerned.

I'm sure he knows how the papers end. Surely, he could understand why I'm reacting the way I am. After all, they went through to be together, and then, that's it. They never got a life together, only the pain of losing each other and a missing child. It's nothing less than hell.

"Hans wants to know what's wrong, oy," Danner translates. "Hans, sie will mehr über Matilda und das Buch wissen."

I glance at Hans—my grandfather—and his gray bushy eyebrows arch with question and confusion. His mouth is ajar, likely wishing he could understand what I'm asking.

"Archie, please, I can't take this confusion. What happened? Was that it? Did she die all those years ago? I don't understand. I was in her bedroom, and she left the shop for me, right?"

"Grace," Archie says, standing from his seat to place his hands on my shoulders. "Take a breath."

"I can't," I croak. "I can't, not after all of this—a week of learning about my family's history just to find out there was no happy ending, even without my mom."

"I understand why you are thinking this way. It's understandable," he says.

"No, you can't make this right with beautiful words. Nothing can make this right. Why didn't he finish the story? I need him to answer."

"Hans, warum ist die Geschichte hier zu Ende?" Archie translates to Hans.

Hans closes his eyes for a moment, then sits up a little straighter within his chair. He seems uncomfortable as he wraps his hands around each cherrywood armrest, squeezing until his knuckles turn white. "I—could—no—end the book without Runa—finding her— your mother."

His broken English is clear enough to decipher, and I'm heartbroken all over again. I'm not what he was hoping for, of course. He spent his entire life searching for Mom and now he ends up with me instead. "I'm so sorry. She passed away a few years ago from cancer."

"Runa starb an Krebs," Archie tells Hans.

"We didn't know what she passed away from, only that she had passed away, but Hans didn't hesitate to send you everything as soon as he found out he had a granddaughter. He was beyond elated, Grace. Of course, he was heartbroken about your mother, but he wanted to reconnect your family so badly and he's able to now," Archie explains.

"Cancer?" Hans asks.

I nod my head, gesturing in agreement with his question.

"My Matilda—she—die—from cancer—uh, drei—" Hans says, holding up three fingers, "years back," Hans says.

"What?" I cry out.

Archie and Danner are both staring at Hans along with me, but Hans is biting the inside of his cheek, shuffling his jaw from side to side as if he's trying to hold back from saying something.

"I miss—her—so very much," Hans says. "I pray—one chance more, and I promised—" he points up to the ceiling, "to God— I not ask more if he let her live—ah—through—"

"The gunshot wound," Archie completes his statement.

"Matilda survived the gunshot wound? Then why did these words stop? Why did the story end? What was the rest of her life like?" I wrap my hands around my stomach, feeling pain for something that happened so long ago, yet it feels like I'm living through it at this very moment. I need relief. I want the hollow, guttural sensation writhing through me to stop.

Archie releases his hands from my shoulders, and they seem to fall by his sides. "I can understand why he couldn't finish the story."

"I thought Matilda wrote all of this?" I ask.

Danner smirks. "Oh, no, Hans wrote Matilda's story from the written pages she gave him after the war was over. He wanted to see life through her eyes, and her eyes only. His previous years were ones he wanted to replace with your grandmother's memories."

"We lived—a wonderful life. My Tilly, she not—give—hope—up, nor ever did she stop—ah— moving," Hans stumbles over his broken English, trying to give me a bit of insight.

"She couldn't stop moving or talking," Danner adds. "That woman —she was full of life. Everyone wanted to be around her. She made people smile. It was her best quality."

"Da," Hans chokes out a soft laugh. "Nothing could get in her way until she became ill." He pinches the bridge of his nose and his chest shudders.

"You know, my mother died three years ago this summer, too. Matilda and she died around the same time," I state, realizing the odd reality. "They are together now."

Hans seems to understand what I'm saying as he reaches for my hands, pulling me back over to the chair I was sitting in when Archie read the last of the words written. "We—now have each other, yes?"

Hot tears pierce the corners of my eyes and my jaw shivers, knowing his question is the same thought going through my head. "Yes, yes, we have each other now."

Hans reaches for the papers in my hand and takes them back. "Then—now, I finish the story. It ends with you. You are a part of the greatest secret of all time."

"Ich brauche einen Stift," Hans tells Danner.

"Da, da," Danner replies, springing from his seat as if in search of someone or something.

"Your grandfather needs a pen," Archie says, grinning against the words.

Danner returns promptly with a pen and Hans reaches for it and doesn't wait more than a second before he places the papers down on the side table next to him and begins writing as if the words are bleeding out of his soul.

Archie whispers softly, likely trying to avoid distracting Hans from what he's writing. "They spent their lives in the bookshop, connecting treasures to families, collecting books of Jewish writers whose words had been thrown into flames. They devoted their lives to helping others in the hope of someday also finding your mother."

"They spent their lives in the shop?" I repeat his words, needing the reaffirmation.

"Yes, they did. Matilda was there when I was born and there for me when my mother passed. We are like family."

"Not the kind of family you are related to," Danner adds. "Because you two are not related, in case I'm not clear."

"Thanks, Grandfather," Archie responds, clearing his throat. I try to keep my focus on what he is saying rather than the humor running through Danner's statement. "Anyway, it wasn't until last year that we heard about the opportunity to send a sample of DNA in the hope of receiving a family match in return. If your mother hadn't taken the DNA test, we would still be in search of her, and we wouldn't have found you."

I have so many questions and I want to blurt them all out in a long string of words until I run out of breath, but Hans seems to be in another world as he writes faster than I've ever seen a person write.

"They always intended to pass the family business down. We all just hoped it would stay within the bloodline," Archie says.

I'm staring at my grandfather, smiling as he scribbles his pen against the paper. My phone is vibrating in my back pocket, and I'm very aware that I'm in Germany—far away from Boston. I'm not sure how I could leave Dachau or go back to America.

The second my phone stops buzzing, it starts again. I pull it out of my back pocket and find Carla's text messages popping up at an alarming rate.

Carla: I have been very patient, but please, just tell me you are alive and safe.

With a smile I can't hold back, I type a response against the keypad.

Me: I'm perfect, and I'm with my grandfather. He has my freckles, or I have his.

Carla: Oh my God, Grace. I'm crying my heart out for you right now. Reading this—it's everything. I can't wait to hear the entire story. When are you coming home?

"Is Carla checking on you again?" Archie asks.

"She sure is," I tell him. "And she wants to know when I'll be coming home."

Hans stops writing. Danner repositions himself in his seat, and Archie leans back down to reclaim his chair.

"There is no rush to decide on the shop," Archie says. "Hans has made that clear throughout this process." While I believe the words to be truthful, all three men look as if they are holding their breath, waiting for me to say something that will offer them relief.

"There isn't a decision to make," I say.

Hans releases the air he was holding onto, then presses his lips together as if trying to hold back his emotions. With his hand on his chest, I can clearly read the gratitude sparkling through his eyes. Archie tries to fight off a smile teasing the left corner of his lips. He folds his hands behind his back and bows his head.

After a long minute of silence, Archie lifts his gaze and straightens his shoulders. "Grace, let's take a moment and let Hans write. Follow me out to the garden. It's beautiful out back," he says, standing from his seat while reaching out to me.

We walk in silence out through the back sliding doors, finding tall green hedges with beds of flowers lining a large grassy area with white marble benches. "I'm very overwhelmed," I say.

"I can see that and understand why, but, Grace, you shouldn't feel pressured to decide today. A life takes a lifetime to put together, and this is your life, not Matilda's or Hans's."

"How could I walk away?" I ask.

"From a place you have called home?" Archie replies.

I shake my head and fold my arms across my chest. "No, from the first place I feel like I have ever belonged."

"It's only a place," he says.

"What would you do?" I ask, looking up at his unfocused gaze.

"I'm not sure, Grace. I wouldn't wish a decision like this on anyone. There is a lot to consider, but I can tell you one thing: no matter what decision you make, you will never lose Hans, my grandfather, or me. We are your—"

"You're not family, Archie. Remember what your grandfather said?"

He tries to hide his smile by running his hand down the side of his face. "Right. Well, in that case, whether you stay or go back home, I'm not sorry that I met you." He takes my hands and leans forward to kiss my cheek. The spicy scent of his aftershave makes me want to take in a deeper breath than my lungs will allow. The desire to be held tightly within his arms is intense, and I wish life could be like a fairy tale sometimes, but I know better.

He's still looking at me as he pulls away and I wonder if he can feel my pulse in my wrist because it's racing so hard, I'm out of breath. Archie cups his hands on my cheeks and leans back in to steal a kiss that causes an eruption of flutters to engulf every part of my being. I'm not sure I'm breathing and even less sure if I will ever feel the need to take another breath.

"I changed my mind about what I would do," he says, pulling back. "I'd at least stay a little longer to think things through." He smiles and kisses me once more, something short and sweet, leaving me wanting to relive this moment again and again.

"I was thinking the same. I definitely need more time. But time will only make it harder to walk away."

I've seen things I wouldn't wish on the worst Nazi I crossed paths with. Despite all the suffering, loss, displacement, and physical ailments, nothing compares to watching the love of my life writhe in pain. Guilt has run through me, knowing I pleaded with God to keep her alive, because now I wonder if it's my fault she is living in pain, here in this hospital.

Matilda barely survived the gunshot wound, but by some miracle, the doctors were able to remove the bullet that somehow missed all her major organs. The blood loss was the biggest concern, but they say she is out of the woods now and that she will recover, albeit each minute feels like years as I hold her hand in mine, an image, a thought, and a wish I had for so long while I was caged between the iron walls of Dachau.

We trade ignorance for bliss, and immortality for brutality, but there isn't a good reason. It's best to assume there is a lesson to be learned, but all I have learned over the past six years is how capable humans are of hating one another. We are all the same inside, and yet we are at war with each other for the beliefs we own, the color of our skin, and the type of blood that runs through us. I want to hope that to learn of such hate would cause more love, but only time will tell. I know I would sacrifice myself again to teach a lesson for future generations.

"You know, you won't be able to write anything for me to read tonight if you hold my hand all day," Matilda says, her voice choky with a hoarse rasp.

"Oh, you hush. How can you still be so bossy in this condition? I told you it's time to let me take care of you for a change, yes?"

"I'm tired of lying in this hospital bed," she groans. "I want fresh air."

Fresh air; another luxury. I watched people walk into a building where Nazis would deny them oxygen and instead desecrate them with gas.

"The doctor said you should be able to go home in a few days," I say to Matilda. "We're almost there."

A sigh of exasperation unravels from her lungs, but she winces against the pain. "Hans, if I had a book to read, this hospital stay would go by much faster," she says.

I tilt my head to the side, looking at this beautiful woman with her eyebrow raised, who can say so much with just a few words. I haven't told her I can't find it in me to write. The act of scribbling words on paper is an escape and there isn't a part of me that wants to escape any one moment when I'm with her.

"What we have already written, it's our story, and there is nothing more to add until it's over. That won't be for a very long time."

"Your words kept me alive," she says.

"And you kept me alive, even in those few notes I received, it was enough, and it came when the worst was in front of us." The chance of survival each day seemed to be against our odds. Whether dying of starvation, typhus, or being plucked out of a crowd to deport, nothing was in our favor.

I still smell the carnage mixed with sweat and odors of prolonged filth. I remember the feeling of trying to smile at a rare joke but realizing I had no strength to move the muscles in my cheeks. I would look around at the others and remember my early school years when we would learn about human bones by studying a skeleton hoisted onto a metal pole. We would play with the wobbly bones when the teacher wasn't looking. I regret doing that. If I had known I would someday see those bones among the bodies walking around beside me —gangly and lacking muscle like that skeleton in the classroom—I would have shown the classroom display more respect than we were given in the camp. That skeleton still had teeth. Many of those in my block lost theirs from malnutrition and rot. I was lucky to keep mine.

I was also one of the youngest men besides Danner—maybe age was in my favor.

"Hans," Matilda says, squeezing my hand, "where is your mind?"

"On you, of course," I lie shamefully.

"No, it's not. There's a window within your pupils and I can see right through you," she replies with a weak grin.

I brush a few strands of hair away from her face and run my hand down the side of her cheek. "I'm right here. There is nothing to see through."

"You're an awful liar, Hans," she says.

"Fine. I'm still upset with you for pushing me out of the way of the bullet. You're in this bed because of me. Death was not chasing you, Matilda." It has come for almost everyone I love already. Adding me to the list of casualties to join Mama, Papa, and Danya would have been easier.

A fury runs through Matilda's eyes as she tries to sit up a little more in her bed, wincing against the pain. "That's not fair, Hans. You have lost everything, including your parents and Danya. We both know they would want you to live a life they couldn't, and I will not allow that to be taken from you too."

The lists of names were blurry at first because I didn't want to discover the worst. The Nazis kept such intricate and precise records of who perished, from what and where, that there was no question of who survived and who didn't. The feeling of being grateful for surviving in the camp was stolen from me the moment I read their names among the other deaths. Loss is something we had all come to terms with, and if there was anything to be found, it would be one measure of a miracle. I knew this, but I prayed very hard for that miracle. Maybe we're only allowed one per lifetime.

"I could have lost you, Matilda. Then what? Then I would have truly lost everyone and my purpose in life—what then?"

Matilda presses her lips together and looks to struggle while swallowing a lump in her throat. "Your purpose is to reconnect our family so our nonsensical accomplishments will set a new tone in this horrible world. Runa and whatever she makes of her life results from us. Whether we live or die right here and now, we have done something spectacular, and that was my thinking when I thought it was the end of my story. It was a moment of awakening."

I hate that she always makes perfect sense. Still, she should not be lying in this bed for me. "I guess we have all had those moments. They define us," I agree.

"Precisely."

"Matilda, there's something I've been thinking about these last couple of days."

"Just something? I can only imagine what you haven't thought of over the last couple of days," she replies with a teasing smirk.

"Hear me out. I want to change the name of the shop. Since we are bringing in these wonderful books that are taking up most of the space, it should be known to anyone passing by."

Matilda's lips twist to the left, as if she isn't sure about my idea. I know she was very attached to Galina, and I wouldn't want to interfere with her respect toward the shop, but we are keeping the items alive—the treasures and unique items—and it should be a landmark for those who are lost and looking for a place to belong. "I don't know, Hans," she says.

I paint my hands across the air in front of her. "Runa's Wunderbare Bücher—Runa's Wondrous Books. Her name means secret, and the books we have are all full of wonderful words. It can be her shop."

A tear skates down the side of Matilda's cheek, a rare sight from the woman whom I claim to be the strongest of them all. "Yes, yes, yes. I love the idea and Galina would say so too. I wasn't sure if you wanted to stay here forever, in Dachau," she says, glancing down at her fingers toying with the white linen sheet covering her body.

Her statement has a lot of truth and the thought has gone through my mind many times over the last two years.

I stand up from the chair and pace over to the window, staring out into the intense sunlight. "If no one stays to make this town good again, it will forever be a prison and I don't want that."

"People will wonder why we stayed," Matilda says from behind me.

"So, we tell them the truth: In honor of those who didn't make it, we will stay and guard their graves and give new life to the grounds they are a part of. They can be the foundation to a world without hate, and the root to a beautiful alternative way of life. We will memorialize their lives as a fresh start rather than a loss in vain of what once was."

EPILOGUE

It was too often that I wondered why my life wasn't moving one direction over another. When we are born in a country, most of us think that's where we should stay forever, but like many who found their way to America with hope of a better life, I was seeking the same. Yet I have found sparks of what I've always wanted here in Germany. I thought I had my life planned out, but I'm glad I was wrong. Plus, I couldn't have been happier to quit my job in Boston. It turns out that Paul was as pretentious as I assumed, and he never suspected I would walk away from his company. After gracefully telling him I wouldn't be returning, there was a long pause and a soft gasp. He pleaded with me to come back, offered me an office with a view, a raise, and a promotion—everything he knew I had wanted so much.

I only wanted all of that before I found out what I truly desire.

It was nice to hear him grovel and apologize, and I was satisfied to walk away on that note.

To do as Mom would have done, I made the decision to clear the air between Dad and myself when explaining my reasons for leaving the country. He was more upset than I thought he might be, but then insisted on visiting. To my surprise, he has come out twice in the last year, and though I don't want to get my hopes up of an everlasting change in our relationship, his attempt to right the wrongs of our past means the world to me.

Then there's Carla, the one person I had trouble leaving behind, but the girl seems to have endless air miles saved up, and she comes out here at every chance, searching for her great love story. She said she plans to move out here as soon as she meets her prince.

Even though it's only been a year since I arrived, I can't remember a day when Archie hasn't been by my side. His patience and willingness to help me create a life here is more than anyone has ever done for me. Though it seems our feelings for each other came naturally, and almost all at once, we have an unbreakable bond made of friendship and pasts that have made us who we are. We sometimes feel like we are two of a kind, meant to find each other in a world full of people who don't see life the way we do. He's my Hans and I think I'm his Matilda.

"Are you sure you're ready for this?" Archie asks, holding his hand against the small of my back.

"I'm more than ready," I say, squeezing the book in my hand.

I knock on the door and pull in a deep breath, then unintentionally hold it until the door opens.

"Hallo, kann ich Ihnen helfen?" A woman answers the door and I hear children playing in another room. She looks a bit disheveled, but also nervous at the sight of two strangers. I've learned a good deal of German, but I'm not quite fluent yet and I've found that most others around my age speak better English than I do German thankfully.

"Hi, I'm Grace Laurent. This might sound odd, but my grandmother, Matilda Ellman, used to live in this exact flat."

The woman looks taken aback, as if she knows who I'm talking about, which seems impossible given all the time that has since passed.

"You are Matilda's granddaughter?" the woman repeats my words as if she's worried.

"Yes, did you know Matilda?"

"Why, of course. She would stop by occasionally. My parents knew her well and when they left the flat to me, Matilda continued to drop in. There was something about the attic that she enjoyed visiting, but I'm not sure what it could be—she never really said. It's just a spare room here."

"And the crawl space," I add. "It meant a great deal to her."

"The crawl space?" the woman asks, clearly confused.

I glance at Archie, and by the look of his arched brows, he appears as surprised as I feel. "This might sound odd, but my mother was born in the attic's crawlspace. In fact, I wouldn't be here if it weren't for that little area of this flat."

The woman closes her eyes for a moment and places her hand on her chest. "I've lived here for so long and yet I don't have a clue what you are referring to. Would you like to come in and see for yourself?"

Archie takes my hand and squeezes gently.

"I would be very grateful. This is Archie Alesky, my boyfriend—our families are very close."

"Alesky?" the woman questions as if she's searching through a list of names in her head. "Are you related to Danner Alesky?"

"Oh yes, that's my grandfather," Archie says.

"Of course, he, your mother, Matilda, and Hans used to come by together occasionally after my parents became friendly with them. I can't believe I remember all of this since I was so young. This is unreal."

"We understand, more than I can explain," I say. I cannot believe I'm standing at the entrance to this flat. By the looks of the inside, the worn finish of the dark wooden floors, the dull floral wallpaper lining the kitchen, and the sea-green appliances that look as if they shouldn't work anymore, not much has changed over the years.

"Please, come in. I'm Adriana Windsor. I hope you'll excuse my children's mess. They don't understand the meaning of picking up after themselves yet."

"Oh, please, don't apologize. I'm just appreciative that you are allowing us into your home," I say. "It's so warm and welcoming."

"It's outdated, to say the least," she says with an embarrassed giggle. "Come on, I'll show you to the attic."

We walk by her children throwing foam blocks at one another in the middle of the open area where Matilda talked of her parents' armchairs residing. A little girl and a boy maybe a year or two older are laughing and shrieking. This is a happy home now—one it should always have been. "They're adorable," I tell her.

"And loud," she counters with a tired moan. "Be careful on the stairs, they're quite steep."

And rickety, I want to add, recalling the stories about sneaking over the wooden floor planks that creaked.

The room upstairs is just as described, a place for storage. But I can imagine Matilda's bed against the wall across from the window.

There's an old steam trunk collecting dust where the bed must have been.

"Do you mind if I slide this to the side?" I ask Adriana.

"By all means. It's obvious I haven't needed anything in that silly old trunk for a while."

Archie helps me slide the piece to the side and I run my hand down the wallpaper, feeling for a slight break in the panels.

"This is the crawl space," I tell her, handing Archie the book I was holding.

"Honestly, we had no idea there was any extra storage space up here. I'm in shock," Adriana says. "Are you able to open it?"

I remember reading that Matilda had to lift it up and pull the knob, so I slide the tips of my fingers between the floorboards and the wall and lift before tugging it open. It takes a little effort, but the panel finally separates from the wall.

"Well, I'll be... It's quite the little secret," she says.

The sun is shining through the window just enough to light up half of the crawl space. There are still a few papers clinging to the walls and I wonder if they are Hans's handwritten quotes that Matilda hung up.

"Here, would you like a flashlight?" Adriana retrieves one from the drawer of a dusty nightstand covered with folders of papers.

"Oh, yes, please." I take the torch from her hand and crawl inside the hole. A musty, damp odor mixed with what I assume an old newspaper might smell like fills the space. I find a mess of dusty blankets, pads of paper, and what I can confirm to be Hans's quotes on the wall by the resemblance of his immaculate handwriting—every embellished swoop and swish of his pen matches the written words of his story.

I turn and sit against the wall, closing my eyes to imagine what it must have been like in here—everything that was hidden and brought to life only to be kept as a secret.

Archie carefully crawls in, but looks far more uncomfortable than me, since he's taller. "I can't picture having to live here," he says. "It's just unimaginable."

"Did you say someone lived here in this tiny space?" Adriana responds from outside of the opening.

"It's quite a story," I say, "but it's all here in this book."

Archie hands me the canvas bound book with the embossed

words "The Secret in the Attic" on the front cover and the spine. "This is Matilda and Hans's story. After starting the book over seventy years ago, Hans finally had it published last month. Of course, being the humble man he is, he has requested that we only print a couple of copies. So, we placed one in Runa's Wunderbare Bücher as the heart of all the rare and collected items, and now here, in the very spot where the story began."

With a sense of finality, we leave the book where it belongs in the crawl space and thank Adriana sincerely for allowing us into her home.

Archie pulls me down the hallway in the building, away from the stairs that descend toward the exit.

"Where are we going?"

"There's one more thing we have to see before we leave," he says, opening a metal door at the end of the hall. I follow him through the dark passageway until I hear a croak and moan of another door that opens to a short ladder.

"I almost forgot," I say.

We make our way up to the rooftop where Matilda and Hans used to spend time. The sun is setting, casting an orange glow across the town made up of red and copper hues of the steepled rooftops.

"I can see why they came up here." I walk closer to the edge, looking out over the short wall. "They must have felt free up here."

"Grace," Archie calls from behind.

I twist around, finding him glancing down at his feet. "What's wrong?"

"Nothing is wrong at all. I—I want to spend the rest of my life with you. I know it's only been a year, but I think about Matilda and Hans's story and how it always should have been, and I want that—I can't imagine sharing a life with anyone else but you."

I feel blown away, listening to what Archie is saying. It's not that I haven't thought of what might happen between us, but we've connected on such a deeper level that I couldn't imagine us ever growing apart.

"You are a star in the sky out of millions," I reply. "I feel like the world has jumped through hoops of fire to bring us together and I could never leave you—this—what we have."

"I'm relieved to hear this," he says, his lips quivering into a tight-lipped smile. He seems nervous, and I don't understand why, but at the same time there's an enchanting look within his eyes that matches the feeling in my heart.

"Did you think I would leave?"

"No, but Hans gave this to me, hoping you would say yes. So, it would be very awkward to hand it back," he says through nervous laughter. Archie reaches into his pocket and pulls out a beautiful ring. "He gave this to Matilda as a symbol of their love and life together. I think we can keep that love alive."

I throw my arms around Archie's neck, shaking while holding onto him so tightly that I can't stand the thought of letting go.

"I didn't get to ask you if you would marry me?" he whispers into my ear.

The question breaks me, and I fall into a mess of tears, feeling so many emotions all at once. "Yes, without an ounce of doubt, this is what I want more than anything in the world."

After a long moment, I release my grip around his neck and, with unsteady hands, he lifts mine to slide the ring onto my finger. Just as he does, a little yellow bird lands behind him on the stone wall. He turns his head in search of what I'm staring at.

"The little bird of hope gives us its blessing," Archie says. "What more could we ask for?"

I sniffle and stiffen my jaw to stop my chin from trembling. "Nothing—there's nothing more to ask for when we have everything."

A LETTER FROM SHARI

Dear reader,

I'm so grateful you chose to read *The Bookseller of Dachau*. The World War Two stories I write about are very near and dear to my heart due to my upbringing and heritage. As a descendant of two Holocaust survivors, I feel the best way I can honor my grandmother and great-grandmother's sacrifices and struggles is to pick up the pieces from where they left off and carry forward the memories of a time that should never be forgotten. While the subject matter is difficult to write, there isn't a better feeling than gaining a new level of gratitude and understanding for where my roots began.

If you enjoyed *The Bookseller of Dachau* and want to keep up to date with all my latest releases, just sign up at the following link. Your email address will never be shared and you can unsubscribe at any time.

www.bookouture.com/shari-j-ryan

I truly hope you enjoyed the book, and if so, I would be very appreciative if you could write a review. Since the feedback from readers helps me grow as a writer, I would love to hear what you think, and it makes such a difference helping new readers to discover one of my books for the first time.

There's no greater pleasure than hearing from my readers – you can get in touch on my Facebook page, through Twitter, Goodreads or my website.

Thank you for reading!

xoxo

Shari

www.sharijryan.com

 facebook.com/authorsharijryan
twitter.com/sharijryan

ACKNOWLEDGMENTS

The Bookseller of Dachau was a journey I'll never forget. The characters and locations will always have a place in my heart.

Bookouture, thank you for bringing me into your incredible publishing house. I'm so fortunate to be around such exceptional talent and support. Thank you!

Christina, thank you for offering me a chance to work with you on this novel. I have learned a great deal and will be forever grateful for the time you have spent editing and guiding me on how to make this book the best it can be. I look forward to continuing this journey with you!

Linda, thank you so much for your endless support on my publishing endeavors and always being a shoulder to lean on when in need. Your friendship means the world to me.

Freesia, thank you for being my rock when I'm frazzled and clearing the path ahead of me so I'm not walking blindly into walls covered with sticky notes.

Tracey, Gabby, Elaine, Heather, and Emily—I couldn't ask for a better sounding board than the five of you. I'm forever grateful for the time and support you offer me, but most of all, for your friendship. To know I can chat about fictional characters as if they are sitting next to me offers me so much motivation and excitement. I don't know what I'd do without you ladies!

To the wonderful bloggers and readers: Being in this community has given me a different outlook on life, and I can't think of a better industry to be a part of than this one with all of you. Thank you for your support and encouragement to continue living out my dream.

My friends—the ones who watch me turn red, then listen to me chatter about my invisible friends in books: Your support is everything to me.

Lori, you're the best sister in the universe and I'm so lucky to have you as my forever #1 reader. Love you!

My family—Mom, Dad, Mark, and Ev—thank you for your endless support and checking on me to make sure I'm never late with a deadline. To know you have faith in my ability to tell these stories means more than I could ever explain. I love you all.

Bryce and Brayden—my wonderful boys—I hope this book will be a way for you to understand where you came from and to know you have heroic blood running through your veins. Both of you have proven to me you can accomplish anything you put your mind to, and you make me proud every single day.

Josh, my other half—for the last ten years of my writing career, you have been my biggest supporter, and have given me a hand to hold when I think I've lost my way or when I find a new, exciting way. You motivated me to begin this journey all those years ago, and I hope you know I've come this far because of you, too. Having you by my side makes me feel like the luckiest girl in the world. I love you so much!

Made in the USA
Middletown, DE
28 December 2021

57200771R00161